AS LOVERS REUNITE

It seemed an eternity to Julia before the outside door opened and Marcus came through it, his eyes locking with hers as he closed it behind him.

Her feet barely touched the floor as she ran to him; he folded her into his arms and said, concerned, "Tears? Why are you crying?"

"I was just thinking about the chance we're both taking. This is so dangerous," she murmured against his chest.

"Say the word and I'll go," he replied, holding her off to look at her.

Julia dropped her eyes. "I can never say that word, Marcus. Why?"

"I think there's a good reason."

"What is it?"

"Fatum nos coegisse credo," he replied. "I believe that fate brought us together."

She looked up at him and nodded.

"Then why question what we both sense to be the work of the gods?" he said. "Accept it as a gift."

Julia buried her face against his hard shoulder. "It's difficult to live so much of my life without seeing you. When I'm not with you I think—oh, terrible things."

"And when you are with me?"

"Then I forget the rest of the world."

He bent his head to kiss the side of her neck. "I'll make you forget it completely," he said softly, his lips soft and caressing. "All of it. Just give me the chance. . . ."

DOREEN OWENS MALEK
THE RAVEN
AND THE
ROSE

ZEBRA BOOKS
KENSINGTON PUBLISHING CORP.

ZEBRA BOOKS are published by

Kensington Publishing Corp.
850 Third Avenue
New York, NY 10022

First Printing: December, 1994

Printed in the United States of America

One

"Here's your shield, Centurion," Lisander said. "I rebound the edge with new leather. I think it will hold. Take a look."

The tall dark man accepted the shield from the Greek slave and examined the workmanship carefully, then nodded.

"This will do. You can put it in my supply chest."

The slave departed with the shield, and the soldier went back to lacing up his sandal, sighing heavily.

Marcus Corvus Demeter was tired of war. He had joined the Roman army when he was seventeen, and he'd been fighting continuously for the last eleven years. The front of his body was covered with scars from various campaigns against barbarian tribes. The muscles of his forearms were as hard as flint from hauling a forty-pound

pack on the march, as well as carrying a
leather-clad shield and a six-foot lance into
battle. There was no extra flesh anywhere
on his frame, as the army consumed little
more than wheat biscuits and water laced
with vinegar during a campaign, and while
the soldiers were at rest in winter quarters
they maintained almost the same diet.
There had been some opportunity for the
temptations of the vulgar city to find their
way onto his bones at social events, but
Marcus never ate much at leisure either.
Like all Roman soldiers, he prided himself
on staying in top fighting trim and disdained the chubby city dwellers for their
excesses.

He finished strapping on his sandal
and stood erect, topping the others mill-
ing around the barracks by at least a
head. Demeter was from the Roman province of Corsica, had a Greek name, and
looked it. He was dark and handsome, in
the Macedonian way, with glossy black
hair, smooth olive skin, and large almond-
shaped brown eyes. His arched nose,
along with his coloring, had earned him
the name of *Corvus,* Raven. He was the
descendant of Greek sailors who had
plied their trade across the Mediterranean
three hundred years earlier, intermarrying
with the Etruscans living on the sunswept

islands to the west of Italy. He stood out from his fellows for his height and for his exceptional courage, which had won him many accolades from his general, Julius Caesar, now the unacknowledged dictator of their country.

Marcus automatically checked his weapons as he dressed, the sword sheathed on one side of his leather belt and the short knife on the other, thinking about the uneasy state of the Roman Republic. The Senate still sat, the magistrates still issued edicts, and the citizens still voted, but since the death of his rival Pompey four years earlier, Julius Caesar alone had ruled the most powerful nation in the known world.

And there were many who were not happy about it.

"Marcus, do you want to come along with us to the forum?" Septimus Valerius Gracchus called to him, tossing him a ball of amber, which the men used in the storage chests to scent their clothes. "Cicero is giving another speech denouncing Mark Antony."

Marcus looked at his friend, who was a tribune, and the scion of a noble house, one of the hundred or so patrician families with three generations of magistrates in their past. Septimus would be expected to run for public office and serve in the Senate in order to inherit his father's considerable wealth. But while he was doing his obligatory term in the army he was on an equal footing with Marcus, who had saved his life in Cordoba and marched beside him for many hundreds of miles. Their friendship had endured through Gaul and Iberia and Britannia, where the natives painted their faces blue with woad and, like their continental cousins the Gauls, fought with a fierceness that astonished even the seasoned Romans.

Marcus and Septimus had survived many hazards in their years together.

Marcus shook his head. "I'm tired of that windbag," he replied. "Every time I walk through the forum he's tearing apart yet another one of Caesar's friends. Pompey was murdered in Egypt, his cause is dead. Hasn't anyone told that speech-maker yet?"

Septimus grinned. "Don't you find Cicero amusing?"

"No." Marcus tossed the ball of amber into his clothes chest and dropped the lid.

"I've told you before, Marcus, you must learn to develop a sense of humor," Septimus said, wagging his finger at his companion. Shorter and stockier than Marcus, with unexceptional features, he was nevertheless attractive, with the easy charm and confidence of the well born. "That's what comes of growing up in the provinces. We city dwellers have learned to take these orators lightly."

A ten-year-old boy ran breathlessly into the barracks and skidded to a stop in front of Marcus.

"Marcus Corvus Demeter," he said hastily, impressed with the importance of his mission, "Imperator Caesar requests your presence at noon at the *porta publica* of the Senate."

"Take it easy, Appius," Septimus said, ruffling the boy's hair. "Your father will not disinherit you if you walk at a stately pace to deliver your messages."

Appius was a magistrate's son learning warfare as a page to the army.

"Does the Imperator need an escort?" Marcus asked, fastening his deep red cloak, its garnet color adopted by the practical Romans to conceal the bloodstains of battle. It hung over his short-sleeved, knee-length tunic of a similar red, which was covered by a leather breastplate and skirt guard. His metal helmet was decorated with a standing ruff of garnet feathers. He picked it up and placed it under his arm.

The boy nodded eagerly. "To the *Aedes*

Vestae. You are to report to Tribune Drusus
Vinicius at the outer gate of the camp for
your orders."

"Caesar must be changing his will
again," Septimus said, laughing. "I only
hope that means he'll be leaving some of
his money to me."

"At least he's consented to an armed
companion," Marcus replied. "He has too
many enemies to wander around without
his bodyguard the way he often does."

"You'll take good care of him, I'm
sure," Septimus said. "Well, I'm off now.
Remember you're coming to my father's
house for *cena* tonight."

Marcus nodded. *Cena* was dinner, the
only formal meal the Romans ate. They
were great snackers, snatching a flat bread
filled with cooked vegetables while conducting business or a honeycake from a
vendor on the way to the forum in the
morning. But *cena* was a formal and elaborate meal, a relaxation from the cares of
the day and a chance for the family to get
together and discuss the local gossip, of
which the people were inordinately fond.
Guests were frequently invited, and it was
an honor for a provincial like Marcus to
be asked to the home of Senator Valerius
Gracchus.

But Marcus was a war hero, and had saved the life of the Senator's only son.

"Hurry, hurry," Appius said, dancing in place. "Caesar will be waiting."

Marcus smiled at the boy. "It's not noon yet, but you've done your duty, *caligula,*" he said, using an affectionate term, "little boots," to describe the child. "I'm sure Lisander can find some work for you to do."

The boy dashed out, and Marcus pushed his way through the military throng in the Campus Martius courtyard to the northern guard house, where Vinicius gave him his orders. When not at war, the army barracks in winter quarters was like a men's club, where the soldiers came and went at their leisure and in fact could live elsewhere if they pleased. Only a direct order such as the one Marcus had just received interrupted the respite meant to restore strength for summer, the season of war. As soon as the red flag was seen flying from the citadel above the temple of Janus, the men reported for duty. And once they took the *sacramentum,* the soldier's oath, only death or the end of the war could release them from it.

In May, Caesar was planning to invade Parthia.

Marcus walked out into the street, which was a narrow warren winding through close buildings and leading to a main artery, the Via Flaminia. The Campus Martius, or field of Mars, was named for the god of war and lay between the River Tiber and the city proper. As Marcus walked toward his destination he observed the life of the metropolis teeming around him.

The scene was one of ceaseless bustle and dust and incredible noise. Carriages were barred from the city during the day, but the litters which were their substitute clogged every passage, the nobles within them peering out through the curtains at the enclosing crowd. Businessmen hawked wares from stalls, and citizens lingered on street corners to discuss that consuming Roman passion, politics. Slaves of all sizes and races hurried everywhere, running errands, trailing their schoolboy charges, carrying supplies and babies and bundles and jugs of water. Two Senators in white togas striped with reddish purple, preceded by their *lictors,* or assistants, cut a path through the more dully dressed rabble, avoiding the morning Senate session to make their way to the forum and listen to Cicero. People parted ranks when they saw Marcus; in a city with no standing police force, the army was often called in to settle disputes, and his centurion's uniform bespoke authority.

"Corvus, look sharp!" someone called to him, and as Marcus turned he caught an object tossed in his direction. It turned out to be a ripe bundle of figs tied together by their stems with a piece of thin twine.

"From Judea," the fruit seller said, saluting him. "The best. Enjoy them."

Marcus reached for the bag of coins at his belt, but the vendor waved him away.

"Pro bono," he said. "For your past services to the state. Just make sure you keep the barbarians away from Rome on your next campaign."

"I will try," Marcus replied, always amazed when some stranger recognized him. He did not think of himself as well known, but in a brutal world where a country survived or succumbed on the strength of its fighting force, highly successful soldiers were national celebrities.

Marcus stopped at a stall which boasted a hand-lettered sign reading IN JUST TODAY FROM POMPEII. Fresh trout and carp and flounder hung on hooks above urns of *garum*, the fermented fish sauce the Romans used with everything in their cooking, and flasks of must, the pressed grape husks that served as filling in desserts. He moved closer to examine the wares and bought a bottle of *garum* marked *Optime,* "the very best," to bring as a gift when he attended dinner that evening. He stowed it, and the figs, in the capacious pockets of his cloak, and then walked on, pausing beside a stable to wipe his brow with the back of his arm. The day was a warm one for February and the sun was arcing overhead.

The smell of horse dung made him wrinkle his nose. Romans venerated cleanliness, and did their best to maintain it, despite the refuse problems associated with so many people living in cramped quarters. The teeming *insulae*, or low-rent apartment houses, flimsily built and often on fire, were the source of the worst contamination. There was no running water above the first floor and tenants dropped offal into the streets from the roof during the dark of night, since there was a stiff fine for littering. The *insulae* were behind a row of shops on the Via Sacra, but Marcus fancied he could smell them, too. They were a sanitary challenge to the entire city, the subject of much Senatorial legislation concerning the best way to improve them.

From what Marcus had seen of the living conditions there, he doubted that passing laws would make much of a difference. People who could not afford anything better would flock to the *insulae* no matter what restrictions were enacted. Civic pride was a national mania, but it was at odds with the desire of every Roman citizen to live within the city, which meant clogged streets and crowded houses. From the estates on the Palatine hill, where property of a quarter of an acre was considered sumptuously large, to the tiniest cell of the *insulae*, the population battled disease and dirt, but remained in place. Refuse was hauled away by slaves pulling wagons, homeowners and shopkeepers were required by law to sweep their properties every day, and a vast system of drainage ditches swept away liquid waste and carried it underground, but it often seemed to the city-bound residents that the litter was increasing despite their efforts.

Marcus squinted in the sunlight and looked around, turning toward the sound of running water. The Romans countered the heat and dust of their environment with the purity and renewal of water. In the massive public baths, in four aqueducts which carried millions of gallons of bubbling freshets down from the hills, in the thousands of fountains, public and private, which sparkled and murmured in the Italian sunlight, they brought the source of cleanliness close to home. Rome was a city which streamed with water.

Marcus walked over to the fountain nearby and splashed his face. The statue at the center of the marble basin was of Diana, goddess of the hunt, her hair bound with a leather thong, a quiver loaded with arrows strapped to her back. Water cascaded from her outstretched hands into his. As he turned away he sidestepped a slave bending to look at a poster tacked to the footing. It advertised a gladiatorial show.

The people pressing in around Marcus as he dried his face with the hem of his cloak made up a human rainbow. In the crowd he saw blacks from Carthage and Utica in North Africa, emancipated Gauls with ruddy complexions and bristling red hair, dark-eyed descendants of Etruscans like himself, golden Greeks from Corinth with pale complexions and Alexandrian ringleted hair, all of them wearing the toga of citizenship. Racial prejudice did not exist in Rome. It was civic prejudice that was the Republic's flaw. There were only citizens and noncitizens, and the former regarded the latter as one step above chattels. Therefore it was the ambition of every slave and freedman to attain *civitas*, citizenship, which allowed one to vote,

register in the census, participate in the
swell and murmur of public life. Until
that was achieved you were a slave to be
ordered about and dominated, cared for,
if you were lucky, but merely in the way
a faithful dog is maintained by its master.

Marcus had been born a citizen, which
forever separated him from the rabble
that swirled around him as he made his
way past a grove of statues and the prae-
tors' tribunal to the *curia*, where the Senate met. Only citizens could wear the
toga, the long draped cloak which distinguished the important people from the
rest; the latter, dressed in simple woolen
shifts, outnumbered the former three or
four to one. Slaves were mostly members
of conquered tribes who'd been captured
as booty. They were brought back in
chains to Rome by the victorious legions
to be sold at auction. Since Rome's conquests ringed the Mediterranean, which
its citizens called *mare nostrum*, "our sea,"
there were slaves everywhere.

Marcus, like most citizens, gave little
thought to the slaves. There was always
the hope they could become citizens,
through a noble deed, purchasing liberty
after many years of saving, or emancipation by a grateful master. But the majority did not attain freedom, and they lived

out their days serving those whose only difference from them was membership in a republic which boasted the most powerful and victorious army in the world.

Marcus himself was a prime example of why the Roman army drove all before it and swallowed enemies like a tidal wave clearing a shore. Discipline was the keynote of his life. Like all Roman soldiers he could march sixteen miles a day on sparse rations and then build a camp at night before he went to sleep. He was a war machine, trained and expert in the art of battle; everything else in his life was secondary. He had not seen his family for years, had no friends outside the army, and had never been in love. His attitude toward women had always been utilitarian: desire was expected, procreation necessary, but letting the emotions overmaster the soul seemed foolish, even shameful. He was handsome, not to mention a highly decorated soldier, and he had never lacked female companionship. But a special attachment was something he'd never had the time or the inclination to pursue.

Marcus lifted his tunic away from his neck with a forefinger, then grimaced as he bent to remove a pebble from his sandal. Lately an unfamiliar loneliness had

been stealing over him, making him somehow dissatisfied with the Spartan existence
which had previously sustained him. Maybe
he had just been at war too long, or perhaps it was time for a change in his life.
He didn't know, but this new feeling left
him vaguely unsettled and searching for
something more, something different.

He didn't like it.

Marcus glanced around him, taking in
the color and confusion which had always
made him glad to return to Rome. Corsica was a rural backwater by comparison,
and he looked forward each year to winter camp near the city, from which a short
walk would take him into the bustling
throng that eddied around him now. A
builder lumbered by, leading a string of
mules laden with materials, and two dogs
snapped at each other in his wake, snarl-
ing over a bone. A funeral passed on the
other side of the street, its hired mourn-
ers rending their garments, as a poet read
his latest work aloud before a bookshop.
In a covered portico to the left a painter
did portraits, selling them to the passersby, and a merchant offered pearls and
bronzes from India as well as Tyrian purple dye to color the toga hems of the
wealthy. Marcus took it all in, wondering

why it didn't cheer him as it always had in the past.

"Good day, Centurion," said the stable owner as he walked past Marcus, leading a horse into the street. "Are you in the market for some excellent horseflesh? I have a new Arabian that's a beauty. Free stabling for the winter until the army goes on the march."

Marcus shook his head, smiling. "I've heard about you, Postumus. You're always trying to pawn some nag off on an un-suspecting soldier. By the time the horse comes up lame the army is in the Alps and you're in the Suburra spending your sesterces on the Aquitanian whores."

The stable owner made a sad face. "My reputation is undeserved. The competition spreads vicious rumors. I'm surprised an officer like yourself listens to such gos-sip."

"You stung my friend Septimus, old man," Marcus replied, laughing. "You picked the wrong mark, he has an influ-ential family and a big mouth."

"I sold Septimus Valerius a very fine mare. It's not my fault if he ran the ani-mal into the ground."

Marcus bit his lip. "The animal had rickets."

"That's a lie."

"Septimus goes into the forum every morning since the army's been in camp to tell everyone about it," Marcus added, folding his arms, grinning.

The stableman yanked the horse he was leading after him and stalked off, mumbling to himself.

Marcus chuckled, then glanced up at the sun and noticed that it was almost overhead. The *apparitor* standing on the steps of the old *curia* would soon give the signal for the trumpets to be sounded, announcing the noon hour. The Senate session would then end. He went on his way again, briskly this time, his garnet cloak dangling down his back from its metal shoulder clasps, his hobnailed leather sandals clicking when they struck a stone.

He did not want to keep Caesar waiting.

Julia Rosalba Casca entered the Atrium of the shrine of Vesta and set down the copper vessels she'd been carrying, filled with water from the sacred spring of Egeria, near the Porta Capena. It would be used for the ceremonial sprinkling and sweeping of the altar to Vesta. Julia performed the water carrying twice a month, sharing the duty with the other Vestals, and she was always glad when it was over and she was back at the temple. The noise and the crowds of the city gave her a headache. Even though her litter was preceded by a *lictor* and she was guarded at all times, there was something unnerving about the press and clamor of all that humanity, reminding her of everything she was missing as she passed her life in the quiet and seclusion of the temple.

Julia was seventeen, and had been in the service of Vesta for seven years. She'd been taken from her family just before her tenth birthday and solemnly admitted to the Vestals by the chief priest. He had cut off her hair and, addressing her as "beloved," pronounced the solemn formula of initiation. Since then she had lived in the opulent hall, or Atrium, of Vesta which adjoined the temple and learned to perform her duties; the study comprised her first decade of service. During the second she would practice them fully and during the third instruct the new Vestals. At the age of forty she would be free to go, but in fact few Vestals ever left the service, since after so many years marriage and children were unlikely and it was difficult to give up the privileges and honors of a Vestal's life. They lived in great luxury and were attended by many servants in return for their guarding the sacred fire of Vesta, the perpetual flame thought to keep the city of Rome free from plague and foreign invaders; but to be worthy of this honor the Vestals must remain virgins. They faced death by public execution if they violated their vow of chastity.

Julia barely remembered her initiation into Vestal service. It seemed so long ago. What she remembered was that she had not been consulted about the decision. Her grandfather, Gnaeus Casca, had pressed her father to dedicate the life of his younger daughter to Vestal service. This was considered a great honor and would bring even more distinction to an already distinguished family. Julia's older sister, Larthia, had been married to a provincial governor when she was fifteen, so it fell to Julia to fulfill the Vestal role.

She had thus been denied the future comforts of marriage and children when she barely had her second teeth.

There were compensations, to be sure. The Vestals were national icons, treated with veneration when they appeared in public or to officiate at ceremonies. They were kept at State expense in high style. The Atrium Vestae, where they lived, was marble floored and hung with Persian silks. Its tiled bathhouse was fed by a hot spring; and a staff of seamstresses, hair-dressers, and German masseuses lived at the Atrium. Each Vestal had her own suite of rooms with an antechamber for her personal maid. Vestals were given the best education in order that they might record wills and official documents for a population that was largely illiterate. Julia commanded several languages, Greek and Persian as well as Latin, and she could play stringed instruments, dance and sing, and recite the ancient poetry of Homer and the modern poetry of Virgil.

But whenever Julia went out in public, she would look longingly at the young wives buying fish for dinner, at the young mothers shepherding unruly children. Her gaze would linger on them as her *lictor* walked before her litter, clearing a path for the Vestal through the bowing crowd.

At times, she would have to glance away, her vision clouded by tears.

"Madame, you must come quickly!" Margo said, appearing around a corner, whispering urgently. "Imperator Caesar is coming to the Aedes to make an altera-tion to his will and Livia Versalia has re-quested you to attend and take notes."

Margo was Julia's Helvetian maid, cap-tured when her tribe was conquered in Switzerland. She'd been brought back to

Rome and sold into service at the temple. Assigned to Julia shortly after Julia's arrival, Margo was ten years older and had attended the young Vestal ever since. The two women were close, their bond not exactly friendship, not really that of mistress and slave either, but the unique relationship that existed between a child of privilege and the servant who had raised her.

"You must change clothes immediately," Margo added, hurrying alongside Julia as she scurried through the passage which connected the temple to the home of the Vestals immediately next to it. "This is a great honor, to be asked to attend such a conference. You should look your best."

Julia had seen Caesar before, from a distance when he marched in triumph after his military victories, and just once close up the previous autumn when he first came to the temple to file his will. He was always changing that document, however; he'd been married several times, had many dependents, and his personal fortune fluctuated wildly.

"I wonder what this summons means," Julia said, as they turned into the hall leading to the private chambers of the Vestals. Like many Roman structures, the building had no windows facing the street, so the passage was illuminated by flickering torches, even during the day.

"It means the Chief Vestal knows that you will take the best notes for the transcribers. Augusta Gellia made such a mess of the last will she did that Livia knew she would have to give someone else a chance. I'm just surprised she would use you, since your second term doesn't begin for three years. You must have impressed her. I'm so proud of you."

"Don't draw conclusions yet, Margo. If Livia isn't happy with my performance today it's the last time I'll be assigned this particular function." Julia removed her *palla*, the outer garment which was wrapped around the body in many folds, and handed it to Margo as they entered her suite. Several lesser servants, already summoned by Margo, hurried in behind them to help Julia change her clothing and dress her hair in the elaborate, formal style the occasion demanded.

A short time later Julia was ready. She was wearing an ivory sleeveless tunic and a *stola* girdled below her breasts by a *zona,* a belt woven of gold thread. A sky blue, gold-trimmed *diploidion,* a wide scarf draped over one shoulder, was fastened at her waist by a circular gold pin imprinted with the image of Vesta. Julia's long red-gold hair, uncut for the seven years since her initiation, was pinned up and intricately dressed, the crown of her head encircled by *vittae*, braided strips of cloth of gold which fell in loops over each shoulder.

Margo nodded approval and then handed Julia a stylus and a pile of wax tablets. Julia would take notes on the tablets and then they would be given to an official transcriber, a Greek slave who transferred documents to parchment.

"Go," Margo said, urging Julia toward the door. "Livia Versalia will want to speak to you first."

Margo was right. The Chief Vestal was already seated in the recording room of the Aedes, surrounded by labeled scrolls inserted into niches reaching from the floor to the ceiling. She was composed and alert, her eyes sweeping over Julia in measured fashion as the younger woman entered.

"Do you feel equal to this task, Julia Rosalba?" Livia Versalia asked, her expression inquiring. "You know from your training that I take the place of the goddess and bear witness under oath, therefore I may not record what takes place here. That task is left to you. Drucilla Pontifica, my first choice to replace Augusta, is ill today and the Imperator did not give us advance

word of his desire to change his will again.
You are young and inexperienced, but your
tutors tell me that you are the quickest
with languages of any of the novices and
that you write a clear Latin hand which is
easily read. Is that so?"

"I hope I may acquit myself admirably,
madame," Julia said quietly.

"You did not answer my question,"
Livia said dryly.

"I write well and take excellent notes,"
Julia said flatly, meeting the older woman's
gaze.

Livia nodded. "I know you have received instruction in this procedure, but
let me review for a moment. You are an
umbra, a shadow, in this proceeding. You
will record what is said, but you will not
speak unless spoken to and you will pass
the tablets immediately into my hands as
soon as Caesar is finished talking. Is that
perfectly clear?"

Julia nodded.

Livia permitted herself a small smile.
"Sit down, child. I'm sure you will do
well."

Julia sat, glancing covertly at the Chief
Vestal as both women waited for Caesar's
arrival. Livia Versalia was thirty-eight, two
years away from her retirement as a Vestal. She was a tall and handsome woman,

her dark hair lightly threaded with gray, her face unmarked by the cares of the outside world. When she left the Vestals in two years she would have, among many other privileges, lifelong accommodations in the Atrium Vestae; the right to travel through the city by carriage and to be buried at state expense (both royal prerogatives); freedom from taxes and from the stricture of most Roman laws; the best seats reserved at theaters and athletic contests; and the power to pardon any criminal she met in the street on the way to execution. She had risen to her current position through dedication and attention to the most minute of details, and she was not about to jeopardize her standing when she was near to concluding her duties in a blaze of glory.

Julia knew that she would be observed during this meeting by a very watchful eye.

Livia noticed her stirring and said, "It won't be long now. The Imperator is always prompt."

Julia nodded and arranged her long skirt carefully over her knees.

Busy men usually were.

Caesar swept into the Aedes Vestae with Marcus at his side, both men intent on accomplishing this mission and then moving on to other things. In the absence of Caesar's usual bodyguard, Marcus was exceptionally alert, but there was no one in the torchlit entrance hall of the temple except Junia Distania, the second oldest of the Vestals and their official greeter. She bowed her head when she saw Caesar and then gestured for the men to follow her to the recording chamber, the first door on the right past the marble statue of Flavia Publica, a retired Chief Vestal.

Both women in the room rose when Caesar and his companion appeared in the doorway; Junia Distania vanished promptly, her task at an end.

Julia looked at Caesar, who commanded first attention in any setting. The dictator was fifty-six, his face heavily seamed from the sun of a hundred campaigns, his hawk nose dominating it. He had been balding since youth and was vain about it; his graying dark hair was combed forward onto his forehead to disguise a receded hairline. He was dressed in his heavily decorated general's uniform, the coins on the gold chain about his neck signifying the wealth of the territories he had conquered. His deep-set brown eyes scanned the two Vestals, missing nothing.

"Greetings, beloved daughters of Vesta,"

he said, giving them the traditional salutation.

Both women bowed their heads.

"I have brought along my most trusted centurion, Marcus Corvus Demeter of the first cohort, to witness my words today, as our law requires at least two witnesses and Livia Versalia will, of course, serve as one."

Livia bowed her head again, and Julia looked at Caesar's companion. When her eyes met his she froze.

The man was taller than Caesar by a head, and much younger, not more than thirty. His cropped hair was thick and black, his clean-shaven face tanned, his figure slim and erect, the limbs exposed by his soldier's tunic muscular and strong. His eyes were a curious color, a light golden brown, almost amber, and Julia felt herself flush deeply as they studied her.

Livia coughed, and Julia realized that she was standing rooted, her arms folded inside her *diploidion,* staring at the centurion. She turned away immediately and gazed at the floor, trying to disguise her confusion.

"Shall we begin?" Caesar said briskly, and Livia gestured toward the marble-footed table where he would give his deposition. Caesar and the soldier with him sat,

and Julia took her place at the smaller recording table to their left.

Julia listened to Livia taking her oath
and then administering a similar oath to
Caesar's companion. Julia stole glances at
the younger man periodically, her stylus at
the ready in her hand, and twice she
caught him looking back at her intently
and she quickly glanced away. Her heart
was beating fast in her chest, and her fingers around the inscribing tool were damp.
She ducked that hand into her lap and
wiped her hand on her gown, then brought
the stylus up again.

By that time Caesar was ready to talk,
and Julia kept her head down, scribbling
in an effort to keep up with his direct,
well-modulated speech. He spoke from his
own notes and had obviously given much
thought to the changes he wanted to
make; everything was laid out very carefully, and it took him only a short time
to convey the alterations to his previous
will. When he was done he looked at
Julia expectantly and Livia said, "Please
read the deposition back to the Imperator, Julia Rosalba."

Julia obeyed, and Caesar nodded in
agreement when she was finished.

"Fine," he said, and rose, leaning forward to place the signet of his general's

ring against the soft wax on Julia's tablet. The centurion did the same with his legionary's ring, giving Julia an excellent view of the top of his dark head. Livia said in conclusion, "The transcriptions will be ready for your review and formal signature in two days' time, Imperator."

"Excellent," Caesar replied. He smiled at Livia and then at Julia.

"What is your name, young lady?" he asked.

"Julia Rosalba Casca," Julia replied quietly, with downcast eyes.

"Casca! Not the daughter of my longtime rival," Caesar exclaimed in surprise.

"Granddaughter," Livia supplied.

"Ah, I see. Well, you may look up at me, little Casca," Caesar said.

Julia obeyed, noting that the centurion was also watching her fixedly.

"White rose. Your name suits you. Pale skin and eyes the color of an Alpine spring," Caesar said. "Well, you can tell Casca from me that his politics are anathema, but his son has made a beautiful woman." Caesar swept from the room, and the centurion followed him, glancing once over his shoulder at Julia before he left.

Livia patted Julia on the shoulder. "You did very well," she said, accepting the tablets Julia handed her.

Julia didn't trust herself to reply.

"Nothing to say?" Livia asked.

"I was very nervous," Julia replied hastily.

"Yes, I saw that, but it's to be expected. Caesar is a very great man."

Julia knew that her nervousness had had little to do with Caesar. She'd been much more disturbed by the handsome centurion with the compelling amber eyes.

"What is this marking here?" Livia asked, pointing to the second tablet.

Julia started, as if Livia could read her thoughts, then answered a few questions about her shorthand as Livia examined her work.

"You may go," Livia finally said, already having decided which transcriber to assign to the job. "Aren't you due to sacrifice tomorrow?"

Julia nodded.

"Then rest tonight and purify your thoughts. You must have a clear mind and a calm spirit to address the goddess."

"Good day, Livia Versalia."

"Good day, daughter."

Julia left the recording room and returned to her chamber, where Margo was waiting to help her change back into less ceremonial clothes and undo her hair.

"I heard that you more than satisfied

expectations, Margo said, draping Julia's *diploidion* over a gilt chair.

Julia looked at her in amazement. "Have you had a message from the gods? I just left Livia myself."

"Junia Distania was in the hall waiting to escort Caesar out of the temple and heard the end of the interview. She came straight to me after the men left."

Julia shook her head in disgust. "You should be a spy for the Iberians, Margo."

"It reflects badly on me if you fail in your duties," Margo replied, unoffended.

Julia shook out her loosened hair and asked casually, "Do you know the man who came along with Caesar, the centurion of the first cohort?"

Margo stared at her. "Are you joking? You don't know who that was?"

"Caesar said his name when they entered, and I thought it sounded familiar."

"That was the hero of the Cordoba campaign, Marcus Corvus Demeter."

Julia nodded thoughtfully. "Yes, now I remember."

"I should think you would. Didn't you see the triumphal procession on Caesar's return from Iberia? Demeter rode in the back of the Imperator's chariot, along with Mark Antony. Demeter is a most decorated and famous soldier, Caesar's fa-

vorite. Why don't you know this, Julia?
Everyone else does."

"I saw the procession from the Vestals'
box, but Antony and the other soldier
were wearing full armor, it was impossible
to recognize anyone. All I remember is
two tall men and a shorter one with a
laurel wreath on his head."

Margo frowned disapprovingly. "You
should pay more attention to politics,
Julia. Your family is prominent, and it's
part of your heritage to follow these
things. After the Cordoba campaign Demeter has been seen everywhere at Caesar's right hand. If he keeps on this way
he will certainly have the right to an image long before he is an old man."

"What else do you know about him?"
Julia asked.

"Oh, that he was born in Corsica, son
of a freedman farmer. He joined the provincial legion when hardly more than a
child. It is said that he rose through the
ranks quickly from so many acts of brav-
ery that Caesar took personal notice of
him and put him in the first cohort."

"Why is he named for the Greek goddess of grain?"

"There are many Greeks in Corsica,
have you forgotten your lessons?"

"Why do they call him Raven?"

"For his coloring, I suppose."

"How old is he?"

Margo stopped folding garments and looked at Julia sharply. "Why are you so curious?"

Julia shrugged, as if the matter were of no consequence. "He appeared to have Caesar's complete trust."

"As well as the infatuation of every silly young woman in Rome. Be careful, Julia. It would not be seemly for you to pay too much attention to an eligible young officer."

Julia threw up her hands in exasperation. "You were just chiding me for not knowing who he was!"

"Awareness is one thing," Margo said loftily. "Fascination is another."

Julia tossed her braided belt at Margo and said, "You're being ridiculous. Go now and get the *suffibulum* for the sacrifice tomorrow."

Margo stared her down archly.

"Go!" Julia said.

Margo bowed and left the room.

Caesar and Marcus descended the vast temple steps toward the dictator's litter, which was draped in purple silk and waiting in the street. Four towering German slaves in short green tunics stood ready to grasp the wooden hand rests and carry it.

Caesar looked over at his young companion and said, "Why so solemn, young Corvus? Are you sad that I didn't leave you a magnificent bequest in my will?"

Marcus smiled slightly and shook his head.

"Or is it that little Vestal who caught your eye?" Caesar studied him perceptively.

Marcus looked at him briefly, then away.

"Ho, so you *were* smitten! Struck by Jove's thunderbolt!" Caesar chuckled. "Too bad, my boy. Put that one out of your thoughts. The white rose has already been plucked, by the goddess herself. Rosalba is not for you."

Marcus still said nothing.

"I do admit it is a shame," Caesar added, "for one such as that never to know the embrace of a man's body or the suckle of children. Still, the Vestals serve a strong purpose for the state, and they're richly rewarded for it. I have a soft spot for them myself. Did you know they interceded for me when Sulla put a price on my head for refusing to divorce my first wife?"

"I heard something about it. I didn't know the Vestals were involved."

"Oh, yes. The Chief Vestal, not Livia

but her predecessor Flavia, used her influence to keep me alive when I was a young lad and needed friends. A favor like that one doesn't forget. Anyway, it was before you were born and the troubles of those days are long gone. We have new ones to deal with now." Caesar narrowed his keen dark eyes. "Don't you ever wonder why I take you with me on these personal missions, rather than that extra legionary bodyguard the Senate has fitted out for me?"

Marcus hesitated. "I thought you found the formal bodyguard ostentatious," he finally said.

Caesar smiled thinly. "A diplomatic answer. The truth is there are few people I can really trust. The Senate is filled with my enemies, everyone knows this and each day there are new plots hatched against me. To take the reins of the state means to make of oneself a target. You are one of the few men I know who doesn't want anything from me."

Marcus smiled again. "You make me sound very stupid, General."

Caesar shook his head. "All you want from life are the just rewards of a good soldier, and as long as I am alive I shall see that you get them."

Marcus put his hand on his sword hilt as they reached Caesar's litter.

"Go to the Suburra tonight and find a companion who will make you forget all about the white rose," Caesar said, clapping his centurion on the shoulder as the slaves bowed low.

Marcus sighed. "I am tired of *quadrantariae* with transparent tunics and kohl-rimmed eyes, stinking of Persian perfumes, their berry-stained lips whispering lies."

Caesar shrugged. "Such is the lot of the soldier. If you want to do better, take a wife."

Marcus grinned. "I cannot support a wife on army pay. The raise you authorized to two hundred twenty-five denarii a year hardly makes any of us in the legions wealthy."

"You can support an army on the booty you carried back from Gaul and the Iberian campaign," Caesar said dryly. "There's not a man in your legion who didn't return to Rome rich in plate and coins." He pulled back the curtains of his litter and climbed in, looking out at Marcus for the last word.

"Go out tonight, son, and have a good time. You need the relaxation," he said.

"I will. I'm dining tonight at the home of Senator Valerius Gracchus."

"Good. Gracchus sets a fine table. Give him my compliments." Caesar pulled the litter curtains closed and tapped the roof for the slaves to proceed.

Marcus fell in behind the litter, thinking that as much as he respected Caesar, he was going to disregard the general's advice in this instance.

He planned to see the golden-haired Vestal again, no matter what he had to do to arrange it.

Two

Larthia Casca Sejana dismissed her hairdresser and stared moodily into the polished silver mirror she held. She didn't know why she was conducting this elaborate toilette. Her husband was dead (he had scarcely noticed her when he was alive) and now her sole reason for going on seemed to be to uphold the memory of his sacred name. Although she was young and attractive, with thick light brown hair and wide gray eyes, her life had degenerated into a matron's round of entertaining his business contacts and pledging portions of his fortune to various charities.

She was miserably bored.

Larthia picked up a utensil from her dressing table and plucked a hair from her left brow, examining herself critically. She was several shades less vivid than her firehaired, green-eyed sister Julia, but she was still far too pretty to spend her life as keeper of the memory of Consul Sejanus. The only compensation of her current role was that as the consul's widow she'd been able for some time to handle her own money and operate free of the *patria potestas,* the authority of her father. That worthy gentleman had sold her to the Consul Sejanus, and her younger sister Julia to the Vestals, and then had succumbed, it was said, to a jug of poisoned wine. He'd found both of his daughters advantageous positions before a slave he had flogged took revenge by slipping a tincture of mercury into his after-dinner libation.

Her husband was dead, her father was dead, so the only man she still had to deal with was her grandfather, Casca, whom she wished would die. He was coming to visit her shortly, and she did not want to see him. She was tired, restless, and bitter, over three years the widow of a much older man who'd been far more interested in bedding twelve-year-old slave boys than sleeping with his wife. By some miracle he'd left her pregnant when he'd gone to assume the governorship of Cilicia, and she had begged off accompanying him on account of her condition. She had lost the baby, which might have been some comfort to her, and then made excuses not to join Sejanus until he died of some barbarian fe-

ver. Now she had his fortune, but couldn't
have a good time with it because her
grandfather Casca, the *paterfamilias,* still
lived, and claimed the father's authority
over Larthia that his son had relinquished
when he died. She was snared by the ster-
ile fate of the honorable Roman widow,
though still less than twenty-two years old.

Larthia had never accepted the submis-
sive role of Roman women. Controlled
completely by the men in their lives, first
their fathers, then their husbands, they
were free to direct their own destiny only
if they were lucky enough to outlive their
mates and strong enough to resist the considerable social pressure to marry again.
She'd been lucky, and she was strong, but
Casca, though old, still exerted his influence, and Larthia was afraid of him.

His whole family was afraid of him. That
was why Larthia had married Sejanus at
the age of fifteen, because her grandfather
had wanted a political alliance with the
wealthy Consul, even though the latter's
sexual proclivities were well known. Her
sister Julia's fate, also dictated by the family, had been even worse. Larthia had some
chance of autonomy if her grandfather
died, but Julia was trapped for thirty years
in the life of a perpetual virgin because
her father had not been man enough to

object when Casca put her name forward for the honor.

All of it was sordid, and none of it was fair.

"Decimus Gnaeus Casca awaits you in the atrium, mistress," the old slave Nestor announced from her bedroom doorway.

Larthia sighed and rose. She moved quickly through the vast house, which had been decorated tastefully and expensively by Sejanus' previous wife, and in which she still felt like a guest. She saw her grandfather waiting for her in the *atrium,* or entry hall, flanked by the masks of Sejanus' ancestors hanging on the frescoed walls.

Larthia bent and kissed the hand he offered. "Grandfather," she said. "Welcome."

Casca was in his sixties, older than any man had a right to be. His thin white hair barely covered his pink skull, and his elaborately draped toga was bleached snow white in order to make its purple border more vivid. Under it his tunic sleeves were fringed, and the tunic itself, visible at his waist, had two vertical bands of purple woven into the cloth.

Larthia found his affectations ridiculous. He was too ancient to be a dandy.

She led him inside to the *tablinum,* or parlor, where they reclined on a plush

couch, the carved arms of which were inlaid with African ivory.

"How is your health?" Larthia inquired.
It was the standard first question, and she
gestured for Nestor to come forward as
her grandfather recounted his recent visit
to a physician who prescribed juniper
wood wine for his sciatica.

"Would you like some refreshment?"
Larthia asked Casca, who shook his head.

She waved the servant back, and he
bowed his way out of the room.

They made small talk for a little while
longer, until Larthia grew impatient and
said, "Grandfather, why are you here? If
you've come to put forward another can-
didate for my remarriage, I'll say again
that I am not interested." She took great
satisfaction in resisting him as much as
she could. He would make sure she paid
for it if she did anything scandalous that
disgraced his name, but he couldn't legally force her to marry again.

At least Sejanus had left her that much.

Casca shook his head. "No. I have no
energy to spend on debating with you
now."

Larthia suspected she knew the reason.
He was too busy plotting against Caesar
to waste his time scrambling for influence
through marital intrigues. That had been

his occupation in former, more settled times.

"Well, then, what is it?"

"I have purchased a bodyguard for you."

Larthia stared at him. "A what?"

"You heard me."

"Grandfather, that's absurd. I have hundreds of slaves, several of them always accompany me when I go out, why do I need a bodyguard? Who would wish to do me harm?"

Casca rose and began to pace; he looked worried, and it crossed Larthia's mind for the first time that maybe the old man really did care about her.

"Do I have to instruct you about the current situation? Do you spend all of your time inspecting fabrics from Persia and grooming your hair with Jerusalem aloes? Rome is split into factions! I am not popular with some of them! They might take their differences with me out on you."

'Why don't you say what you mean? You're opposing the ruling faction, led by Caesar."

"Caesar is nothing less than a dictator. I want the Republic back," Casca said.

You hypocrite, Larthia thought. He wanted his own power back, and Hades

could take the Republic. Casca was jealous
of Caesar and always had been.

"Caesar doesn't want to be a king. He
thrice refused the crown proffered by
Mark Antony at the festival of the Lupercal," Larthia said reasonably.

"Caesar already is a king, he doesn't
need a crown to prove it," Casca replied
darkly.

Larthia sighed. "So your solution to this
internal strife is to buy some slave to follow
me around the shops and watch me buying
oysters from the fishmongers? Really,
Grandfather, I fear that you have lost your
mind."

"Not just some slave, Larthia. Verrix, a
prince of the Arverni."

"The who?"

"The Arverni, the Celtic tribe which
led the Gallic rebellion against Rome
eight years ago. This man was captured
near Vienne on the Rhone River when
their leader, Vercingetorix, was defeated.
Verrix escaped soon after by killing the
officer guarding the captives and was at
large until last autumn, when the centurion who had first captured him recognized him working on a construction gang
in the Quirinal. He was taken into custody and condemned to death, but escaped again only to find himself betrayed

to the authorities by a companion. He was scheduled for crucifixion when I found him."

"Why did you buy him? He sounds like a criminal," Larthia said with distaste.

"I bought him because he's tough and smart, and nothing is more important to him than his freedom."

"How much did you pay for him?" Larthia asked, playing along with the game.

"Five hundred denarii."

Larthia stared at him. He had paid a fortune for a condemned man. He really *must* be losing his mind.

"And what do you imagine will keep him from bolting again?" she asked logically.

"The promise of his freedom."

"I think he must know the value of Roman promises by now," Larthia said cynically.

"I have already drawn up the papers and filed them with the Vestals."

She looked at him.

"It's true," he said. "They specify that if he guards you for three years, and you are alive and well at the end of that time, he is to be freed. The emancipation papers will survive as part of my will if I die in the interim."

"Grandfather, this is nonsense! I am not taking this man into my household under any conditions, and that's final."

"Yes, you are, Larthia. If you refuse I will disinherit you and any children you might have."

"I don't need your money, old man. I have the fortune Sejanus left me."

"What about your male children? They will not be citizens if I refuse to recognize them, either in person through the acceptance rite or through my will."

Larthia eyed him levelly. That was the law, of course, another device for keeping Roman women in line.

"Why is this so important to you?" she demanded.

"I want something of my family to survive, Larthia. Julia will not have children, but you will."

So she was right. His motive was self-interest, after all. "You haven't succeeded in getting me married again, have you?" she pointed out to him.

"You'll marry again after I'm dead."

"You seem certain of that."

"I'm certain that you plan to hold out until I'm gone just to spite me."

Larthia looked away from him.

"You seem to think your resentment of the arrangements I made for you and your sister has been lost on me. It has not. But I did what I thought was necessary at the time. I am asking you to grant me this indulgence so I can rest easy knowing that your life is not in danger and my dynasty will endure."

"You obviously have great faith in this barbarian."

"I have great faith in his desire to be free. He'll guard you or the Greek Medusa if he knows that his slavery will be over at the end of it. He was a leader of his tribe, you know, fought us like a Nubian tiger from what I hear. The yoke of slavery sits very heavily on his shoulders."

"And he is just taking your word for it that you've already filed his emancipation papers with the Vestals?" Larthia inquired dubiously.

"He went with me when I did."

"He reads Latin?" she asked, surprised.

"He does now. He had eight years to learn."

Larthia shook her head obstinately. "I know I shall dislike giving up my privacy," she said.

"He's a slave, my dear. He'll be at your command, but I beg you to take him with you when you go abroad in the city. I did not want to tell you this, but I see you need convincing. There have been two attempts on my life, and I fear you may be next."

"Attempts on your life?" she whispered, listening closely now.

"Yes. And it is well known that you are the sole survivor of the Casca house likely to bear children and carry on the name. My sons are dead, my grandson, your cousin Gaius, was killed in Gaul, and Julia is a Vestal. Please do this for me."

Larthia was silent; she was stubborn enough, and angry enough at his past manipulations, to oppose the idea, but if her life really was in danger . . . She wasn't ready to cross the River Styx with the ferryman just yet.

"Well?" Casca said.

"You can send him to me."

"He's here, waiting in the *atrium.*"

"Already?"

"I felt certain I could convince you. I have the ownership papers ready to transfer him to you right now."

Larthia shook her head in amazement. The old man was always one step ahead of her.

"I suppose you should bring him in, then," she said wearily, with a gesture of defeat.

Casca stepped into the hall and signaled, and shortly thereafter a blond giant entered the room. He was followed nervously by Nestor, who as Larthia's master of slaves was clearly taken aback by this new addition to his staff.

Larthia waved Nestor into the corner of the room abruptly. She would deal with him later.

"Verrix, this is your new mistress, my granddaughter, Larthia Casca Sejana," Casca instructed the giant in Latin. "You will protect her with your life, as we have discussed. Your *fides*, loyalty, will be only to her now."

Verrix inclined his head, but Larthia had the uneasy feeling that she should be bowing to him. He carried himself regally, as if he were the master and she the slave. He was the most physically imposing human being she had ever seen, even though he was dressed in the long barbarian trousers Romans disdained, his homespun tunic belted at the waist. He was tall, taller than the average Roman to be sure, but it was the breadth of his shoulders and the solidity of his frame that made him seem bigger than he actually was. His hair was the color of ripe wheat, wavy and long, his brows and lashes a shade darker. They emphasized the brilliant blue of his eyes, the shade of rosemary, *rosmarinus*, the dew of the sea.

Larthia stared at him openly. She had often heard that the Celts of Gaul and Britain had beautiful eyes, and now she saw that it was true.

"Verrix," Larthia said finally, clearing her throat, aware that she should say something. "What does that name mean in your language?"

"High king," he replied, and somehow, even though he was barefoot and dressed in rags, the reply was appropriate.

"I understand that my grandfather saved you from imminent execution by paying an exorbitant amount for your life price," Larthia added.

"I would have taken my own life before suffering crucifixion," Verrix replied in excellent Latin, albeit with a slight guttural accent. "I heard what happened to my uncle Vercingetorix when he was led through the Roman streets in chains during Caesar's Gallic triumph, put on display like a Carthaginian elephant, and then murdered. I will determine the manner of my own death."

"Vercingetorix was your uncle?" Larthia asked, glancing at Casca. Both remembered the rebel chieftain who had led the Gallic tribes in revolt against Rome almost a decade earlier, posing the most significant threat to colonial rule the Republic had ever experienced. One of Larthia's most vivid childhood memories was of watching the parade of the conquered Gauls, their pale-haired leader in leg and foot irons, but proud still, staring back defiantly at the jeering Roman crowds rather than gazing at the ground in resignation like the rest of his people.

"I was given the short version of his name to honor him," Verrix replied.

"But you were able to escape when he was taken captive?" Larthia asked.

"He remained with the survivors in order to bargain for their lives. He instructed me to flee and return to the home camp in Gaul to secure reinforcements to launch a counterattack. By the time I got there it had been destroyed by the Aedui, Roman allies, who burned it to the ground."

"But surely it was unwise for you to return to Rome as a wanted man."

"My family was dead, my tribe destroyed. I had to live, but had no wish to remain where there were so many painful memories. I came here because it would have been unexpected. People generally fail to see what is right under their noses. There were so many Gauls in Rome after the war that I blended in with the crowd."

Larthia could not imagine him blending

into any crowd. "And you were at large until a short time ago? How did you live?" she asked.

"By my wits. I have a strong back; I was taken on as a day laborer by a builder from Ostia. I learned to read and write your language, and was prospering until a centurion recognized me and had me arrested for the murder of your Roman officer."

"The builder is Ammianus Paulinus," Casca said dryly. "He is notorious for hiring runaway slaves at cut wages, he never checks for freedman's papers. He is fined for it each time a new *aedile* takes office, but Paulinus gives the lowest bids for public structures so he stays in business."

"How were you caught?" Larthia asked Verrix.

"By chance. I was placing a cornerstone, and Paulinus called the centurion, who is an acquaintance of his, over to see the quality of the workmanship. The officer had been one of those in charge of the prisoners in Gaul during the rebellion; he was a friend of the man I killed. He recognized me."

"By your size?" Larthia asked.

"And this," Verrix replied, touching the thin twisted band of bronze which encircled his muscular neck, the rounded ends of which stopped just short of meeting at the base of his throat. Larthia could see a pulse beating there, steadily, strongly.

"What is that?" she said.

"My torque. It denotes my tribe and clan. The Roman soldier recalled it from our last meeting."

"Does it come off?" she asked.

"Never."

"Who betrayed you to the authorities after you escaped the second time?"

"A woman," he said shortly.

Larthia exchanged a glance with Casca. "Is she still alive?" she asked Verrix dryly.

"As far as I know," he replied coolly.

Verrix and Larthia were eyeing each other warily, like two sparring partners.

"Do you have any further questions?" Casca asked his granddaughter impatiently.

"Very well," Larthia said to the slave suddenly, ignoring the older man. "You will accompany me when I go abroad and protect me, and also undertake whatever duties Nestor assigns to you within the house. Understood?"

Verrix inclined his head.

"Where have you been living?"

"In the *insulae* behind the Via Sacra."

"Nestor will send someone over there to pack your things," Larthia told him.

"That will not be necessary, mistress,"

Nestor said, speaking for the first time. "He brought a bundle with him."

Verrix suddenly looked at Casca, as one equal might gaze at another.

"When does my term of three years begin to run?" he asked the older man.

"Today," Casca replied.

"Three years of me may be more than you can stand," Larthia said slyly.

"I can stand three years of anyone to be free. If I run again, you will only look for me, especially since your father's father paid such a high price for me. If I stay the term I need never look over my shoulder again."

"Three years is a long time," Casca said.

"More so to you than to me, Consular Casca. I am young yet. I have time."

Larthia waved her hand dismissively, ending the exchange. "Nestor, take Verrix to the slave quarters and give him the single room nearest the kitchen. See that Helena gets him something else to wear and some food to eat. I expect to go shopping near the forum in the morning. You may begin your duties then, Verrix."

Nestor looked dubious, but did as he was told. Once the two slaves had left,

Larthia said to her grandfather sharply, "He's arrogant, that Celt."

"So much the better. A cowed slave would flinch at every shadow. This one is bold."

"I'm sure he's dangerous, too. He was wanted for murder, wasn't he?"

"He killed his captor to escape during wartime. Any Roman soldier would have done the same."

"Why are you defending him?"

"I was not defending, merely explaining." Casca adjusted the shoulder drape of his toga fussily. "Well, I must be off to the baths to refresh myself for the evening. I am dining with Marcus Junius Brutus tonight."

Larthia nodded expressionlessly. Her grandfather's influential friends had never impressed her.

"I hope you will be satisfied with my gift," he said, and bent to press his cool lips to her forehead.

Larthia accepted the kiss without moving and then watched as Casca left the room.

What did the old man mean by placing this giant in her household? Her grandfather was so devious that she couldn't take his word for the coming sunrise. Was he telling the truth when he said he merely wanted to protect her?

What, exactly, was Casca up to?

Verrix looked around the spare room he had been assigned and then sat cross-legged on the floor. The cell was the size of an incense box, but at least it was all his. He had passed the main slave quarters with Nestor, and that room was set up like a huge dormitory, long rows of beds with just a thin curtain separating them. He assumed he had been given this spot so that he could be on call for the mistress at all times without disturbing anyone else. It had the disadvantage of being right next to the kitchen; he could hear the cooks in there banging pots while preparing the evening meal. But after seven years on a construction gang he was impervious to noise and didn't care where he slept.

Verrix was surprised, in fact, to find himself still alive. He had prepared for death so often since the failure of the Gallic rebellion when he was eighteen, that to slip away from Cerberus one more time made him all the more determined to survive. And now the prospect of freedom dangled before him tantalizingly, like the fox's grapes hanging just out of reach. But to grasp the prize he had to keep that little minx alive for three years, and during that time he just might kill her himself.

Larthia was a type he particularly disliked. Most Roman women were kept behind closed doors and under the thumbs of their husbands, but the wealthy widow was the conspicuous exception. In his years of observing Roman culture he had seen such matrons out on the town many times, leading an entourage of slaves and ordering all of them about curtly. It made him recall with a pang the women of his tribe, working alongside the men even when heavy with child, valiant to the last when the Romans and their minions swept across the river and razed everything. All of them were gone now, most dead, the survivors scattered like himself.

No, he didn't care much for Larthia Casca Sejana, but he would keep her breathing in order to get the emancipation papers that were his only escape from a future of slavery. He had known the situation when Casca bought him. The only surprise was the physical appearance of the lady in question. He still confused Latin suffixes, had thought she was

Casca's daughter at first, and so had expected a fortyish matron with grown children, not a slender slip of a girl years younger than himself. She must have been married off when she was hardly out of childhood to a monied old coot; he had learned that was the custom with the Roman aristocracy. Now she had her husband's fortune, his massive house, his troops of slaves; but she had her grandfather, too, standing on her neck and making sure she didn't stir off the mark. So she spent her time throwing money away on trifles and growing more irritable and dissipated by the day.

Verrix stood abruptly at a knock on his door. It swung open immediately.

"Come with me," Nestor said, jerking his gray head in the direction of the kitchen. "I want you to help me stoke the stove. You have a strong young back and mine was bent long ago."

Verrix followed the stooped and shuffling man, who had grown old in the service of the Casca family and had then come with Larthia to her husband's house when she married.

Verrix understood that his new life was about to begin.

* * *

Marcus entered the luxurious atrium of the Gracchus estate on the Palatine and handed his helmet and cloak to a bowing servant. The impressively large house was of concrete faced with stone, rectangular in shape, with two floors. Its entry hall roof was open to the stars appearing through a skylight, and to the left the room was lined with cupboards containing masks of the Gracchus ancestors cast in wax. Ranged all around the walls were costly vases and Oriental tapestries, and underfoot was a mosaic of intricate pattern, many tiny tiles inlaid with mortar depicting a pastoral scene of gamboling nymphs and shepherds. Marcus followed the servant through the hall into the *tablinum*, a slightly raised open parlor flanked on either side by the *alae*, alcoves which contained shrines to the *Lares*, household gods.

Senator Gracchus and his son awaited Marcus in the *tablinum*, where they reclined on brocade couches, golden cups in hand. Marcus looked around at the engraved twin candelabra sitting on a side table inlaid with lapis and decorated with green enamel intaglio. The intricately frescoed walls, the hanging tapestry depicting Minerva springing full grown from the brow of Zeus and the waist-high

Greek urn painted with a scene of the mythical Minotaur filled out the room's decor. He smiled at Septimus as he joined the two other men.

"Greetings, my friend. I must say I am dismayed to find you in such miserable surroundings."

Septimus laughed. "Quite a change from those rainy camps in Gaul where we shivered under canvas, eh?" he said.

Marcus nodded, accepting a cup from another servant who appeared instantly from a side door. "Where is the rest of the company?" he asked.

"Already in the dining room with my wife," the Senator answered. "Septimus thought it would be more pleasant to have a short time alone here before joining the crowd. He says you're something of a celebrity and often get pawed by admirers."

"Septimus exaggerates," Marcus replied shortly, taking a sip from his cup.

"Oh, I don't know," Gracchus said. "My wife conducts a sophisticated salon, and she's invited half of Rome here to view the conquering hero. You might be considerably more popular than you had anticipated."

Marcus shot Septimus a desperate look which communicated volumes.

"Now, Father, don't scare him off, you'll

give Marcus the impression he's going to be the centerpiece at dinner," Septimus put in hastily.

"Am I?" Marcus asked pointedly.

"Of course not. Please pay no attention to my father. You're here as my guest, to enjoy yourself and nothing more," Septimus said jovially.

"How do you like the wine, boy?" Senator Gracchus asked Marcus.

"Very good," Marcus replied.

"How would you know, Corvus, you never drink," Septimus grinned.

"You could drink less, it wouldn't hurt you," the Senator observed sharply to his son.

"Oh, I could never aspire to the perfection enjoyed by my friend here," Septimus responded, taking a long swallow of his wine. "He is a true Greek in spirit, faithful to his family name. 'Everything in moderation.' "

"Except warfare," Senator Gracchus said.

"And love," Septimus added sagely. "Isn't that what young Horace says?"

"Oh, that stripling Horace, another friend of Brutus. I am tired of that gang and their mouthpiece, Cicero," the Senator said.

"But you will stay on good terms with them, as well as with Caesar's group."

Septimus smiled wickedly. "My father remains neutral in all political controversies, Marcus. That is how he hangs on to his money."

"A wise course," Marcus said.

"But you are Caesar's partisan, I understand." Gracchus directed the comment to Marcus.

"He was and is my general, Senator Gracchus. I owe him a soldier's loyalty."

"He's much more than a general now," Gracchus said. "In our country politicians have always done military duty. I remember when Cicero was consul of Cilicia before the late Sejanus took over that territory. But Caesar aspires to more, he already calls himself Imperator."

"Any victorious general may claim that title," Marcus said testily.

"True, but it is also an indication of his ambitions. When he shared power with Crassus and Pompey he was more amenable to compromise. Now that he is alone I'm afraid the time will soon come when we all have to choose sides, and that will be a very bad day for Rome."

The Senator's wife entered the room, saying, "Here you are, Marcus. Everyone has been looking for you. And how handsome you are in your uniform!"

"Good evening, Lady Gracchus," Marcus said.

"I told him not to wear his toga because I wanted the women to see his legs," Septimus teased.

"You are not amusing," his mother said sternly, motioning for the men to rise. She was a handsome woman in her late forties, wearing a sleeveless tunic of coral silk with a deep, rounded neck which left her slim arms bare. The *diploidion* draped over one shoulder and fastened with a pearl-studded brooch was of a lighter peach color, complementing her fair complexion. Her hair was elaborately dressed, pulled back from her face into a heavy braid around the crown of her head and then falling in a sweep of curls onto her neck. She extended her hand to Marcus graciously as he approached her.

"For you," he said, handing her the amphora of Pompeiian *garum*.

"Oh, how nice! Thank you, Marcus, you are always so thoughtful. I've taken charge of the seating arrangements myself, my steward always disappoints me with his plans," she said, tucking his arm through hers. "I've tried to put you with amusing people, but of course one never knows. I hope the dinner won't be too interminable, but we'll have a chance to chat together afterward. You can tell me what my son has been up to, it's the only way I have of finding out his doings. He never talks to me."

She led the way to the more sumptuous of the mansion's two dining rooms; the one at the front of the house, off the atrium, was for entertaining large groups, and the smaller one at the back near the kitchen was for family dining. As Marcus entered the formal dining room, called the *triclinium,* or "room with three couches," he saw that everyone else was already reclining on the silk-trimmed settees, awaiting the first course. The usual dining room seated nine, with three diners on each couch using a central table, but as this was designed for large parties there were at least fifteen couches in the hall and close to fifty guests. The hall itself was marble floored, with Doric columns supporting the roof at regular intervals. The walls were hung with embroidered tapestries and lit by flaring torches. Slaves in the blue livery of the house of Gracchus bustled about filling cups, as the guests were already indulging and at such gatherings the wine was frequently of more interest than the food.

Marcus was placed with Septimus and another of his friends, Caelius, while one Cytheris, an actress, and Terentia, the older sister of Septimus, were seated at either end of the couch. Only the men reclined during dinner; the women remained seated. As the first course, cold boar with pickled vegetables, was handed round, it became clear to Marcus that Septimus and his mother had engaged in some not too subtle matchmaking. Septimus spent the whole time talking to his sister and his friend, forcing Marcus to make polite conversation with Cytheris on his left. Several times Marcus saw Septimus glancing over to see how things were going.

To outward appearances, they were going well enough. Cytheris was a henna-rinsed, sloe-eyed beauty who had made a name for herself performing the old comedies of Plautus. Smiling congenially, Marcus listened to accounts of the woman's recent stage triumphs while he passed up a stew of oysters and turbot and shrimp, served with a vinegar and white pepper relish. The main dish, a peacock roasted in its feathers, was followed by wild fowl stuffed with corn and garnished with goose liver, shoulder of hare, and broiled blackbirds with wood pigeons. The parade of food, carried to the tables on platters by a stream of servants, seemed endless, and Marcus finally rose, made his excuses to his companion, and strolled around to the extensive gardens at the back of the house.

This pleasant retreat was walled off from neighbors by a dense cane hedge and overhung by a large portico. The park was filled with marble statues, splashing fountains, and topiary trees, its rows of flowers and evergreen shrubs bordered by paved walking paths. It was a restful place, and Marcus lingered there, thinking, until he heard a step behind him and turned to see Septimus.

"What are you doing hiding out here?" his friend demanded. "Dessert is being served, honey glazed pastry filled with crushed mulberries. My mother's cook is very proud of it."

"I'm not hiding. I just wanted to get away from that din in there and enjoy the night air. The women are so smothered in perfume, and the torch wax so impregnated with incense, that I could hardly breathe."

Septimus leaned against a polished column supporting the portico and sighed. "Well, you've left Cytheris high and dry. I don't think that's ever happened to her before tonight, she seems quite bemused. I can't believe you abandoned her. Don't you think she's pretty?"

"Everyone thinks she's pretty. Everyone's slept with her, too. She's a notorious tart, Septimus, haven't you heard?"

"Of course I have. That's why I had Mother place you next to her. When did you become such a prig, Marcus? I thought she would show you a good time!"

"I don't want a good time."

"Then you *need* one. You've been so morose lately I just wanted to give you an opportunity to relax. I remember sporting with you in any number of brothels, I didn't know you had turned celibate. At least Cytheris is on the stage, not the street."

"There seems to be little difference in her case. Granius Metellus says he got the pox from her."

"Oh, that's just a story Granius tells. I think he says things like that to disguise his real preference, and it isn't for fullgrown women."

Marcus shrugged dismissively. "It doesn't matter. I was not rude to her, Septimus, I just needed to be alone."

Septimus put his hand on Marcus' shoulder. "What is wrong? Is there something I can do to help?"

Marcus looked at him. "Perhaps there is."

Septimus waited.

"Do you know the upcoming schedule of the Vestal Virgins?" Marcus asked.

"The schedule of the Vestal Virgins?" Septimus repeated stupidly, staring at him.

"Yes, when they perform the sacrifices, when they travel to the sacred spring for water, you know what I mean. Your father is the Senate counsel to the Vestals, isn't he? Can you get the information for me?"

"Why in the name of Jove do you want to know?" Septimus demanded.

"I am interested."

"So it would seem. What, may I ask, is responsible for this new devotion to the goddess Vesta?"

Marcus was silent.

"Did you meet a woman while observing public sacrifice at the temple?" Septimus inquired. Then his expression changed. "Marcus, you must be joking. Not one of the virgins!"

"Yes. I met her when I went to the Aedes with Caesar to change his will."

Septimus merely stared at him in amazement.

"Don't look at me that way. I want to see her again. Will you help me?"

"Corvus, you are deranged. Put her out of your mind. The idea is impossible."

"I haven't done anything. I just want to observe her from a distance."

"To what purpose? To torment your-self? There is no future in it, my friend. If you defile a Vestal, *she* will be buried alive for breaking her vows, and even your illustrious army career will not save *you*. I don't care how many successful cam-paigns you have seen or how many times you have received the laurel or carried the bay leaf in a triumph, the Senate and the magistrates will give you a life sentence to the mines in Numidia! And you will be expected to throw yourself on your sword, unable to bear the shame of it."

"You're getting a bit ahead of things, Septimus. I want to have another look at her, that's all."

"And moon around the temple like a lovesick schoolboy? That will undoubtedly enhance your glorious reputation."

"Watching a public sacrifice will hardly be making a spectacle of myself. There is always a crowd at such events, and I will be one of many."

Septimus shook his head. "I don't like it, Marcus."

"Can you do it?"

Septimus shrugged.

"Well?"

"A copy of the Vestals' schedule is on my father's desk. He gets it every term to coordinate the Senate sessions with their events."

"May I see it?"

Septimus stared into the distance and sighed.

"Septimus?"

The tribune shook his head. "I know I will be sorry I ever got involved in this."

"I only need to see it briefly."

Septimus held his finger under Marcus' nose. "I have to put it back before dinner is over, I don't want him to miss it."

Marcus nodded.

"Wait here."

Marcus stood looking out over the garden for what seemed like a long time before he heard Septimus return. He whirled to see his friend holding a sheet of parchment covered with the careful lettering of a Greek scribe. He snatched it.

"Careful with that!" Septimus hissed.

Marcus held the paper up to the light of a torch burning in a corner of the portico.

"She's sacrificing tomorrow morning at dawn and going to the spring in five days," he said.

Septimus peered over his shoulder, matching up the times with the names. "Julia Rosalba Casca?" he whispered.

Marcus handed him the paper.

"You are truly insane, Marcus. Do you have any idea who she is?"

"The loveliest woman I have ever seen."

"The most dangerous woman you have ever seen. She's the younger daughter of the late Tullius Casca and the grand-daughter of Decimus Gnaeus Casca, Caesar's great enemy!"

"I care nothing for politics, Septimus, surely you must know that."

"You'll care if it comes to civil war, as it certainly may. Aside from the fact that she's a Vestal, and untouchable for that reason, she's allied with the house and family of your mentor's bitterest rival."

Marcus said nothing.

Septimus held up his hand. "I will not be a party to this madness."

"I'm not asking you to be a party to anything. You have done enough just getting me this information."

"And I should return it before dinner is over," Marcus said, casting a glance back toward the house. He took a step and then hesitated. "Marcus, be careful. I am not joking. This is serious business."

"I understand that," Marcus said.

"I don't think you do. You were not raised in Rome, and you don't know the reverence given to the Vestals or the extreme outrage which follows when one of them is accused of wrongdoing. I saw a Vestal buried alive at the Campus Sceleratus when I was a young boy, and believe me, I have never forgotten it. She was convicted on the testimony of slaves, slaves who can be bribed, who can be tortured until they will say almost anything, but nothing could save her. It was a truly horrible death."

"I will not put the Rosalba in danger," Marcus said softly. "I just want to see her."

Both of them heard a sound from inside and Septimus held his finger to his lips, then slipped back into the house through a side door. Marcus smiled and nodded when the slave who had made the noise came out and threw a pan of water into the garden.

Then he went back to his thoughts.

Julia bent her head as Margo draped the *suffibulum*, a rectangular piece of white cloth bordered by a purple stripe, over her head and then fastened it on her breast with an ornamented brooch. The servant straightened the veil and then stepped back, nodding her approval.

"You are ready. Go now, and walk quickly. Dawn will be breaking soon."

Julia left her suite, picking up her temple guard as she walked through the Atrium and then through the altar door of the temple. Inside a crowd had already gathered, even though the first streaks of red were just showing in the sky and it would be several minutes before the light streamed through the rose window in the stuccoed ceiling and slanted onto the altar.

Then the sacrifice could begin.

The salt cakes and wine and oil were already in place near the sacred fire, which burned brightly at the foot of a three times life-size statue of the goddess. Julia took her place in front of the altar and bowed her head, waiting for the rays of the sun to fall into place and allow her to begin.

When the moment came, she raised her arms, and a hush fell over the expectant crowd. She began to chant the prayers for the safety of the Roman state as she broke up the cakes and dropped the pieces into the fire, which consumed them immediately. Then she poured wine, followed by oil, onto the fire, stepping back as the flames leaped up and she felt their warmth on her skin. The crowd responded with a murmur of awe.

Julia bowed low and continued the prayers until the fire died down again, then sprinkled the altar with spring water, a ceremonial cleansing that was performed at each new moon. At the conclusion of the sacrifice she lay prostrate before the altar and begged Vesta to protect all Roman citizens, wherever in the world they might be, and then rose to turn and face the crowd, a signal that they might then petition the goddess for their personal intentions.

At the front of the group, taller than everyone else and dressed in full uniform, was the centurion she had seen at the revising of Caesar's will.

Julia held his gaze for a long moment, her heart beginning to pound, and then deliberately looked away. She forced her gaze to include the whole assembly before she turned back to the altar, bowed, and then exited into the hall which led to the Atrium.

Once there, she leaned against the wall, feeling weak and disoriented.

Why had he come? She had never seen him at a sacrifice before. Was it a coincidence or was he there because they had met in the recording room of the Aedes? And if that was so, what did he hope to accomplish by viewing her sacrifice?

He must know that any relationship between them was impossible.

But she knew it, and she was still trembling like a cornered hare, so much so that her temple guards were staring at her with concern.

She waved them away, then gathered her skirts into her hands and ran all the way back to her room.

Three

Verrix lounged at the entrance to the stall where Larthia was having her portrait painted, his tall frame blocking the sun.

"Will you tell that barbarian to move?" the artist said testily to Larthia. "I can't even see what I'm doing."

"Verrix, stand to one side so that Endymion can take advantage of the light," Larthia called obediently to her bodyguard.

Verrix took two steps to the left and resumed his watchful pose, his eyes on the street. Endymion mixed two colors on his palette to achieve the shade he wanted and asked in a low tone, "Where did you get him?"

Larthia sighed. "My grandfather bought him for me."

"Why?"

"He's supposed to be protecting me

from Casca's enemies," Larthia replied resignedly.

"Well, Jove knows the old man has plenty of those," Endymion said. He tilted Larthia's chin up and added, "What did you call him just then?"

"Verrix."

The Greek rolled his eyes. "Rix, rax, rux, they all have names like that, they're flooding into Rome from the Gallic colonies every day. Even when they supposedly speak Latin I can't understand a word they're saying."

Larthia laughed. "Who are you to talk? You're from Crete and have an accent yourself."

The Greek freedman shrugged. "At least I'm not a slave anymore, and I have a marketable skill. These people are just a burden on the tax rolls, they work for almost nothing so that Roman citizens suffer."

Verrix, who could surely hear some of their conversation, maintained a neutral expression as his eyes methodically scanned the street.

"He would make a good model, though," Endymion added, eyeing the slave judiciously. "He's perfectly proportioned. I don't suppose you'd lend him out to me for my sculpture class."

Larthia shot the artist a sidelong glance.

"Endymion, his job is to protect my body, not display his own. You'll have to find some other unfortunate who will pose for the meager wages you pay."

"Pity," Endymion said, daubing paint on his canvas. "I'm going to be as successful as Praxiteles one day and getting a reputation as my model could make him famous."

"Not everyone wants to be famous," Larthia replied, her tone muted.

"No?"

"No, Endymion. Some of us just want to be happy."

Verrix shifted his blue gaze from the bustling street to his mistress' face, but she was gazing into the distance, maintaining her "model" pose.

"There, I think that should do it," Endymion said with satisfaction. "We'll let that set, and then if you come back in three days I'm sure I can finish it."

"May I just have a peek at it?" Larthia asked.

"No. You can't see it until it's finished." Endymion recapped his vials of vegetable tints and dropped his fur-tipped brushes into a cup. "But I do think you will be very pleased."

"Let's hope the tanners' guild will be very pleased. They're paying for it."

"Oh, yes, that's right, I'd forgotten. Are you their new patroness?"

"My husband was their patron before he died. I'm continuing the tradition."

"You don't sound very happy about it," Endymion commented, wiping his hands on a cloth and dropping a cover over the painting. The wet paint was protected by a wooden frame which kept the cover from touching it.

"Every guild in Rome is clamoring for my patronage," Larthia replied, standing and shaking out the skirt of her gown. "It's not my name they want, but the Sejanus money."

"They want both, Lady Sejana. Finances and publicity are equally important to ambitious tradesmen."

"Speaking of finances, don't forget the discount you promised me for coming to your stall."

"You'll get it. Letting the passersby see you sitting here posing is worth far more to me than painting you in the comfort of your parlor."

Larthia nodded wearily, picking up the hem of her *diploidion* and tossing it over her shoulder. "I will see you in three days, Endymion, first thing in the morning."

Endymion bowed.

Verrix stepped aside as Larthia moved past him, out of the artist's stall and into the busy street. She walked a short distance and then stopped to examine a pile of silks displayed on a broad wooden table.

"When did these come in?" she said to the tradesman, a dark-eyed Parthian with a curling black beard and a tiered and braided headdress.

"Just this morning, mistress," he replied in execrable Latin, bowing.

Verrix stood behind Larthia, his arms folded, as she examined the bolts of cloth.

"What color is this?" she asked, holding up a sample of material.

"Lapis lazuli, my lady Sejana, and may I say you honor my humble establishment with your presence. The cloth is dyed with the ink of the tentacled sea creature called *oktopous* by the Greeks. The dye is very fast and makes a beautiful shade."

Larthia handed the bolt of cloth to Verrix, who looked startled, then sullen as he shoved the rolled material under his arm.

"And this?" Larthia asked, fingering a small piece of cloth of gold.

"Ah, a fine choice, you have excellent taste, my lady. That piece was handmade by my wife, interweaving the silk with the gold threads on her own loom."

"How much for both pieces?" Larthia asked.

"Three sesterces," the Parthian said rapidly.

Larthia shook her head.

"Two," the tradesman said.

"One," Larthia offered.

"Done."

Larthia removed the silver coin from the drawstring purse at her waist and handed it over, then accepted the second bolt of cloth and gave it to Verrix. He added it to the first one, his face set. Larthia walked on to the fruit stall next door and poked a pile of dates to test for ripeness.

"From Galilee," the fruit seller said, hovering. "The most succulent, from the choicest palm trees."

Larthia made her purchases, walking along the lane from stall to stall, handing everything she bought to Verrix. By the time she returned to her litter his arms were loaded.

She climbed into the litter and settled back, pulling the curtains closed. In the next instant a curtain was whipped back again and Verrix had dumped her purchases in her lap.

The two bearers looked at one another in astonishment and then away, waiting for Lathia's reaction.

"What are you doing?" she gasped.

"What does it look like?" Verrix responded.

Larthia glared at him, opened her mouth, then remembered the presence of the other servants.

"I'll deal with you later," she said shortly. To the bearers, she directed, "Take me home."

Verrix walked behind the litter as the bearers wove their way back to the Sejanus estate. Once Larthia was ensconced on a couch in her *tablinum* she dismissed the other servants and then said to Verrix in a deadly tone, "What was the meaning of that rebellious display in the forum?"

"My purpose is to protect you from harm, not to trot at your heels like your little dog carrying whatever trinkets might catch your eye."

"Your purpose is to do whatever I tell you to do!" Larthia responded angrily. "In Gaul you may have been a prince, my arrogant giant, but in this house you are a slave!"

"I am very aware of my position in this house," he replied stonily.

"I don't think you are," Larthia said,

rising from the couch. "I could have you flogged for this, or prescribe any other punishment I choose, even sell you."

"You won't sell me," Verrix replied.

Larthia gaped at him, unable to comprehend such insolence. "Oh, no?" she finally managed to croak.

"My presence is keeping your grandfather off your back. And more than that, you need me. You are afraid."

Larthia swallowed, her eyes locked with his.

"Afraid of what?" she said.

"Afraid that Casca might be right, and you are the target of his enemies. I have been in Rome some time, and I know that these politicians employ gangs of young ruffians to do their bidding. The toughs roam the streets at night and hang about the centers of commerce during the day, studying the habits of their victims. We saw one such group today near the Via Sacra. Were they following you? Did you notice them?"

Larthia's eyes narrowed. "You are not the only bodyguard in Rome," she said quietly. "Every colonial rousted from his homeland by the recent wars is looking for a job."

"But I am the only one who has your grandfather's confidence, and again the only one so highly motivated by the thought of his potential freedom that he would die to protect you," Verrix responded evenly.

Larthia stared back at him, silenced.

Verrix waited patiently.

"You do think you have me at a disadvantage, don't you?" she finally observed quietly, forcing herself to hold his cool blue gaze directly.

"No, mistress," he replied. "I think I have an accurate understanding of our relative positions, and yours is still far superior to mine."

Larthia took a deep breath, then exhaled slowly. "Just so you understand that," she said firmly.

He bowed his head.

"I am dining with my sister at the Atrium Vestae this evening," Larthia continued. "You will accompany me there. You are dismissed until then."

Verrix bowed again and backed out of the room.

Larthia resumed her seat slowly, staring at the space where the slave had been.

"So, did you see her?" Septimus asked, sitting on the edge of the pool as a slave scraped his back with a strigil.

"I saw her," Marcus replied, rolling over in the steaming water and pushing his wet hair back from his face.

"And?"

"And she is incredibly lovely," Marcus said.

Both men were naked. They were lolling in a pool fed by a stone pipe emerging from an exterior wall and heated by a hypocaust extending beneath the floor of the bath. Under his feet Marcus could feel the scraping of coins tossed into the spring outside as an offering to the deity of the baths and then carried inside with the rush of water. The goddess Minerva, depicted holding an owl and helmeted for war in a carving on the bronze dome above their heads, was the target of this largesse. It was an act of extreme impiety, punishable by the gods, to remove any of the money.

Marcus rubbed his arms briskly; the air was getting just a trifle chilly, and he sank into the water. The domed ceiling could be raised or lowered to control the room's temperature. The walls surrounding the men were lined with ceramic tiles, and the floor skirting the edge of the pool was terra-cotta flagged. Slaves stood at the ready to scrape the bathers' skin clean, hand out towels, or perform a massage in the adjoining cool room.

"So what's the next step?" Septimus asked. "Looking for a prostitute who resembles her?"

Marcus said nothing to this standard advice; he merely leaned back on his elbows at the edge of the pool and watched the steam rising off the water.

"I'm going to the Suburra tonight," Septimus added, extending an arm for the slave to scrape. "Why don't you come with me? I hear there are some new offerings from Phrygia. They're said to be quite tasty."

Marcus shook his head.

Septimus grabbed a towel from the slave's arm and threw it at his friend. "You are no fun anymore! You've become such a tiresome bore since you saw that woman. I'm going in for a massage. Are you coming?"

"I think I'll soak here a while longer," Marcus replied, closing his eyes.

"I'll meet you in the changing room, then," Septimus said, turning away.

"No, on the western terrace," Marcus contradicted. "I want a cup of wine."

"I hope you're not taking to drink over this girl," Septimus called jokingly. He stood and walked into the *tepidarium,* the slave padding softly after him. There he stretched out on a stone slab and the slave began to pound his flesh rhythmically.

Marcus sank beneath the surface of the water again, sighing as the hot water soothed his aching muscles. He and Septimus had spent the early afternoon playing handball on the Campus Martius, then relaxing in the solarium of the baths, the southern terrace which allowed the sun to caress the tan-worshipping Romans to a golden brown. A brown skin was associated with health and virility, linked as it was to a soldier's outdoor life, and a pallid complexion was the sign of effeminacy.

The solaria all over the city were very busy.

Marcus finally emerged from the water and, bypassing the *tepidarium* where Septimus reclined, walked to the cold pool and rinsed off briskly. Then he headed to the lockers to dress. He slipped into his uniform quickly, nodding briefly to other bathers who caught his eye in the crush of men. Once dressed, he went outside to the western-facing terrace and sought a vendor, buying a cup of golden wine from the Abruzzi district of Italy. He sipped it slowly, watching the sun sink below the hills as the departing crowd chattered behind him, heading home for the evening meal.

What was he going to do? He could not forget the Vestal; his visit to the temple that morning had inflamed his itch rather than soothed it. Even swathed in the heavy veil she wore for sacrificing, she was so ethereally beautiful that the sight of her took his breath away.

He had a plan, but it would draw him deeper into dangerous territory, and the rational side of his nature counseled against putting it into action. Still, the mental debate was mostly an exercise; no matter what his good sense told him, he knew that he had to speak to her, touch her, turn her pristine image into reality.

He had seen the Vestals' schedule. He knew that she would be going to the sacred spring near the Porta Capena again in just three days. Although she would surely be guarded, her companions shouldn't be much of a problem for a man like himself, who'd been victorious in hand-to-hand combat against all manner of opponents for the last decade.

Marcus knew the route, and the exact spot where he could intercept her.

He drained his wooden cup, then returned the vessel to the vendor, who

scoured it with sand and rinsed it with
water before setting it back on his rack.
When Marcus turned away he saw Septimus coming toward him, his hand raised
in greeting.

Marcus smiled at his friend, resolved to
keep his scandalous thoughts to himself.

"Margo, did you get these lampreys from
the *piscinae* on my grandfather's estate?"
Julia asked, examining the platters of food
set out for the *gustatio*, or appetizer. "My
sister is especially fond of those."

"I did exactly as you requested, mistress," Margo replied patiently, as Julia
fluttered around the anteroom of her
suite in the Atrium Vestae, making sure
that everything was in readiness for
Larthia's visit. The Vestals were not permitted many guests, so this was a special
occasion. Only female relatives could be
received in a Vestal's private apartment;
male relatives and all others had to be
seen in the common room off the main
hall, in the presence of Livia Versalia or
Junia Distania, the official greeter. A
chance like this to talk in private with
someone close to her own age was a rare
treat for Julia.

"And the honeyed wine?" Julia said.

Margo indicated the ornamental jug on the table. "Are you sure you don't want me to remain and serve you?" she asked.

"No," Julia said firmly. "I am perfectly capable of pouring wine and passing a tray of sweetmeats across a table. You may retire to your room."

Margo bowed and retreated, and seconds later Junia Distania entered with Larthia fast on her heels.

"Little Rosalba, how well you are looking!" Larthia said, embracing her sister and kissing her on both cheeks. Junia bowed and left, and Larthia looked over her shoulder to make sure she was gone before saying, "I don't know how you can bear it here, this place is loaded with spies."

Julia made a face. "Larthia, how you exaggerate." She indicated a chair of carved mahogany drawn up to the serving table, and Larthia sat in it.

"Do I? What about that servant of yours who is always lurking in the shadows, taking notes?"

"I dismissed Margo for the evening."

"Good." Larthia reached for a shelled walnut and popped it into her mouth. "This place is deadly dull, Julia, I always feel like I'm entering a tomb when I come here. How do you tolerate such a cloistered existence?"

Julia sat across from her sister and said dryly, "I have no choice. Do you have anything else complimentary to say before I pour the wine?"

Larthia shrugged dismissively. "You know how I've always felt about your life being tossed away in the service of some statue in a temple," she commented.

"Lower your voice," Julia hissed. "Such statements can be construed as heresy, not to mention treason. And my life has not been tossed away; I'm still breathing."

Larthia reached for a silver serving spoon and helped herself to several of the eels. "You can't tell me you're happy here," she said insistently.

Julia did not reply as she lifted the jug of Falernian wine and poured it into two goblets. Larthia picked up her cup and sipped from it gingerly, then took a bigger drink.

"Very good," she said approvingly, nodding. "I like honeyed wine."

Julia nodded. "It was too strong, the Falernian generally is, so I asked Margo to temper it."

Larthia sat back and surveyed her sister, a younger, more sanguine version of herself. "You must be wondering why I sent word that I wanted to come and see you."

Julia waited.

"Our grandfather has supplied me with a bodyguard," Larthia said.

"What, a slave?"

"A slave."

"You already have hundreds of slaves, Larthia, what do you mean?"

"He's a Gaul, to be exact, but his assignment is to watch over me when I go out to make sure I don't come to harm."

Julia stared at her sister. "Is someone trying to hurt you?" she asked.

"According to grandfather, it's a possibility."

"Why?"

"His politics, and I suppose my late husband's. Caesar's faction is growing in power every day, soon he will be sole dictator in name as well as practice. Casca thinks that the Caesarian gangs could go after me to get to him. The Senators and the other politicians are too well protected, but a lone woman out shopping with just a set of bearers and an old man like Nestor might be a target."

"Have things gotten that bad?" Julia murmured.

Larthia shrugged. "Apparently so."

"Caesar doesn't seem that ruthless," Julia said.

"He hasn't gotten where he is with displays of kindness. He eliminates without a qualm anyone who stands in his way." Larthia swallowed another sip of her wine appreciatively. "How do you know him?"

"He's been to the temple a few times to file and amend his will. The last time he came I took the dictation."

"You took Caesar's dictation? Aren't you a little young for that distinction?"

Julia smiled. "Livia Versalia found herself unprepared. Caesar came on short notice, and I was the only one available."

"What is he like in close quarters? I've only seen him at banquets when my husband was alive. He just greeted the women and then moved off to talk politics with the men, so it was difficult to judge his personality."

"I was only with him a short time myself, but it's clear he's . . . powerful. With the Vestals he was very charming and courtly, of course."

Larthia nodded. "That's the type you have to watch. Did he come alone?"

Julia rose from the table and turned away, fiddling with a water jug on a stand nearby. "No, he had a centurion of the first cohort with him."

"The Raven?" Larthia said, sitting up alertly. "That Greek aide of his? What's his name? Demeter!"

"Yes," Julia replied, not meeting her sister's eyes.

"Isn't he something? They say there's hardly a space on his body that isn't marked from some campaign." She chuckled. "Quite a few ladies in Rome would like to find out for themselves."

Julia turned back to the table with the water jug. As she added some liquid to her cup the jug flew out of her hand and splashed to the floor.

Larthia bent immediately to help her, staying her hand as Julia began to pick up the pieces of the shattered terra-cotta vessel.

"Don't bother with that, leave it for the servants. Come back and sit down; you haven't eaten anything."

Julia sat again, bringing forward a platter of salted bass, already cut into pieces for finger food. She offered it to Larthia, who took a piece and then watched as Julia sipped from her cup of diluted wine but ate nothing.

"Are you feeling well?" Larthia asked.

"Why do you ask?"

"You seemed distracted."

"Do I?"

"Yes, you certainly do. You're jittery as a street cat, you're smashing crockery, and you seem to be fasting."

"I'm just not hungry."

"But this is delicious, you should try some."

Julia shook her head.

"All right. It looks as though the timing of my visit was fortuitous. You appear to be bothered by something, and there are shadows under your eyes as if you didn't sleep well last night. What could possibly be haunting you in this glorious haven of peace and tranquillity?"

Julia looked up at her suddenly, and Larthia saw with concern that her sister's eyes were full of tears.

Larthia dropped the piece of fish in her hand and leaned forward across the table. "By all the gods, what is wrong with you?"

Julia swallowed hard and whispered, "It's that centurion you mentioned, Caesar's aide. The one they call Raven."

Larthia watched her, transfixed. When Julia said nothing further Larthia nodded encouragingly.

"I met him when he came here with Caesar," Julia went on. "And then this morning, when I sacrificed, he was in the crowd, watching me."

"Did he speak to you?" Larthia muttered, looking toward the door, which was ajar.

"No, but—"

"But what?"

"The way he looks at me . . ." Julia closed her eyes and swallowed with difficulty.

Larthia got up and glanced into the hall, then shut the door. She rejoined Julia and said in a low tone, "This is what's been bothering you? The way he looks at you?"

"Not just that. The way he makes me feel."

"And how does he make you feel?"

Julia put a hand to her throat. "Since seeing him I can't eat," she whispered, "I can't sleep . . ."

Larthia examined her sister intently. "Maybe his presence at the sacrifice was an accident."

Julia shook her head. "He never took his eyes off me. I can feel them still. And now I think the next time I go out to that altar . . ." She stopped and bent her head.

"Do you want him to be there?" Larthia asked softly, grasping the situation immediately.

Julia bit her lip and shook her head, then she shrugged helplessly.

Larthia reached across the table and took her hand. "You know how perilous this is. You can't encourage a flirtation with this man, I don't care who he is. Your very life is at stake."

Julia nodded sadly.

"You must remember how opposed I was to Casca's choice of this life for you, but you're committed to it now. If you violate your vows you'll pay the price."

Julia wiped her eyes. "Larthia, I haven't even spoken to him," she said.

"Something significant has happened, or you wouldn't be in this state."

"I just didn't expect to feel this way. Once I entered the service I accepted that certain aspects of life would not be available to me."

"You entered the service when you were ten years old! I was only fifteen, but I did my best to avoid this fate for you; you know how successful I was. Surely, though, you didn't think that your training or your celibacy would exempt you from feeling desire."

"Is that what I'm feeling? Desire?"

"Of course. I've seen this Demeter, he's a very attractive man. And he's also a celebrated war hero. How could you fail to be impressed?"

"It's more than that. Men have come here before to record wills, it happens almost daily. But once I saw him, I couldn't take my eyes off him."

"And it seems he feels the same way about you."

Julia was silent.

"He must know the penalties for pursuing a Vestal," Larthia said quietly. "Is he that reckless?"

There was a knock at the door and both sisters jumped involuntarily.

"Come in," Julia called.

Margo entered, bearing a tray.

"Livia Versalia presents her compliments to the esteemed widow of Consul Sejanus," Margo announced, placing her burden carefully on the table in front of Larthia. It contained delectable pieces of honey-glazed fruit, apples and figs and pears cut into slices and placed ornamentally around a centerpiece of whole oranges from the province of Judea.

"Return my compliments to the Chief Vestal, with my thanks," Larthia replied.

Margo bowed and retreated, closing the door behind her as she left.

"Do you think she heard anything?"

Larthia asked anxiously, looking after the servant.

"Even if she did, Margo wouldn't say a word to endanger me," Julia replied.

"Are you sure?"

Julia nodded. "I may not be sophisticated in the ways of the world you inhabit, Larthia, but within the confines of these walls I know which people I can trust."

Larthia looked at the dessert tray without enthusiasm; she had lost her appetite, too.

"What are you going to do about this centurion?" she asked Julia.

Julia closed her eyes. "I may never see him again."

"But you think you will."

Julia lifted one delicate shoulder. "I think from his history that he goes after what he wants."

"What is his history?"

"I don't know much of it, only that he is the son of a freedman farmer from Corsica."

"But to come from that background and rise as high as he has in the army bespeaks a determination that he will now apply to his pursuit of you, is that it?" Larthia supplied.

Julia met her eyes and then looked away.

"His career must mean a great deal to him. He's the confidant of Caesar, a line officer of the Imperator's elite first cohort. Do you imagine that he will throw all that away in order to chase a forbidden woman?"

"I guess it does sound ridiculous, doesn't it?" Julia replied, sighing.

"A little."

"I don't know, Larthia, but seeing him there watching me when I was sacrificing, I was so shocked . . ." She stopped and smiled gingerly. "I suppose I am making too much of it. Maybe it was a coincidence, or maybe he was just curious and wanted another look at me. That doesn't mean anything further will come of it." She laughed a trifle shakily. "I fear I am spending too much time by myself. Brooding allows one to magnify a small incident and turn it into a big problem."

"I will come and see you more often," Larthia said, smiling too. "If I request permission of Livia personally I'm sure she will allow it. It's clear that you need company. I'm not doing anything except planning parties, posing for guild portraits, and fighting with my new bodyguard."

"You're fighting with him?" Julia said, grinning, taking pity on this anonymous slave who had the nerve to thwart Larthia's whim of iron.

"Oh, he's impossible, but Casca has sicked him on me and I seem to be stuck with him."

"Tell me about him," Julia said, glad to change the subject, and Larthia complied.

When Larthia emerged from the Atrium Vestae a short time later, the square outside the temple was deserted except for her bearers and Verrix, who were waiting for her at the bottom of the steps. A few revelers on their way to the Suburra appeared around a corner as she said goodbye to Junia Distania, and Verrix placed his solid body between them and the path to his mistress until they had vanished from sight.

Larthia climbed into her litter without looking at him and then tapped its roof for the bearers to start moving. She sat staring straight ahead, her curtains closed, the increase in the amount of noise surrounding her telling her that they had moved from the quiet temple square into the main thoroughfare. This was jammed with the wagons of tradesmen: fruit sellers and wine merchants and rug vendors who were prevented by law from bringing the carts containing their wares into the city by day. So once darkness fell the streets came alive with the creaking of wheels, the neighing of horses, and the cries of slaves transporting goods for their masters. The occasional private litter mingled with this traffic, its bearers dodging wagon wheels as they crossed intersections to seek out the gravel side paths set aside for pedestrians.

Larthia was thinking about her visit with her sister, wondering where the latter's fascination with the celebrated centurion might lead, when a crescendo of shouts alerted her to the presence of danger. She looked through the litter's curtains to see a runaway horse bearing down on her, dragging a wagon piled high with African bananas. The slave driving the cart was trying desperately to rein in the terrified animal. Larthia barely had time to take in this nightmarish scene before Verrix leaned into the litter, seized both of her hands and yanked her bodily out of her seat. She had a sensation of flying through the air before she landed on her "dignity" on a grassy verge, Verrix on top of her.

For several seconds neither moved. Larthia dimly heard a splintering crash and then the horse thundering by her, followed by a confused babble of voices. She realized that she was immobilized; Verrix had her pinned to the ground.

It was not an unpleasant sensation. He was big and solid and warm, and she did feel protected. He smelled strongly of the pine soap Nestor issued to the slaves. Soap was an eastern innovation disdained by the Roman upper classes, who preferred to cleanse the skin with a strigil, but Nestor insisted that soap was necessary to counteract the effects of many hard-laboring bodies living together in close quarters. She noticed too that her bodyguard's hair and tunic smelled fresh, and that the skin at the base of his throat where her face was pressed was as silky as a baby's.

Then she realized what she was thinking and said in a commanding voice, "Get off me!"

Verrix sat up immediately, surveying her to see that she was in one piece before looking toward the litter. It was smashed at the side of the street and both bearers were sitting on the ground next to it, seemingly intact but shaken.

"Are you all right?" he called to them.

The men looked at one another and then nodded, standing gingerly, as if testing their limbs.

"You might ask that question of me," Larthia said huffily, arranging her clothing and patting her hair. "I feel as if I've been hit by a German phalanx."

"I hit you," Verrix replied evenly. "It was me or the runaway horse and wagon."

"That slave should be flogged and his owner fined," Larthia said peevishly. "Any man who can't control an animal shouldn't be left in charge of one."

"Her ladyship is fine," Verrix called to the crowd which was lingering to see if there were any injuries. "Go about your business." He extended his hand to Larthia, who took it and tried to stand. Her left ankle gave way beneath her.

"I am not fine!" she barked at him. "I can't walk, I think my leg is broken."

He astonished her by squatting next to her and lifting the hem of her *stola,* then encircling her slim ankle with his supple brown fingers and manipulating the joint.

"It's not broken," he announced, as she gasped at his effrontery, looking around furtively to see who was witnessing this familiarity. To her relief the crowd was dissipating and only a few people were looking her way.

"Take your hands off me this instant," she said between her teeth.

Verrix obeyed, rising in one smooth motion. "I merely wanted to see if the bone was splintered," he said mildly. "I think it's just a sprain."

"Are you a physician now?" Larthia asked sarcastically, wincing as he withdrew his support and she tried to put her weight on the injured leg.

"I saw many such injuries during the rebellion," he replied. "I think I know when a bone is broken, and yours isn't."

"Nevertheless, I cannot walk," Larthia said, enunciating each word clearly as if he were slow witted.

"Then I will carry you," he answered, and before she could protest he had scooped her up in his arms and was striding along the footpath in the direction of the Palatine.

"Leave the litter where it is, the street cleaners will get it later," Verrix said to the two bearers. "Just follow me back to the house."

They fell in behind him, as Larthia had no choice but to let the big slave haul her bodily up to the Sejanus estate. She stared off into the distance, her arms around his neck, refusing to meet his eyes, as he carried her easily, not even winded. She tried not to dwell on the strength of his arms or the breadth of his shoulders under her hands, but since her only experience with men had been the feeble embraces of a bisexual old man, she could not help noting the difference. This was a *young* man, a virile man, and his constant proximity to her person was beginning to make her anxious.

Once inside the house, Verrix set Larthia on a couch in the *tablinum* and then brought a torch from a wall niche to examine her injured member more closely.

"Leave me alone!" Larthia snapped as he bent over her foot. Her nerves were raw, the prospect of another probing by this infuriating man increasing her tension. "I'll send for my physician in the morning."

"You should bathe the ankle in cold water," Verrix said stubbornly. "It will reduce the swelling."

"Then send Nestor for some," Larthia replied wearily. She was achingly tired, her ankle was throbbing, and Verrix looked as if he had just arisen from a restful nap after carrying her uphill for more than a mile. She wanted to hit him.

Verrix went into the hall, and she heard him talking to someone; he returned shortly with a basin. He elevated her foot onto a stool and then slipped the basin into place, easing her ankle into the water.

"Ah!" she gasped, yanking her foot out again and splashing water onto the tiled floor. "That's freezing!"

"Yes, I know," he said, seizing her foot and submerging it firmly. "Unless you want your ankle to look like a Jericho orange in the morning, I suggest you leave it where it is."

Larthia obeyed reluctantly, her expression mutinous.

"You're enjoying this," she said accusingly.

His disgusted expression indicated what he thought of that statement.

"It's all your fault anyway," she added childishly.

He stared at her.

"If you had been looking where we were going, none of this would have happened."

"The horse came around a bend in the road. If you have devised a method of seeing around corners I wish you would let me know about it," Verrix replied.

"You're supposed to be taking care of me!"

"I thought I was doing that," he said evenly. "You have lived in Rome far longer than I have. You know you should not be abroad in the streets late at night when deliveries are being made and the gangs roam at will."

"I will not be trapped in this tomb of a house all my life!" Larthia burst out, then looked away from him irritably.

"Then go to see your sister during the day," Verrix said reasonably.

"She is busy during the day. Don't ask me what with, but they manage to keep her occupied."

"It seems to me you have enough to do," Verrix said. "Your late husband's affairs are complex."

Larthia snorted derisively.

"If you are lonely—" Verrix began.

"Don't speak to me that way!" Larthia said tersely, suddenly conscious of the fact that she was confiding in a servant. "I don't care if your uncle was a king or your grandfather a god, you will keep a civil tongue in your head when you address me!"

Verrix stiffened, as he always did when reminded of his servile status, but his expression revealed nothing. Then it changed from perfect blankness to startled consternation when Larthia burst into tears.

He waited a long moment before saying, "Is there anything I can do for you?"

She looked away from him and said, "You can go."

He hesitated. "Are you certain you want me to leave?"

"Yes. Send Nestor to me when you do."

Verrix went into the hall and then back to the slave quarters, where the slave master was giving directions on airing the bedding. The wooden frames were being stripped of their straw mattresses and woolen blankets. The mattresses would be replaced with fresh ones and the blankets washed. Nestor saw to it that this was done regularly; it was a point of pride with him that his slave dormitory was well maintained. He always supervised the process at night because he thought it was bad luck to change bedding during the daylight.

Nestor looked up impatiently when he saw the big Gaul standing in the doorway.

"What is it?" he asked.

"The mistress wants to see you," Verrix replied.

"Where is she?"

"In the *tablinum*. She met with an accident in the street and is bathing her foot."

"An accident?" Nestor inquired, raising one gray eyebrow, his lips pursed.

"A runaway horse smashed her litter, but she escaped unhurt. I carried her back here."

Nestor looked at the younger man intently for a moment and then said, "Go inside and help remove the old mattresses. I'll attend to the mistress."

As Verrix obeyed, Nestor hurried along the corridor leading from the slave quarters to the front of the house. When he entered the *tablinum* he found Larthia wiping her eyes with the hem of her *diploidion* and frowning down at her elevated foot.

"Are you quite all right, mistress?" he asked, although the answer was obviously in the negative.

"I am not. I want you to summon that Greek physician from the Via Sacra near the Diana fountain, first thing in the morning. What is his name?"

"His name is Paris, mistress. He was the house slave of Senator Pilatus Dolabella and was freed in the will when the Senator died."

"Yes, yes, that's the one. I remember that he healed my father's wrist the time it was broken."

"He is very skilled, mistress, I will certainly get him for you as soon as the sun rises. Will there be anything else?"

"I'll need some help to get to my bedroom. I can't walk unassisted."

"Shall I summon Verrix?" Nestor asked.

"No!" Larthia said sharply, and then, in

a milder tone, "I am not heavy. I think you can manage."

"Has Verrix offended in some way, mistress?" Nestor asked. "I will speak to him."

"It's not necessary to speak to him, Nestor, as if that would have any effect," Larthia said dryly, rising with difficulty and putting her arm across the old man's frail shoulders. "Verrix just has a tendency to take charge, and I don't want him taking charge of me again tonight."

She hobbled toward the door as the servant assisted her; they headed in tandem toward her room.

Verrix finished turning the beds in the dormitory and then retired to his room. He lay down on his bed, identical to the ones he had just changed, and stared out his tiny window at the stars blooming in the sky.

He slept poorly in this house. Often he dreamed he was back in Gaul with his tribe, swimming in the icy rivers, making camp in open fields, moving from place to place as the spirit and the harvests directed his people. Then he would awaken in this cell and remember his slavery, his isolation, and his bitter fate.

He hated being at the beck and call of

his conquerors, but he was beginning to feel a little sorry for Larthia, Lady Sejana. Scarred by the early death of her mother, bartered by her grasping father, hideously neglected by her frequently absent and always inattentive husband, confused and unhappy as a result: these things he had learned about her from listening to the other servants. Added to that fund of information was what he had observed for himself. She could not pass a beggar without tossing a coin, she was as solicitous of fussy old Nestor as if he were her father, and that evening on the way to the Atrium Vestae she had given up her litter to a sick child who needed assistance in getting home. This did not make her the good goddess, certainly, but neither was she the self-centered shrew she appeared to be at first glance.

Verrix rolled over and lay with his cheek pressed to the raw woolen blanket, his eyes closed. He had not expected these stirrings of sympathy for Larthia. At the bottom of everything, she was lonely, and he knew very well what that did to the human *animus*. And she was very pretty, very young, and alone in the male-dominated Roman world. But he could not fall into the trap of harboring tender feelings for the lady of the estate. That would lead to disaster.

As Larthia constantly reminded him, he was a slave in this house. In the patriarchal Roman society he had come to know, male citizens could sleep with whomever and whatever they wanted, with impunity. But Roman women were indoctrinated from birth with the necessity of chastity and fidelity, with the importance of upholding their place in society; the typical Roman matron would rather climb into the bath and open her veins than have it known she was indulging in a relationship with a slave.

But of course Larthia was not the typical Roman matron, was she?

Verrix sat up and crossed his arms on his upraised knees. What was he thinking? She had felt soft and yielding in his arms, she had smelled like gillyflowers and crushed verbena, she had clung to him as if he were a raft in a churning sea. None of that meant that she was responding to him as a man; he was transportation in a crisis, nothing more.

He had to remember that.

He lay back down and willed himself to go to sleep.

Four

Marcus lingered in the gray dawn, watching the path along which Julia would come. A thin mist hovered over the spring; the Porta Capena loomed in the background. As the sun broke through the clouds the mist lifted and began to dissolve.

He had prepared well for this moment. Through careful questioning he had learned that the Vestals performed this duty on foot and alone, except for a single guard. The litter used for city travel, and the *lictor* which preceded it, were absent during this most sacred and ancient rite, the drawing of water for the altar of Vesta. The ceremony harked back to the foundation of the colony of Alba Longa, and it was thought fitting to perform it in the most primitive way. The participant walked to the spring and back and hauled the water by hand. The trip presented a rare opportunity to find Julia outside the tem-

ple and well away from the city crowds, and
Marcus planned to make the most of it.

It wasn't long before he heard footsteps
on the path, and he moved out of sight.
He waited until Julia's lighter tread had
passed and then seized her companion,
bringing his forearm across the man's
throat and pressing backward just enough
to seal off his windpipe. The slave struggled like a gaffed fish and then passed
out, slipping bonelessly to the grass.

Julia turned, puzzled by the slight
sounds behind her, then gasped in horror
and dropped the container she was carrying when she saw her guard lying unconscious on the ground.

"Don't be alarmed," Marcus said quickly.
"He'll come around in a short while, and
he'll be fine. He might have a slight headache, that's all."

Julia stared at him, unable to reply.

"Do you remember me?" he asked.

Her expression indicated that she did.

"Please don't be afraid. I didn't want
to accost you, but I have to talk to you
and this seemed the only way to do it."

"Why do you have to talk to me?" Her
voice was low, sweet, well modulated.

"Because I haven't been able to think
about anything else but you since the day
we met," he said simply.

He saw on her face the impact of that statement, and took a step closer to her. She stiffened.

"Don't be afraid," he said again, softly.

She didn't move.

"Are you afraid of me?" he asked.

"No." Then, as he moved closer still, "Yes."

"I don't mean you any harm."

She held up her hand. "This is forbidden."

"It's forbidden for us to have a conversation?"

She looked away from him in dismay. "You know very well what I mean."

He reached for her shoulder gently, turned her to him, and drew her veil back from her face. "You are so lovely," he said, and touched her cheek with the side of his hand.

She closed her eyes. "Please," she murmured.

He stared down at her, marveling at the perfection of her poreless skin, the soft curve of her brow and lips. "Do you want me to go away and never see you again?" he asked.

She did not respond.

"Do you?" he insisted.

"No." It was the faintest of whispers, but his heart leaped at the sound.

The guard stirred behind them and groaned.

"When can we meet again?" he asked quickly. "When you draw the water next time?"

"I am always accompanied," she answered, staring up at him. He was even handsomer up close, his mouth wide and firm, his lashes lush and sweeping.

"Then when?"

She thought a moment. "My elder sister is the widow of Consul Sejanus, she has his estate on the Palatine. Do you know where it is?"

He nodded. "Near the home of Senator Gracchus."

"Yes, that's right. She is hosting a *convivium* for Livia Versalia in seven days. All the patrician families will be represented to celebrate the upcoming new year on the first of March, the Chief Vestal's anniversary of investiture. Do you know anyone who can invite you as a guest?"

"I'll be there," Marcus said firmly.

The guard mumbled something, and Marcus stepped back into the trees.

"You know we both court death if we continue to meet," Julia said softly, putting her hand on his arm to detain him and searching his face.

"I don't care. Do you?"

She smiled for the first time. "At this moment, I confess that I don't."

"I promise you, I will protect you with my life," Marcus said softly. "No harm will come to you from seeing me."

Her smile became sad. "Can you take back my vows?" she whispered.

"Your fate was forced on you," he said roughly. "No one can make a true choice at such a tender age."

"You know the practice concerning Vestals?"

"I have inquired," he said shortly.

The guard sat up groggily, his hand going slowly to his bruised throat.

"How will I find you . . . ?" Julia began, looking back anxiously at the slave, who was blinking and shaking his head.

"I'll find you," Marcus replied, holding up his hand in farewell as he melted into the copse.

The guard sat up and looked around him querulously.

"What happened?" he said dazedly.

"I think someone attacked you, but he's gone," Julia said calmly, and offered the man her hand.

"So it isn't broken?" Larthia said.

"No, madam. You certainly twisted it

badly, and I'm sure it's quite painful, but the bone is intact. Whoever advised you to immerse the ankle in cold water saved you a great deal of swelling and discomfort." The physician rose from a kneeling position and bowed deferentially.

Larthia mentally rolled her eyes, glad that Verrix was not in the room to hear this.

"You should not walk on it for four or five days. Other than that, you will be unaffected once the bruise heals."

Larthia nodded. "Thank you. Please see Nestor for your payment."

Paris bowed again and left the room. Seconds later Nestor appeared and said, "Mistress, your sister, the honorable Julia Rosalba Casca, is awaiting an audience in the atrium."

"Julia?" Larthia was surprised. She had just seen her sister, and Livia Versalia did not permit the Vestals out for socializing very often.

"Yes, madam."

"Well, show her in, Nestor."

Julia entered seconds later and said, "I heard that you had met with an accident, Larthia. I came to see how you are faring." She walked over to her sister and bent to kiss her cheek.

"How kind," Larthia replied. "I seem

to be faring very well. Would you like some refreshment?''

Julia shook her head. "I'm fine."

"Nestor, would you leave us alone, please? I'll summon you if I need anything."

As soon as the door closed behind the servant, Larthia said curiously, "What is going on, Julia? Livia Versalia is not one to permit gallivanting around town, and as you can see I am hardly on my deathbed."

"I'm afraid I exaggerated your injury to Livia in order to gain an audience with you," Julia admitted.

"How did you find out about my mishap?"

"One of the temple slaves was walking by and witnessed it. He knew who you were by the crest on the litter."

"Come and sit here," Larthia said, patting the spot next to her on the couch. When her sister was seated Larthia said in a low tone, "Is it something to do with that centurion?"

Julia flushed, and Larthia knew she was right.

"What happened?" Larthia asked.

Julia recounted her meeting with Marcus at the sacred spring, and when she had finished Larthia said in astonishment, "So you told him you would meet him *here?*"

"It was the only thing I could think of at the time. The guard was waking up and I had to act fast."

"Have you given any consideration to the position you're putting me in, Julia? For permitting the two of you to meet in my house I could be found guilty of a capital crime and have all my property confiscated. I might even be banished."

Julia closed her eyes. "I know. If you want I'll plead illness and avoid the *convivium*. If I don't show up here Marcus will know I changed my mind and you will be guilty of nothing."

Larthia thought for a moment. "How did you persuade Livia Versalia to permit this visit when she knew your guard had been attacked at the spring? I would think that would make her even more cautious than usual."

"She didn't know about it," Julia replied evenly. "I bribed the guard to keep him quiet."

"Bribed him how? You have no money of your own, Julia, it was all placed in a primogeniture trust when you entered the Vestal service."

"I gave him mother's carnelian brooch."

Larthia stared at her sister, open-mouthed, then pressed her lips together tightly. "It must be very important to you to see this soldier again," she finally said.

"I didn't know how much the guard had observed. I was afraid he might be able to provide a description of his attacker if he were questioned about it. Marcus is . . . memorable. His height alone would point to him as a suspect, and I've heard that people in the city often recognize him."

"So you parted with a family heirloom to protect your paramour," Larthia said dryly.

"He's hardly that. I've only exchanged a few words with him."

"Don't minimize the situation. He's made enough of an impression for you to risk your life to see him again."

Julia said nothing.

Larthia settled herself more comfortably and rested her head against the back of the couch. "Perhaps you could tell me how you're planning to conduct a tryst in this house while I'm hosting a gathering to celebrate Livia Versalia's anniversary. It strikes me as a singularly poor time for a romantic rendezvous."

"I was hoping you would help me with that part of it," Julia admitted.

"Since I'm the one with the devious mind?" Larthia asked archly.

"I have no experience with such things," Julia said, shrugging helplessly.

"Well, this may come as a great shock to you, but neither do I. You have never asked, but I was faithful to my husband, much good it ever did me, and since he died grandfather has watched over me as if I were Caesar's wife. Even if I wanted to take a lover, which I haven't, the combined weight of the Casca and Sejanus names has been enough to keep me chaste. I'm hardly the woman of the world you seem to think me, and I'm just as frightened by all of this intrigue as you are yourself."

Julia looked suitably chastened.

"That doesn't mean I won't help you," Larthia said hastily, squeezing Julia's hand.

Julia met her sister's eyes hopefully.

"It seems fair that at least one of us should be lucky in love," Larthia declared, and Julia leaned forward to hug her.

Larthia rang the little silver bell at her elbow.

"I'll order us a little taste of something, and then we'll make our plans."

"Livia Versalia's anniversary?" Septimus said, frowning. "Why do you want to attend such a dull gathering? The politicians will be making tedious speeches, these religious observances are always deadly. I had other ideas for this evening."

"I'm not going to the temple service, just the *convivium* afterward. I will be attending as Caesar's representative, to present his compliments. He is very grateful to the Vestals for past favors and wants to show his respect, but he will be in Ostia tonight and unable to join the festivities." Marcus tried to keep his tone casual; he was afraid his voice would reveal the anxious time he had spent waiting for this evening to come.

"And he asked you to go in his place?" Septimus said, impressed.

"Well, no. I offered to attend."

"Why?" Septimus studied his friend, puzzled, and then his expression cleared. "I see. The widow of Sejanus is hosting the event, and that little Vestal you've been trailing is a Casca, too. The Sejana's sister, if I'm not mistaken. Is that correct?"

Marcus reached for an olive from the tray at his elbow, but said nothing.

Septimus shook his head, amazed, rising from the couch in his father's *tablinum*. "She'll be there, won't she?" he insisted.

"All the Vestals will be there."

"You're playing with fire, Marcus."

"So you've said, and I don't need to

hear it again. Will you go with me or not?"

"Why do you want me along? Lovemaking is for two, as I remember it."

Marcus said nothing, but Septimus read his expression accurately.

"You want an ally near at hand if there's trouble?" Septimus asked.

"I'm not expecting any trouble."

"You might have some if you seduce a consecrated virgin in the Sejanus house," Septimus said dryly.

"I won't be seducing anyone, Septimus, I'm not a complete fool."

"No?"

"No," Marcus replied firmly.

"Then what are you planning?"

"I'm not planning anything."

Septimus threw up his hands in exasperation. Marcus was like a sphinx of Egypt when he didn't want to talk, and this was evidently one of those occasions.

"Will you go with me or not?" Marcus demanded.

"I'll go with you," Septimus said shortly. "My father was planning to attend, but if I go in his place he will be able to spend the evening with his mistress, and that will certainly please him. Now can we change the subject before this leads to an argument?"

"By all means." Marcus reached over to a side table, picking up a flyer on the gladiator Senator Gracchus was backing in an upcoming contest. "Which man do you like in the games beginning on the Ides?" he asked. "The Samnite or the Thracian?"

"The Samnite is a *retiarius*. The net and the trident make a man clumsy, they're no match for the Thracian's fancy footwork. My money's on the Thracian."

They went on to talk lightly of the sporting event, but his lingering concern was still plain on Septimus' face.

"Good evening, Centurion," Larthia said smoothly, taking Marcus' arm as he entered the atrium of her house. "Although we have never met I, like all citizens of Rome, have heard of your many splendid deeds. I was dismayed to accept the Imperator's regrets, but comforted when he said you would be coming in his place."

"Thank you," Marcus said.

"And of course the son of Senator Gracchus honors us with his presence. Welcome, Tribune."

"Good evening to you, Lady Sejana," Septimus said, smiling. "An offering for the *Penates.*" He placed a cake of incense on the altar of the gods of plenty in a recess of the frescoed wall.

Larthia bowed her head. "Come inside and join the gathering." As Septimus walked ahead she leaned forward to whisper in Marcus' ear, "She is already in my bedchamber. She feigned a dizzy spell and has retired to have a rest."

Marcus looked startled, then nodded and squeezed Larthia's elbow. He had not realized that Julia would enlist her sister in their conspiracy.

"I will come for you when it is best for you to slip away," she added in an undertone, leading them through the hall and into the large dining room.

It was clear to Marcus at a glance that the cream of Roman society was present. Senators in their striped togas, great ladies glittering with jewels, celebrated artists and businessmen and theatrical performers filled the luxurious room. Censors in plain purple togas and retired generals in purple togas edged with gold mixed with the Vestals who dotted the crowd, standing out in their pale saffron formal robes. The usual attire for evening dinner parties was relaxed, colorful tunics, but since this occasion was connected with Livia Versalia's official function everyone was decked out in the robes of public office.

Marcus saw Cytheris, on the arm of a fabulously wealthy Parthian rug and tapestry dealer, and she favored him with a dazzling smile.

"I see that your erstwhile admirer is here," Septimus murmured to him dryly. "She must imagine that you are pining away to see her with that foreigner. I understand he paves the walkways of his garden with sesterces."

Marcus shot his friend a withering glance.

"Help yourselves to the refreshments," Larthia said, gesturing to the slaves walking through the reception and carrying trays loaded with golden goblets, as well as sausages, honey cakes, and bits of salted carp. "I must see to my hostessing duties. The guest of honor is holding court in the *tablinum.*" Then she went on in a louder voice, "Senator Trajan, how kind of you to come." She released Marcus and walked over to the man she had just greeted, still limping slightly, leaving Marcus and Septimus on their own.

"I don't know about you," Septimus said, "but I need a drink." He lifted a goblet from a tray as a slave went past and took a long swallow of the wine. "Look at this group. If a fire broke out here tonight Caesar wouldn't have to fight to be top dog. He'd be the only contender left alive."

Marcus smiled grimly, sorely tempted to go looking for Julia himself, but he knew that would be rash. The house was very large and he couldn't run around trying doors until he found the right one. He would just have to be patient until Larthia returned and showed him the way.

"There's your ladyfriend's grandfather, Decimus Gnaeus Casca," Septimus said, nodding in the direction of a white-haired Senator wearing a chalk-bleached toga adorned with broad bands of purple and gold, indicating his former status as a *praetor*, or judge. "What an old scoundrel he is. It seems to me the sister we just saw must be more like him than your precious Julia."

"Have you known him long?" Marcus asked, watching Casca curiously.

"All my life. He was *praetor* when my father sued the corn factors for holding back their supply until the price went up. Now that my father is an *aedile* he consults with Casca frequently about town planning."

"While the esteemed Senator Gracchus keeps well in with Caesar at the same time," Marcus replied, laughing.

"Of course," Septimus replied, grinning

back at him. "Well, I suppose we had better go and pay our respects to Livia. Where is the *tablinum* in this mausoleum?"

"I imagine where the line is forming," Marcus replied, wondering how he could possibly be polite to the Chief Vestal while anticipating a tryst with one of her charges. The thought that Julia was under the same roof with him, but inaccessible at the moment, was driving him wild.

"Let's go and get it done," Septimus said.

They moved through the crowd, dodging servants and guests alike, then joined the line waiting to see Livia Versalia. A *convivium* was more like a reception than a banquet; guests remained standing and talked with one another while helping themselves to food and drink rather than reclining during a meal. Septimus entertained Marcus with acid comments about many of the partygoers as they moved closer to their destination.

Livia Versalia, seated in an ivory chair, wearing her gilt-edged saffron robes and the laurel wreath of the Vestalis Maxima, was receiving congratulations on the anniversary of her investiture as Chief Vestal. At her feet was the pile of offerings brought by the guests in hopes that she would intercede for them with the goddess.

"Septimus Valerius Gracchus," she said, offering her hand to Septimus as he reached her.

"I am honored to give greetings to the *amata vestae,* the beloved of Vesta," Septimus said, holding the woman's hand to his forehead.

"Thank you," Livia said graciously.

"Food for the sacrifice," Septimus added, placing a bundle of salt cakes wrapped in leaves of the date palm at her feet.

Livia bowed her head.

"And Marcus Corvus Demeter," she said, when Septimus stepped aside.

"Greetings, Lady."

"It is pleasant to see you again so soon after your visit to the Aedes with Caesar."

"I am here in place of the Imperator, who sends his greetings and this token of his esteem." Marcus handed her a gilt-framed concave mirror and said, "From the prytaneum of the Greeks, to rekindle the Vestal fire in the new year."

Livia smiled. "Our Caesar knows his ancient history," she said, turning the artifact over in her hands.

"He is well versed in many things," Marcus said.

She nodded. "True. Please tell him for me that he was missed here this evening, but that his handsome and gracious representative was well received."

Marcus bowed and withdrew.

"Another admirer of the Raven to add to the fold," Septimus said, sighing deeply. "I do believe that we'll have to form a guild for you."

Marcus scanned the gathering for Larthia but was unable to see her.

"Will you stop looking through the crowd like a Persian policeman searching for a suspect?" Septimus said wearily. "Our hostess said she would be back. Until she arrives your object should be to blend into the scene; your basilisk stare is as obvious as a Vestal at an orgy."

Marcus ignored him, continuing to peer into the distance with the acute visual perception he had developed on night watch in the army. Suddenly he froze and narrowed his eyes.

"What is it?" Septimus asked, following the direction of his gaze.

"Do you see that man standing by the statue of Venus with his arms folded? The one wearing the homespun tunic?"

"How could I miss him? He's the biggest thing in the room," Septimus said.

"I know him."

"Know him? He's a slave, a Gaul by the

look of him," Septimus replied in a bored tone.

"Yes. What I'd like to know is what he's doing here. The last time I saw him I turned him in as the escaped prisoner who had killed Antoninus Mellius. He was condemned to death for it."

"Antoninus?" Septimus said, interested now. "He's the one who killed Antoninus?"

Marcus was already moving toward his target when Larthia sidled up to him and took his arm, saying, "You may come with me now. The guests are all well into their cups, I doubt that you will be missed."

Marcus stopped, still glaring at Verrix, who was watching Larthia, his expression unreadable.

"What is that man doing in your house?" Marcus demanded of his hostess.

"I beg your pardon?" she said loftily, her eyes widening at his rudeness.

"I turned that slave in to the authorities for killing a Roman soldier in the course of an escape. The tribunal gave him the death penalty, and now I see him, free as air, lounging around this party like a male courtesan! I demand an explanation."

"He's not lounging, he's on duty. He's my bodyguard." Larthia attempted, futilely, to steer Marcus out of the crowd. She had dismissed as inconsequential the references

Verrix had made to the centurion who had identified him when he was captured. Now she realized with a sinking heart that Julia's inamorata was that same centurion who had recognized Verrix from the Gallic campaign! This was a dire complication she had not anticipated. Worried that Marcus would make a scene, she tugged on his arm, but his feet were planted.

"Your bodyguard! This is an outrage. That man is responsible for the death of a Roman soldier, a good friend of mine. Did you know his history when he came here?"

"Lower your voice," Septimus said to Marcus in an advisory tone, looking around him apprehensively. "You are beginning to attract attention."

"My grandfather paid his life price and presented him to me for my protection," Larthia said hastily.

Marcus looked down at her, and she saw the face he showed to Rome's enemies. His eyes were compassionless.

"Is it not the duty of a Roman soldier to escape when captured?" Larthia said desperately, echoing the argument her grandfather had made to her. "He merely did exactly what you would have done in his place."

She saw that Marcus was unmoved; only

his reluctance to shove her out of the way was holding him where he was.

"It will not help your cause with my sister if you make a scene in my house on the occasion of Livia Versalia's anniversary," Larthia said through a false smile, waving to Endymion, her portrait painter, as he passed with a goblet in hand. "She is waiting to see you right now. Who is more important to you, Julia or a runaway slave who managed to elude crucifixion? You decide."

Marcus looked once more at Verrix, then down at Larthia. "Take me to Julia," he said.

Releasing her breath audibly, Larthia glanced at Septimus in relief and took Marcus by the elbow.

"A sensible decision," she said, nodding amiably at her guests as she steered him through the crowd. "Now as far as anyone can tell we are just going for a stroll through the gardens. Please at least try to look as if you are enjoying yourself, my reputation as a dazzling hostess is at stake."

Marcus complied, smiling down at her.

"That's better," she said softly, leading him through a labyrinth of marble-floored, torch-lit halls and then out to the gardens, which were even more elaborate and extensive than those belonging to her neighbor, Senator Gracchus. From this distance the party chatter was a subdued murmur, the clatter of slaves in the kitchen nearby a louder counterpoint to the voices and laughter coming from the interior of the house.

"Julia is in there," Larthia said, pointing to a small door facing out to the portico. "My husband, on those rare occasions when he was actually at home, liked to sit out here and then retire to his chamber without walking through the rest of the house. The door opens to my bedroom."

Marcus started toward it immediately.

Larthia put her hand on his arm.

"Your life is taking a dangerous turn, Centurion," she said quietly.

"Yours, too," he replied. "Why are you helping us?"

Larthia was silent a moment, looking back toward the house, bright with torchlight, the windows along the back open to the night air.

"I have asked myself that same question," she finally said. "Am I restless and bored, participating in this intrigue because my own life is so colorless? While that is certainly true, I think there is more to it."

Marcus waited politely, impatient for

Julia, but mindful that the young woman before him had made his meeting with the Vestal possible.

"I was fifteen when Julia was dedicated to the Vestals, old enough to know what she would be giving up when she entered the service and what her future life would be like. Julia was ten, the sweetest and most innocent child you ever saw. Perhaps I didn't do enough to stop it."

"What could you have done?"

"I was affianced to Sejanus at that time, he was a powerful man. If I had interceded with him then, before we were married and he quickly grew tired of me, I might have been able to help her. But I was too afraid of my family, of my father and grandfather. I hesitated, and Julia was swallowed up by the temple before she knew what had happened to her. The honor her investiture brought to the Casca family was much more important to my relatives than the bleak fate of one small child."

Marcus said nothing.

"I have thought upon it many times since then," Larthia added softly. She looked back at Marcus. "Be good to her," she said. "She wants you very much. Make sure her time with you is worth the risk she is taking."

Marcus pressed her hand and then

walked swiftly across the portico, heading for the door Larthia had indicated.

Larthia watched him go and then went back inside, to her guests.

Julia was standing near Larthia's bed when the door opened. She looked up, saw Marcus, and flew into his arms.

He held her for a long moment, his throat closing with tenderness, savoring the sensation of her slim body pressed to his. Even through the voluminous Vestal robes he could feel the warmth and softness of her skin, the silken fall of her hair against his arm through her diaphanous veil. At length he held her off and drew the veil down to her shoulders, sinking his fingers into the thick red-gold mass of her hair.

"Have you been waiting long?" he said huskily.

"It seemed long," she replied, her wide eyes searching his face.

"I had to wait for your sister to bring me in," Marcus said apologetically.

Julia smiled and held his hand to her cheek. "I can't believe you're here," she said softly.

"Julia, did you think I might not come?" he asked her incredulously.

"I didn't know what to think. Sometimes, while I waited for this night, it seemed I had dreamed our meeting by the spring, that I wanted it so much I'd imagined it."

"I'm no phantom," he said, taking her hands and leading her to Larthia's bed. They sat on its edge and faced one another.

"When Larthia brought me in here she told me that my life was taking a dangerous turn," Marcus said, twining Julia's fingers with his. "But I'm a soldier, and my life has been full of dangers. Facing them is my trade." He looked down at their joined hands and then up into her face. "Your life has been very different. I wonder if you've considered what continuing to see me will mean."

"I've considered it," Julia replied.

He hesitated, aware that he wasn't making himself clear. "Julia, so far we've done nothing more than talk. You can walk away from me now and have no worries about your future."

"But I can't walk away from you, Marcus," she replied, saying his name for the first time. "I knew that in the recording room of the Aedes the day we met."

He pulled her into his arms again. "Then we have to make plans," he said against her ear. "Will your sister allow us to continue to meet here?"

"Yes," Julia whispered.

"How?"

Julia drew back and looked at him. "I feigned illness tonight, not only to enable me to retire from the party but to set up a reason to meet with Larthia's physician in the future."

"Why?"

"I can tell Livia Versalia that I must come here on each *nundina* to receive his ministrations. The doctor lives just across the Via Sacra, but it would not be seemly for me to go to his home for treatment. Livia will accept my meeting with him here."

"Wouldn't she expect him to come to the Atrium Vestae to see you?"

"Males other than relatives are not permitted intimate contact with a Vestal within the temple or the Atrium. We must always go out to see physicians."

"And how will you keep the doctor quiet?" Marcus asked, concerned.

"I plan to see him as a patient," Julia said reasonably. "He is greedy enough to be well paid every eight days for treating imaginary ailments. I will work hard to be a convincing actress." She smiled and put her head on Marcus' shoulder. "And when he leaves, I will then see you."

Marcus chuckled. "Brilliant as well as beautiful."

"It was Larthia's idea."

"The words apply to your sister as well."

"She is taking a big chance for us," Julia said.

"It's my guess that Larthia could take on the Persian horde and come out the winner," Marcus said dryly.

Julia giggled.

"How will I wait for another market day before seeing you again?" Marcus asked, nuzzling her hair.

"I know it's a long time, but I didn't want to risk sending messages back and forth to set up meetings," Julia whispered. "This way, you'll always know when you'll see me."

"It will never be often enough," Marcus said, bending his head to kiss her.

Julia accepted the pressure of his mouth on hers, her lips parting slightly, then clutched his shoulders as he drew her closer and embraced her more fully. His mouth was moving caressingly from her lips to her neck when the door to the hall opened and Larthia burst into the room.

"Out!" she said breathlessly to Marcus. "Livia Versalia is on her way in here right now to check on Julia. Go out the door to the portico!"

Marcus leaped to his feet, releasing Julia so suddenly that she fell back on the bed.

"Next market day, at sunset," Julia said, clutching desperately at his hand.

"For pity's sake, Julia, let him go!" Larthia hissed. "She must be almost here!"

Julia drew back and Marcus fled across the room and out the door. It had just closed behind him when Livia tapped softly on the door leading to the hall.

"Julia Rosalba?" she called. "May I come in?"

Larthia waved Julia into a prone position on the bed and waited until her sister had arranged her clothing. Then she pulled the door open and greeted Livia with a wide smile.

"Well, the guest of honor! I think my sister is feeling better, Livia, the rest must have done her good."

Livia advanced into the room, the hem of her gown whispering along the marble-tiled floor. She walked to the side of the bed and studied the prone figure of the younger woman lying there.

"I don't know, Larthia, she looks flushed to me. Don't you think she looks flushed?"

Larthia, who knew very well why Julia's cheeks were rosy, said hastily, "Perhaps she has a touch of fever."

Livia seemed concerned. "The Pontine Marsh is a terrible source of contagion this time of year."

"You could send her to see my physician, Paris, he's very good. She could meet with him here at my house. Would you like me to arrange it?"

Livia nodded, putting the back of her hand to Julia's forehead. "Yes, I would. Thank you, Lady Sejana."

Larthia winked at Julia behind Livia's back.

"I take the welfare of my ladies very seriously," Livia said briskly. "Julia Rosalba, spend the remainder of the evening resting, and I excuse you from your duties tomorrow. We will arrange for you to see the Greek healer as soon as possible. I'll send a litter for you tonight so you won't have to go back to the Atrium with us in the *currus*."

"Thank you, Livia," Julia said from the bed.

"Now we must rejoin the party," Larthia said to Livia, putting her hand on the Chief Vestal's shoulder and directing her toward the door. "I'm sure the guests will want to say good night to you before they go home."

Larthia looked back at her sister reassuringly as they went through the door, then made small talk with Livia while they walked back to the gathering, where the partygoers were indeed taking their leave. Larthia left Livia to say her good-byes, then grabbed a cup of wine from a passing slave and drank from it deeply.

She was not as steady as she appeared; when Livia almost walked in on Marcus and her sister, her heart was in her mouth. She swallowed hard and forced a smile to her lips when her next door neighbor, Portia Scipiana Campania, appeared and extended her plump hand.

"Lovely *convivium,* Larthia, I'm sure Livia Versalia is most pleased."

"Thank you."

"My dear, I must speak to you. I've noticed something this last week and this evening, too, and I've been intrigued."

"Really?" Larthia said, wondering apprehensively what was coming.

Portia nodded. "Why is that huge slave following you around everywhere you go?"

Larthia looked at Verrix hovering in the background and groaned inwardly. Portia was the wife of a *quaestor,* or tax collector, and a notorious gossip. Whatever she told Portia would be the equivalent of writing on a broadsheet to be posted in the forum.

"He's my bodyguard," Larthia replied,

deciding that a simple version of the truth was best.

Portia's eyes widened. "Are you in danger?"

Larthia shrugged dismissively. "I am humoring my grandfather. He's worried about the political unrest and thinks I may become a victim of his battles with Caesar."

"Surely we are more civilized than that," Portia said, drawing the hood of her evening coat over her head.

"I would hope so," Larthia replied, nodding at a departing guest who waved in farewell.

"Is he a Gaul?" Portia asked, looking in the direction of Verrix, who remained immobile against a wall.

"What else? Don't you see the torque?"

"He's very comely. Hair the color of ripe corn, and those pale eyes. The Gauls are handsome people."

"You forget what he looks like very quickly when exposed to his personality," Larthia said darkly.

"I know they make difficult slaves," Portia said, shaking her head resignedly. "My husband says that they are virtually intractable. Not like the Greeks, who seem to be philosophical about their servile status and adapt to it. The Celts fight their fate tenaciously to the very end."

Larthia nodded, noting with alarm that Verrix seemed to be listening to what they were saying.

"Well, I must be going," Portia said. "I have to find my doddering husband, who is doubtless getting drunk on Lesbian wine with that fool Titus Labienus. Thank you again for a splendid evening. Good night."

Larthia managed to stay on her feet long enough to get rid of the remainder of her guests and see Livia Versalia into her carriage. With the departure of the rest of the Vestals, who followed behind Livia in another conveyance, she was released from her role as hostess. Walking around her house wearily, she was directing the cleanup operation when she saw that Verrix was wearing a very mutinous expression.

"What is wrong with you?" she finally said to him impatiently, turning to face him with her hands on her hips, in no mood for his nonsense.

"May I have a word in private, mistress?" he asked, making the last word sound, as he always did, like blasphemy.

Larthia waved him wordlessly into an anteroom and shut the door.

"I heard what that woman said about me," he announced immediately.

"What woman?"

"That fat woman in the blue hooded coat."

"What she said is of no consequence to you."

"Does it make you feel superior to discuss me as if I were some special breed of canine?" he said furiously. "Gauls are intractable, Greeks adapt—we are people, Lady Sejana, not hunting hounds!"

"You are slaves," Larthia said. "Bear it in mind."

"Oh, I see. Am I going to hear about flogging again? Shall I get you the lash?"

"For your information, I spared you from a fate far worse than flogging this very night. If I wanted you to suffer I would have turned you over to that centurion, Demeter. He was very eager to get his vengeful hands on you."

Verrix looked back at her, stone-faced. "I saw him," he said shortly.

"Is that all you have to say?"

"I did what was necessary to escape from Roman captivity," he said shortly. "His friend was killed in the process."

"That's not how he sees it."

"That's how it was."

"He would have seized you in front of everybody if I hadn't stopped him."

"I don't need a woman to intervene for me," Verrix said shortly.

"I didn't intervene for *you*," Larthia said nastily. "You represent a substantial investment to my grandfather; I want him to get his money's worth."

Verrix stared back at her, inwardly seething but silent as a tomb.

Larthia met his gaze, uncomfortable with his anger. Why did she care what he thought? It bothered her that she did.

"Why do you pay attention to that stupid Campania woman's chatter anyway?" Larthia said in irritation. "Everyone knows she's a brainless babbler."

"You were paying attention to her."

"I was making conversation."

"You were agreeing with her!"

Larthia stared at him.

"You nodded!" he said furiously.

"I was trying to get rid of her! I wanted her to go home, wanted all of them to go home. If she had said that she was about to sprout a peaked crown and turn into the goddess Juno I would have nodded!"

Verrix glared at her, but again said nothing.

"Why am I having this conversation with you?" Larthia asked herself aloud.

"Why do I always do this?" She closed her eyes, opened them again, and announced, "I am going to bed. Nestor will find something for you to do."

He turned immediately to go, but for some reason she couldn't afterward fathom she stopped him at the door.

"Verrix, why did my interchange with Portia bother you so much?" she asked, her tone of command now altered, almost conciliatory. "You must be accustomed to the Roman attitude toward slaves by this time."

He turned slowly to face her.

"It's not the Roman attitude toward slaves," he said. "It's yours."

"I am a Roman woman."

His gaze fell away from hers. "I want you to think of me as a person," he said quietly.

Larthia looked back at him in silence, her heart beginning to beat faster.

"I want you to think of me as a man," he added, even more softly, and left.

Larthia swallowed hard, putting her hand out to touch the shelf next to her. The terra-cotta jars and pots stored there rattled with the sudden motion.

She was startled to find that she was blinking rapidly. Was her younger sister's emotionalism contagious? Like Julia, she seemed always to be on the verge of tears lately. She tilted her head back to prevent the kohl lining her eyes from running.

What was it about Verrix that drew her? He was a slave, yet she couldn't seem to remember that. She knew in her heart that she really thought of him as her equal, as if his former status had clung to him through the defeat of his people and his subsequent enslavement. And in a way it had. He didn't think of himself as a servant, merely as a man forced by circumstances to guard her until he was able to resume a free life. His attitude had communicated itself to her, and he knew it. He was able to read her mind as if she were speaking her thoughts to him.

Larthia closed her eyes again, pressing her lips together. She should sell him, convince her grandfather somehow that Verrix had to go. But already that thought was abhorrent to her.

She had grown used to the stability of his presence; Verrix did make her feel secure, exactly as Casca had intended. And if she were really honest with herself she had to admit that she liked having him around just to look at him. He was handsome, and he was also everything her husband had not been: young, virile, and overwhelmingly interested in her.

But he was also a slave.

Larthia started as the door opened and Nestor stopped short, surprised to see her.

"Are you all right, mistress?" he said, looking around the closet as if for an explanation of her presence there.

"Yes, yes, I was just searching for the storage jars for the *garum,*" Larthia said hastily, turning away to wipe her eyes with her fingers.

"They're in the kitchen, mistress, on the floor of the cold pantry."

"Of course, of course, I'd forgotten. What did you want, Nestor?"

He reached up past her head and took a jar off a shelf. "Just this."

Larthia nodded.

"Since we have a moment away from the others, mistress, may I speak to you about something?"

"Certainly," Larthia replied, glad of the distraction from her troubled thoughts.

"It's about Verrix."

Larthia sighed inwardly. So it was not to be a distraction after all.

"Go on," she said shortly.

"He takes direction poorly," Nestor said.

"Has he refused to obey an order you gave him?"

"No . . ." Nestor answered hesitantly.

"Then what?"

"He always argues with me, tells me that something may be done better another way, tries to instruct me . . ."

"Well, is he usually right?"

"That's not the point!" Nestor said, agitated. "I am in charge of this house. When I say 'Do this' to a slave, it should be done. Without discussion."

"I see." So Nestor was feeling territorial. Well, she was feeling tired and short tempered. She'd had enough of contentious servants for one night.

"I will tell Verrix to obey you without question," Larthia said briefly. "Is there anything else?"

"I was going to come for you shortly to look over the wine inventory. The guests drank more tonight than was expected. Would you like to do it now?"

"Fine." Larthia followed the servant out of the closet and into the hall.

Julia sat at the window of Larthia's room and played her meeting with Marcus over and over in her mind; his every touch, gesture, word was committed to memory. She got up and walked, then sat, then rose once more. She was so exhilarated that it seemed she would never rest again.

Why was she willing to risk her life for a man she hardly knew? She couldn't understand it logically, but at the same time she didn't care. She just wanted to feel again the way she had felt when he was with her.

She was clear about her decision to continue seeing Marcus. Unlike Livia Versalia, Julia was not religious. She believed in Marcus far more than she did in the goddess Vesta. She had not chosen her present life and had no qualms about abandoning it. Her only concern was the danger to Marcus and herself in pursuing a relationship forbidden by custom and by law.

It would be an eternity until the next market day. She needed the time to talk to him and get to know him; she yearned to hear everything about him, his family, his past, his hopes and dreams. These brief meetings snatched under trying circumstances only whetted her appetite for more.

Desire was like a rising tide within her; it shocked her in retrospect, but at the time Marcus kissed her she had wanted to climb inside his clothes. Her distant awareness of their surroundings had faded into nothingness. If he had pressed her back onto the bed she would not have stopped him.

Each time she saw him she was amazed again that this man wanted her enough to flout the law and put his illustrious career in jeopardy. He looked like the Etruscan kings who had founded Rome, whose representation she had seen everywhere since childhood. He had the same strong nose, finely chiseled mouth, and lustrous black hair. He had walked off a temple frieze or an ancient tiled mosaic and into her arms. She, who had little experience of life and no experience of men, had won the hero of the barbarian campaigns.

It seemed impossible but it was true.

Julia paced the bedroom, dimly aware of the sounds of the party breaking up, the rumble of departing carriages, and the scurrying of servants in the halls. She stopped to examine a crystal bottle of scent on the dressing table, pulling out the stopper and holding it under her nose. Lemon verbena. She replaced the bottle and looked around the room.

Larthia's bedroom was almost bare, furnished with a bed and a chest and a vanity table, a few other necessary items. Romans, even the wealthy ones, saved their display of luxury for the reception rooms where others might view their largesse. The chambers meant for sleep were spare and functional, an outgrowth of the Roman attitude that the best of life was lived in public.

Julia, unable to still her wandering feet, went to the window again. She was staring out at the moonlit portico when Larthia entered from the hall.

"The litter Livia sent for you is here," she announced, removing a pin from her hair to ease her aching head.

Julia went to the door and embraced her sister.

"I can't thank you enough for everything you have done for me," Julia said. "I'm so happy."

Larthia nodded absently.

"Are you all right?" Julia asked, staring with concern at her sister's distracted expression.

Larthia shrugged. "My head is banging like the gong used to summon Hannibal's elephants."

"Are you worried about my meeting Marcus here in the future? We can arrange something else . . ."

"No, no, that's not it. Just a domestic matter." Larthia smiled. "And I'm tired. The party was a lot of work and now there's the clearing up to do."

"I understand." Julia kissed her sister's cheek. "I will see you here next market day. Please ask the physician to come in the early evening."

"What shall I say is wrong with you?" Larthia asked, raising her brows inquiringly.

Julia shrugged. "Fatigue, malaise, loss of appetite. Back pain, everybody has back pain. Avoid anything specific."

Larthia nodded. "I'll walk you to the door."

She stood in the doorway and watched her sister climb into the litter, wondering if the course they were contemplating meant that both of them had lost their minds.

Then she went back inside and closed the door.

Five

Marcus paused in the act of lifting the *pilum* and wiped his brow with the back of his free hand. In front of him, his class of fifty *hastati* watched his every move. They were the youngest legionaries, new recruits, and he was instructing them in the use of the six-foot javelin, the primary missile weapon of the infantry.

Marcus blinked and tightened his grip on the *aumentum,* the leather throwing thong bound to the shaft of the lance. He hoisted it behind his shoulder and threw; as it left his hand he gave it a half turn, which imparted a rotary motion to both maintain its direction and increase its penetrating power. The *hastati* turned their heads as one to follow its progress through the morning air.

Marcus was an expert with the lance. He could throw it more than sixty-five yards with deadly accuracy. The men watched in awe as the missile's pointed shaft sank into the soggy spring earth of the Campus Martius, and the lance remained in place, quivering with tension.

Marcus walked over to it and pointed out its angle of entry and depth of penetration, speaking the plain, elementary Latin most likely to be understood by these men, most of whom employed it as a second language. He was training them as a special favor to Caesar, whose recruits they were, raised in Transalpine Gaul. Called *alaudae,* "the larks," they were the Imperator's attempt to prove that provincials could do as well in battle as the Italian born if properly trained from the time of their entry into the army. To that end he had sent Marcus, who was usually assigned more administrative tasks, to demonstrate the use of the *pilum* to the larks.

Marcus retrieved the lance and then called for the men to come forward, one at a time. He showed each one how to grip the *aumentum* and hold the javelin aloft, thinking that this entire legion could put some of the native Roman soldiers to shame. The larks were all industrious and very eager to learn, conscious of the chance they were being given to win citizenship as part of Caesar's long term recruitment plan. They wanted to find and keep their place in the most ef-

ficient and rigidly organized fighting body
the world had yet seen: the Roman army.
To that end they had been formed into a
supplementary legion, or *auxilium,* to
prove their mettle. If they performed up
to standard their status would be stabi-
lized and their group organized like the
others.

Caesar's legions were subdivided into
ten cohorts each, and each cohort had
three maniples, or tactical units. A man-
iple had two centuries, groups of one
hundred men, commanded by a centurion. Thus each cohort had six centurions, and premier among these six was the
pilus prior, or first javelin thrower, who
commanded the entire cohort. Marcus was
the *pilus prior* of Caesar's first cohort,
summoned to all of his war councils, second in command only to the military tribunes, men of patrician families who
achieved their positions more by right of
birth than military merit. Such officers
would be the last to dispute that the centurions were the backbone and the real
heroes of the army. Marcus' friendship
with the libertine Septimus Gracchus was
an example of the relative standing of the
two classes of officers; the much decorated
career soldier Marcus was a centurion,
and Septimus, the Senator's son doing his

obligatory term in the military, was a tribune.

The recruit grasping the *pilum* let it slip through his fingers to the ground.

"Like this," Marcus said patiently, picking up the javelin and showing the man how to insert his first and second fingers through the leather loop on its shaft. He glanced up at the sun and wondered how much time he would have left to show them the *hasta,* the two-foot-long, double-edged Spanish sword for which the first line of infantry was named. Practice had shown that the javelin was more effective in battle than the sword, so he was concentrating on the *pilum,* but the men had to learn the use of both.

Another *pilum* crashed to the ground, and Marcus knew that the *hasta* would have to wait for another day.

He was having difficulty concentrating on the task at hand. As he lay sleepless in the barracks the previous night he could hear the distant rumble of carts clattering through the city streets, reminding him that the next morning market day began. He was meeting Julia at her sister's house after sundown, and he was preoccupied with anticipation of that event. But by this time throwing the javelin was as natural to him as breathing, so

he could go through the motions without
engaging his mind. He had tutored all of
the men and dismissed them at noon before he looked up from packing his gear
and saw Septimus bearing down on him.

"I'm for the baths," Septimus said, gazing with amusement at the barbarians departing the field, some of them dragging
their *pila* along the ground. "How about
you?"

Marcus shook his head.

"Too nervous about your rendezvous?"
Septimus asked him archly.

"Be quiet," Marcus said sharply. He
hadn't told Septimus about his arrangement with Julia, not wanting to draw his
friend further into illegal activity. But
when Septimus saw that Marcus, who never
avoided a scheduled duty, had traded watch
times at the barracks with another centurion he had been able to deduce the truth
without too much effort.

"Don't worry, they're all gone, there's no
one to hear us. By the way, I consulted the
auspices this morning at home, and they
were favorable," Septimus said, referring to
the practice of checking with the gods to
make sure it was a good day to start something. Romans believed that the success of
an enterprise was determined by the way
it began. "I saw a flock of ravens flying in

formation through the sky, and took it for a sign from Jupiter that your affair will have a happy outcome."

"What does that mean?" Marcus asked dryly. "That Julia and I will both remain alive?"

"Among other things."

"I thought you were trying to warn me off her," Marcus said, as he stowed his *pilum* in his *sarcina*, or kit. This was a bundle tied to a forked pole and carried over the shoulder.

"No longer," Septimus said resignedly. "You are the most determined man I ever met, Marcus, and if you're set on going through with this, all I can do now is help you."

"That's a very sensible attitude," Marcus said, and Septimus laughed, shaking his head.

"Are you sure you won't join me at the baths?" he asked again. "Your lady will be very pleased to find you freshly bathed and scented with aloes."

Marcus grinned. "All right. I suppose it will help to pass the time."

Septimus patted Marcus on the back. "In truth, I envy you, my friend. The last time I had a virgin I was seventeen years old, and I had to go to Parthia for the privilege."

The two men walked off the deserted field dedicated to the military games of the god Mars, their minds far from war.

"Is this where it hurts?" Paris asked, manipulating Julia's spine. Behind his back Larthia crossed her eyes and then looked at the ceiling, her foot tapping impatiently.

"Farther down," Julia replied, wincing as the physician increased the pressure of his fingers.

"There?"

"Yes, I think so," Julia replied, silently begging the indulgence of the gods for her lie.

"And is it always so?"

"No, it comes and goes," Julia said, as Larthia suppressed a giggle, turning away from the scene.

Paris stepped back and let the hem of Julia's shift fall. "This may be a female complaint," he announced. "Does the pain come just before the issue of blood with each moon?"

"Yes," Julia said, seizing on the first plausible explanation that might satisfy the physician.

"And do you have cramping each time?"

"Yes, I do."

Paris nodded. "This results from the lack of childbearing, I've seen it in Vestals before, and in other long-term virgins. I will prescribe an extract of foxglove that will help with the pain, and I will see you again here the first market day after the new moon."

Julia and Larthia exchanged glances. "I would prefer not to wait for so long a time," Julia said hastily. "Could I not see you again next *nundina*? It would please me to know that I have a regular appointment with you, this discomfort has been bothering me for some time."

"Certainly," Paris said smoothly, totaling up the extra fees in his head. "Will it be convenient, Lady Sejana, for me to see your sister here at your home in the future?"

"Yes," Larthia said shortly, tiring of the charade.

"Very well. I will send the plant extract to the Atrium Vestae by messenger in the morning, I will need this evening to prepare it. I shall expect to see you here next market day, Julia Rosalba. Good evening."

"I'll show you out," Larthia said, preceding the physician into the hallway. When she returned a short time later she said to Julia, "I thought he would never leave."

"He gave me a very thorough examination."

"Since there's nothing really wrong with you, it would have been amazing if he found something."

"Did you pay him?" Julia asked.

"Of course."

"How much did he charge you? I will transfer the amount from my inheritance to yours."

"Don't be ridiculous, Julia, we're both risking our lives here, do you think I am worried about a few sesterces?"

Julia studied her sister in silence, then said, "I think I should go, Larthia, this was a bad idea. If I leave before—"

"Centurion Marcus Corvus Demeter is waiting for you in the atrium, mistress," Nestor said from the doorway.

"Thank you, Nestor. You may go." Larthia waited for the servant's footsteps to fade before observing to Julia, "Too late. Now stop fussing and get ready for your visitor. I'll send him in to you shortly."

She left before Julia could protest.

Marcus looked up as Larthia came into the entry hall and greeted him, extending both of her hands to take his.

"Centurion, how nice to see you again so soon!" Larthia said delightedly, mindful of Nestor, who was watering a plant right behind her. "Come into the *tablinum* where we can discuss our business. Would you care for some refreshment?"

"No, thank you," Marcus said, somewhat overwhelmed by this effusive greeting.

Larthia led him into the parlor. She waited until Nestor had passed the door on his way back to the kitchen before saying in a low tone, "In the future you will have to climb over the back wall and enter the bedroom from the patio. Let no one see you. Servants talk. If you arrive at the front door too often they will be saying you're having an affair with *me.*"

Marcus nodded.

"When you leave just walk around to the gardens and go in the back way as you did last time. Julia is waiting for you."

Marcus nodded again.

"Now," Larthia said, "let's pretend to be interested in one another long enough to convince the servants we actually have something to discuss."

Marcus smiled.

* * *

It seemed an eternity to Julia before the outside door opened and Marcus came through it, his eyes locking with hers as he closed it behind him.

Her feet barely touched the floor as she ran to him; he folded her into his arms and said, concerned, "Tears? Why are you crying?"

"I was just thinking about the chance we're both taking. This is so dangerous," she murmured against his chest.

"Say the word and I'll go," he replied, holding her off to look at her.

Julia dropped her eyes. "I can never say that word, Marcus. Why?"

"I think there's a good reason."

"What is it?"

Fatum nos coegisse credo," he replied. "I believe that fate brought us together."

She looked up at him and nodded.

"Then why question what we both sense to be the work of the gods?" he said. "Accept it as a gift."

Julia buried her face against his hard shoulder again. "It's difficult to live so much of my life without seeing you. When I'm not with you I think—oh, terrible things."

"And when you are with me?"

"Then I forget the rest of the world."

He bent his head to kiss the side of

her neck. "I'll make you forget it completely," he said softly, his lips soft and caressing. "All of it. Just give me the chance."

Julia closed her eyes, content to let him lead her down the path she had never trod before this night. He murmured to her as she clung to him, reveling in the strength of his body, the soothing sound of his husky voice. She felt his mouth move to her hair, her cheek, and then to her lips. As he kissed her repeatedly he opened her mouth with his tongue, and Julia responded eagerly, her desire to please him compensating for her lack of experience. He ran his hands down her back, forcing her closer, spreading his legs to take her weight. She moaned when she felt him hard against her, the sound part fear but more desire, and tightened her arms around his neck.

Marcus felt his fragile control slipping; he knew he couldn't move too fast or he would lose her trust, but he had thought of little else but this moment since the last time he saw her. He pulled the veil from her hair, dropping it on the floor. Her *palla* followed soon after, and she stood in her thin gown, her hands fluttering down his spine as he kissed the satiny smoothness of her neck and shoulders. His mouth was open, leaving a trail of wetness on her skin. He pushed aside the neckline of her *stola* impatiently to clear his path.

Julia gasped as he bent her over his bracing arm; she had never been touched like this, held like this, caressed with such primitive urgency, and she dug her fingers into the muscles of his back, sensing the coiled power under her hands. He was the embodiment of every guilty reverie of her adolescence, every daydream inspired by the sight of a muscular body revealed in an athletic contest or the display of nearly naked male slaves being offered for auction. She had never thought a man would come to release her from the prison of her mind and give flesh to her fantasies, yet here he was.

Marcus moved his mouth lower, to her breasts. Julia moaned when through her gossamer tunic she felt his lips on her nipple; his mouth was so hot it seemed to sear her, sending ripples of heat and excitement along her nerves. She arched her back still further, sinking her fingers into his hair and holding his head against her as he laved her through the silken material, nipping and teasing the bud of flesh that had stiffened instantly at his touch. Her small sounds of pleasure inflamed him until, in frustration, he tore at the clasps on her shoulders and roughly pulled the gown down to her waist.

Julia was almost swooning; she swayed in his arms as he took one swollen peak between his lips and covered her other breast greedily with his hand. Her fine skin, dappled lightly with pale freckles like a bird's egg, was the color and consistency of cream, his tan standing out against it. Her breath was coming in short bursts as he increased the pressure of his mouth, running the fingers of his free hand over her upper arms and naked back like a merchant marveling at the sumptuous quality of imported silk. When he slipped his arm under her knees to lift her to the bed she clung to him, easing backward as he fell against her, enveloping her again with his body.

To feel him all along the length of her was a shock, her *stola* a slight barrier between them, his legs bare. He buried his face between her breasts and locked his hands behind her waist. Julia felt his soft mouth and soft hair against her skin, in contrast with the hard muscles of the arms embracing her. His hair gleamed in the torchlight as he turned his head and placed his flushed face against her flat abdomen, his eyelids drifting closed, their lashes brushing his cheeks, where high color made him look as if he were in the grip of fever. And so he was; when she clutched at his shoulders he raised his head to drag his lips along the supple line of one slender arm, his whole body tight with a tension she had created and which looked to her for its release. He pulled her fiercely to him and said into her ear, "I knew it would be like this, Julia. I saw you and I knew."

Emboldened by their mutual passion, Julia drew aside the material of his tunic and kissed the hollow of his throat. He smelled musky, masculine, and she closed her eyes luxuriously as she tasted the salt of his skin on her lips. Eager for more, she reached down for his belt, her head dropping to his shoulder in submission.

Marcus was undone. Groaning, he slid his palms along her sides and pushed her gown above her knees, his hands trembling as he stroked her. She wanted him, she was almost crazy with wanting him; he could feel it in her body which responded to his touch as a lyre to a musician's fingers. She fairly sang under his hands. But she was a virgin, and he was afraid to hurt her. If he rushed her or forced her too far she might be lost to him forever.

Julia looked up at him with heavy-lidded

eyes, her face pink, her brow dewed with perspiration. He could feel the outlines of her body and wanted her naked, her colt-ish legs wrapped around his hips. But he must not rush her. He rolled Julia onto her back and bent to embrace her again, willing himself to take care.

There was a knock on the bedroom door.

They both froze; Marcus could feel the passion drain from Julia's pliant body as "the rest of the world" intruded on them once again.

"Answer," he murmured into her ear.

"What is it?" Julia called in a wavering tone.

"I have the linens you requested, mis-tress," Nestor's voice answered. "Shall I bring them in?"

Marcus drew back from Julia and held a finger to her lips. "I'll go outside," he whispered. "You let him in."

Julia nodded shakily, rearranging her gown with fingers that refused to obey her at first; it took her three tries before she could close the clasp on her left shoulder. She picked up her veil and *palla* as Marcus slipped through the door to the portico. Clothing hastily straightened, she took sev-eral deep breaths and then went to the hall door and opened it.

Nestor stared at her. "Lady Julia! I thought Lady Sejana was in here."

"I was just resting after my visit from the physician. Shall I take those from you?" Julia said, amazed that her voice could sound so normal.

He handed over the pile of folded laundry. "I'm sorry to disturb you," he said.

"It's all right. Good night."

"Good night," the servant replied, and padded off down the hall. Julia closed the door behind him and then leaned against it, her eyes closed, as her heartbeat returned to normal. After several seconds had passed Julia went to the other door and let Marcus back into the bedroom.

"All clear?" he said.

She nodded and then collapsed into his arms. He held her until her trembling ceased.

"Marcus, how can we continue with this?" she finally said, drawing back to look at him. "We have to snatch forbidden moments like fugitives! I resent feeling like a criminal every time I see you, yet there doesn't seem to be any other way for us, and the thought of not seeing you again is unbearable."

"There will be another way," he said firmly.

"How?"

"I don't know yet, but I'll find it." He led her back to the bed, his passion cooled. His only thought was to allay her fears.

"What do you mean?" she said, facing him as they sat down together.

"We could leave Rome, go somewhere else."

"But you know only the army, Marcus! How would we live?"

"I'm not helpless, Julia. I could hire out as a mercenary, for one thing."

"Where?"

"Britannia, maybe. The tribes there are always fighting one another, the petty kings squabble over territory daily. With my knowledge of sophisticated warfare I'm sure that I would be in demand."

"But, Marcus, you are celebrated here, an honored soldier with triumphs in your past. Could you give that up for me?"

He smoothed the golden red hair back from her face gently. "It doesn't mean as much to me as it once did," he said softly.

"Will you be able to bear the disgrace if we are discovered before we can get away?" Julia asked softly. "I know that a Roman soldier cannot endure shame."

"I can endure anything for you," he said.

There was another knock at the door,

and a woman's voice said, "It's me, Larthia."

"Come in," Julia called.

Marcus stood as Larthia entered.

"Was Nestor here?" she asked anxiously. Julia nodded.

"Did he see—" she began, but Julia interrupted. "No. Marcus slipped outside before I answered the door."

Larthia closed her eyes in relief. "I am so sorry. I asked him for the linens, thinking that he would bring them in the morning. His efficiency almost undid all our planning. When he told me he came here and found you I was afraid of what might have happened."

Marcus bent to kiss Julia's cheek. "I must go, Julia. I want to be back in the barracks before the watch changes. I'll arrange to stay longer next time."

Julia nodded.

"Lady Sejana, thank you," Marcus said, and then looked at Julia. "Until next market day," he said, and went through the door.

Julia watched him go and then turned to her sister.

"A close call," Larthia said.

"Yes."

"I should take steps to make sure such a thing does not happen again."

Julia sighed. "What can you do?"

"I can put a guard on this room when you're in here."

Julia stared at her. "You would have to take that person into your confidence. Who can you trust that much?"

"My bodyguard."

"Larthia, what are you saying?" Julia gasped. "He's a Gaul! And a slave!"

"A slave who doesn't get his freedom papers unless he stays in this job for three whole years. He'll do it, and he'll keep his mouth shut."

"I don't know, Larthia . . . I think it's risky."

"I do not. Nothing is more important to him than his emancipation. He won't care if you're sleeping with a soldier or a street cleaner or Pompey the Great, he'll make sure you have privacy if I tell him to do that. It's perfect."

"I'm not sleeping with anyone at the moment," Julia said morosely.

Larthia looked at her.

"Nestor interrupted us at a very critical point," Julia went on unhappily.

"I see."

"Maybe it's for the best. When I think about it . . . making love, I mean . . ." She shuddered delicately. "I'm so hungry for him, yet afraid at the same time."

"But you weren't afraid when you were with him," Larthia said.

Julia reddened. "No," she admitted. "Not at all."

"Have you talked about it?"

Julia's blush deepened. "We haven't wasted much time with talking."

Larthia studied her sister for a moment and then sighed. "You don't know how lucky you are to feel that way. And to be able to act on it."

"Have you ever felt like this?" Julia asked. "About your husband?"

"Of course not, Julia. How can you ask such a question? You know what the situation was there."

"Not really. I was a child when you got married, and later it never seemed proper to come right out and ask you. I know that you . . . appeared to be unhappy."

"I was."

"If you were not in love with him when you married, what about later, when you were pregnant?"

"I was not in love with him at any time, Julia," Larthia snapped.

"Or with anyone else?"

Larthia didn't answer.

"Larthia?" Julia persisted.

"We're wasting time," her sister said briskly. "You should leave too; your litter is waiting. You don't want to make Livia Versalia suspicious."

"Larthia, are you sure it's all right for us to continue to meet here?"

"I am. I'll take care of the privacy problem. You're happy with Marcus, and that's all that counts. I'll talk to Verrix tonight, and all will be well. You'll see."

Julia embraced her sister. "You always make me feel so much better."

Larthia patted her shoulder. "That's my mission in life. Now let's go, I'll see you to the door."

Once Julia had left, Larthia walked back into the house and encountered Nestor walking through the hall with a brass planter in his hand.

"Mistress, let me apologize again for intruding on your sister," he began.

Larthia waved him away. "Never mind, it's forgotten. Please send Verrix to me in the *tablinum* immediately." She walked on briskly, planning what she would say.

A short time later Verrix came into the room where she was waiting for him and said, "Nestor told me that you wanted to speak to me."

"Yes," Larthia replied. "Close the door."

Verrix did so and returned to her.

"Sit down."

He sat across from her uneasily, a puz-

THE RAVEN AND THE ROSE 183

zled expression on his face. Why had she invited him to sit? Servants were generally kept standing at all times.

"I have something to say to you," Larthia began.

Verrix felt his throat closing. She was selling him. He would never see her again. It was over.

Larthia was silent, as if thinking about what to say. Verrix studied her. Why would she bother to call him in here to tell him that she was selling him? He would just wake up one morning and find that he now belonged to someone else, his deal with her grandfather nullified. As a slave he did not deserve an explanation.

"I find that I must take you into my confidence about something," she said slowly.

Verrix began to breathe again. He waited.

"My sister is having a . . . relationship . . . with a centurion," she said baldly.

Verrix had long since schooled his features to conceal emotion, but it was clear this piece of information startled even him.

"Your sister the Vestal?" he said, in a tone which did not quite conceal his incredulity.

"That's right. She will be meeting him in this house every market day."

Verrix said nothing.

"I am trusting you with this information because I need someone to help me. Your unique position among the slaves makes you the most qualified to do so."

"Does Nestor know about this?"

"No one knows but you."

Verrix digested that and then said, "What do you want me to do?"

"It is imperative that this relationship be concealed at all costs. I think you can understand why. Do you know Roman law concerning the Vestals?"

"I know that the penalty for breaking their vows is death," Verrix replied.

"Exactly. And I cannot be everywhere at once. Although I will be taking every precaution to conceal their meetings, I want you to stand guard outside my room when Julia's visitor is here, and I want you to intercede if anything happens that might reveal their relationship. Is that clear?"

Verrix nodded. "What's the penalty for your collaboration with this scheme?" he asked.

"I don't want to talk about it," Larthia said darkly. "But there is something I should add."

Verrix looked at her.

"The centurion is Demeter."

Verrix showed no response.

"I trust that you remember him; he wanted to impale you on his sword when he saw you here at Livia's reception," Larthia stated dryly.

"I am always mindful of the contract for my freedom," Verrix replied evenly. "I will do as you say."

"Fine. Demeter will return next *nundina*. I will notify you when he arrives."

Verrix rose.

"And there's something else," Larthia said.

Verrix halted.

"Nestor has been complaining to me that you're arguing with him. I know he is old and set on his path, but just do what he says and do it his way, please. I don't have time to smooth his ruffled feathers every time he gives you an order."

Verrix inclined his head.

"That will be all."

Verrix left.

When Marcus returned to the barracks he found Lisander, the slave attached to his cohort, waiting for him.

"A message came for you while you were gone," Lisander said soberly, handing him a tightly wound scroll. The seal on the parchment was the "SPQR" of the Roman Republic (*Senatus Populusque Romanus,* "the Senate and the people of Rome.") Marcus noted that this legend was surmounted by the *fasces,* the bundle of rods which symbolized the unity of the Roman people, and that it was shown with an axe, which only the dictator was allowed to include in the symbol.

The message was from Caesar.

Lisander, who had also noted the origin of the letter, was watching his face.

"Who brought this?" Marcus asked.

"Tiberius Junius Germanicus," Lisander replied.

Marcus considered that. Germanicus was the *hastus prior,* or premier swordsman, of the first cohort, also a close confidante of Caesar's.

This must be important.

"Leave me," Marcus said brusquely to the slave.

As soon as Lisander was gone he looked around the deserted barracks to make sure he was alone before he split the wax seal and unrolled the parchment.

As always, Caesar was brief and to the point. "Come to the southern guardhouse at the turn of the watch," the message said. "Let no one see you." That was all.

Marcus glanced outside at the night sky and determined from the position of Polaris, the north star, that the turn of the watch was not far away. The fact that this message had passed from Tiberius to Lisander to him, and they were all three trusted allies of the dictator, told him that Caesar was taking no chances on discovery.

Marcus walked out of the barracks, past the dormitory where many of the soldiers were sleeping, and into the Campus. The marshy earth gave beneath his sandaled feet as he crossed the archery ground, where the circular targets loomed like ghosts. When he heard voices he ducked behind a pile of dummies, canvas bags with stitched-on limbs stuffed with straw, used in Greek-wrestling instruction. He waited there until those conversing had passed.

Romans rose with the sun and retired early, so the only personnel he encountered when he walked on again were soldiers changing the watch. Marcus saw no one else for the rest of the journey. When he reached the guardhouse it was dark, and he hesitated, wondering if he had mistaken the message and the call was for another night. Then a figure emerged from the shadows and gestured for him to come forward.

"We were waiting for you," Tiberius said, and opened the door, following Marcus into the small, roughcast room, which contained about a dozen men. They were crowded around a brazier on the floor, shielding its light with their bodies so that from the exterior the guardhouse would appear to be unoccupied.

Marcus joined the group, squatting next to Tiberius and nodding to the men whose faces were dappled with firelight: Mark Antony, Caesar's nephew Octavian, Lepidus, Artemidorus, and others that Marcus recognized as Caesar's most trusted friends and advisors. All eyes were focused on the dictator as he stood and addressed them.

"I have called you all here because an incident in the Senate today has confirmed for me that the cause of my enemies is very much alive," he said wearily.

The men waited. This was not news.

"You may recall that on the festival of the Lupercal, having just accepted the post of dictator for life, I was seated on the Rostra when the Luperci came running into the forum. Antony, who as priest of the Juliani was one of them, attempted to place a crown upon my head. I rejected the crown and said, 'Jupiter alone is king of the Romans,' and sent the diadem to the Capitol. I thought at the time that this gesture would be sufficient to finally dispel the notion that I lusted for the title of *rex* to add to the others already conferred upon me."

A few of the men exchanged glances and Antony shifted uncomfortably. Caesar was already running the country, but most of those present knew that the Roman people abhorred the idea of an overlord, embodied in the title of *rex* or king. This was contrary to the *animus*, or spirit, of a republic, their cherished ideal, even if the reality had drifted far from the model by Caesar's time. *Primus inter pares*, first among equals, was much more acceptable to the average Roman than a monarchy in which the monarch was thought superior to the rest of the population.

Antony had acted hastily and made a strategic mistake. The people loved Caesar, but they were not ready for a king. Caesar's enemies had only to promote the notion that he wanted the title to gain attentive listeners and increase their following.

"But this morning," Caesar went on in a weary tone, "Lucius Cotta announced in the Senate that it was written in the Sibylline Books that the Parthians could be conquered only by a king, and therefore in view of the upcoming campaign against them I should immediately be given that title."

A groan arose from the group. Octavian spoke up, saying, "Lucius Cotta is a senile old fool. Nobody will pay any attention to him."

"Somebody must have put Cotta up to it," Tiberius suggested darkly. "Casca, maybe."

"On the contrary, I think Cotta was sincere and his news occasioned much discussion," Caesar said. "He is a priest of Jupiter. His interpretation of the oracle's words receives the close attention of the people, who have heard about it already, I'm sure."

A gloomy silence prevailed.

"My point is this," Caesar said. "If I remain in Rome until May, when the army is scheduled to depart for Parthia, there will be more than two months for Casca and the others to inflame the people against me. I propose that I leave with the scouts on March eighteenth and give all this talk a chance to die down. The disadvantage will be that the army will remain in camp here without me, as it will be too early to march east with the full complement. The spring floods will still be running, and the earth will be too soft for a hard march. What is your advice on this matter?"

The men looked at one another measuringly, considering what he had said. Marcus knew that, as usual, Caesar had already made up his mind on the subject, and was only asking his allies for their thoughts in order to make sure he had not overlooked anything in his planning.

"Your presence here could act more as a panacea than an irritant," Antony said reasonably. "You don't want to appear to be running away."

Caesar nodded, then turned to Octavian.

"I think you should go," Octavian said. "Seeing you every day, wearing the Imperator's robes and preceded by lictors carrying the axed fasces, will only fan the flames. Issuing orders from a distance is safer. The effect will be the same, but your enemies will be denied their rallying symbol: you wearing the purple, sitting in a gilded chair and heading the Senate, acting, in their opinion, like a god."

"Marcus?" Caesar said.

"I agree with your nephew," Marcus replied. "Go to Parthia and let the situation settle in your absence. The army will uphold your standard here."

Caesar polled the rest of the group, and it was agreed that he would leave

Rome in mid-March with the advance guard. As the meeting broke up Tiberius took Marcus aside and said, "Where were you tonight? Your slave Lisander did not know."

A line waited by the guardhouse door; the men were departing one by one to avoid arousing suspicion.

"I went for a walk," Marcus replied.

"You must like to live dangerously," Tiberius said. "The gangs have been rampant in the streets lately."

"I kept to the Campus," Marcus said hastily.

"Nothing like a brisk tramp through the marshes to bring on the flux," Tiberius said, laughing. "You're an odd one, Demeter. It must be your Greek blood."

"Maybe," Marcus replied, smiling thinly.

"No, I'm serious," Tiberius said. "All those athletic contests in the nude, I can never decide whether the Greeks are decadent or just careless of their health."

Marcus laughed.

"Well, my turn to go," Tiberius said, and slipped through the door. Marcus glanced back at Caesar, who was engaged in conversation with his sister's son. Marcus decided to wait and talk to him later, then left when he saw through a crack in the door that Tiberius had disappeared and the coast was clear.

Marcus hardly noticed the walk back to the barracks; his head was filled with disturbing thoughts.

Caesar was in trouble. How could he, Marcus, consider deserting his position in the army and running off with Julia when the man who had raised him so high, transformed his life from that of a poor farmer to that of a hero of the state, was relying on him for future support?

Marcus paused to lean against a piling supporting a *ballista,* or stone-throwing catapult, and closed his eyes. A few months ago he would have turned in anyone he knew was considering deserting, would have killed anyone caught in the act. And now he was contemplating it himself! Meeting Julia had altered his goals so dramatically that sometimes he stopped in midreverie and wondered how he could be thinking what he was thinking.

So suddenly, in the moment he had set eyes on her, nothing much mattered to him except their future together.

But his notions of honor had not completely deserted him. Perhaps he could persuade Julia to wait for him until he returned from Parthia. A victory there would assure that the spoils of that ex-

tremely rich country would flow into
Rome, and the Roman people would certainly express their gratitude by finally
giving Caesar anything he wanted. Quib-
bles over titles or which kind of robes he
should wear would mean little in the face
of an ultimate triumph which filled the
coffers of every citizen. That was why
Caesar's enemies wanted to bring the situation to a head before he left for the
summer campaign; they knew if he won
another victory in the wealthy east, their
political cause at home would be lost.

Marcus sighed and forced his feet to
move forward again. He didn't know what
to do; he had never before faced a situation in which his personal desires con-
flicted with his duty. They had always
been one and the same. The notion of a
life without Julia was bleak indeed, but
his conscience would not allow him to desert his mentor when Caesar's need was
so great.

He walked on with a heavy heart.

"Livia Versalia wants to see you," Margo
said to Julia, as the Vestal walked into her
apartment in the Atrium. "She has sent me
twice to check and see if you had returned."

"What is it about?" Julia said, trying to disguise her reaction as she removed her veil.

"I don't know. Perhaps she wants to hear what you learned from the physician."

"Not much. He is sending me some medicine in the morning."

"Medicine for what?"

"Pain."

"What pain?"

"Margo, stop interrogating me," Julia said, with more than a trace of irritation. "I don't know what's wrong, if I did I wouldn't be consulting a doctor."

"You never complained to me of any pain," Margo said.

"I never complained to you, but I felt it."

The servant's silence was strained, and Julia relented when she realized the older woman was worried about her. She went over and put her hand on Margo's shoulder.

"I'm sure it's not serious. Paris thinks it's a female complaint resulting from a lack of childbearing."

Margo's brow cleared. "That sometimes happens."

"Yes, I know. So don't fret, and let me go on to see Livia. She doesn't like to be kept waiting."

Margo adjusted the drape of Julia's *palla.* "We'll talk when you get back," she said, then dropped her hand.

Julia slipped out into the torch-lit hall of the Atrium, the sound of her steps echoing off the marble walls as she headed for the corner suite which housed the Chief Vestal. She passed statues of Jupiter and Minerva, Diana and Mars, all standing on pedestals or enclosed in wall niches. Various Vestals had left offerings of early spring flowers or shafts of grain and ears of corn before the images, hoping to placate the gods. When she reached Livia's door she was admitted by Danuta, Livia's personal slave.

"Is your mistress ready to see me?" Julia asked.

Danuta bowed and indicated that Julia should go inside. As Julia passed her the slave stepped into the hall and closed the door behind her.

Livia's suite was the most luxurious in the Atrium; her floor was decorated with costly mosaics, the walls were hung with rich tapestries, and all of her furniture was inlaid with lapis lazuli, which gave a soft blue glow to the torch-lit rooms. Livia was seated on a silk-covered couch with carved mahogany arms. She smiled when she saw Julia and gestured for her visitor to sit opposite her.

"Greetings, daughter of Vesta," Livia said, and Julia knew that this was not going to be an informal chat.

"Gratia, Mater," Julia responded evenly, returning the formula salute.

"I requested this visit because I am concerned about you," Livia began, looking up as Danuta reentered the room with a tray containing an arrangement of sliced fruit and two goblets of honeyed goat's milk. The servant put the tray on a small table in front of the couch and then looked inquiringly at Livia. Livia waved her away, and she disappeared.

"I'm fine," Julia said evenly, once Danuta had left.

"I don't agree. You have been nervous and distracted, you said the wrong invocation prayers at your last sacrifice. Now I understand you have undertaken a program of physician's visits at Lady Sejana's house in addition to the one which I authorized."

"I confused the days at the sacrifice, I said the prayers for freedom from plague rather than for the general safety of the Roman state. Anyone could make such a mistake. I had never done so before."

"Exactly my point. Something is bothering you."

"I have not been feeling well. I suppose it's made me forgetful."

"What does the physician Paris say?"

"He says it's a female complaint."

Livia arched her brows inquiringly.

"Lack of childbearing," Julia elucidated.

"I see. I have heard this before with regard to our sisters. It seems to be the first idea that comes to a doctor's mind for an unexplained medical condition, since our virginal state is regarded as unhealthy and so must be the reason for everything."

Julia was silent. Livia was shrewd and in her quarter century with the Vestals had seen and heard quite a bit.

She would not be easy to fool.

"Something to drink?" Livia suggested.

Julia shook her head.

"I do not understand why your complaint requires such frequent visits with this physician," Livia went on, taking a sip from her own cup.

"I assume he wants to follow the progress of his treatment. He's recommended an extract of foxglove which will be delivered here in the morning."

"A painkiller?" said Livia, who was familiar with the healing properties of many plants and herbs.

"Yes," Julia responded, wishing miserably that she had never begun this deception. She was a novice liar and therefore not a very proficient one.

"You must be uncomfortable, then," Livia observed.

"Only at certain times."

Livia leaned forward and replaced her cup on the tray. "Very well," she said briskly. "You may continue to see the doctor, but I expect to be kept informed of your progress. Your health is of the utmost importance to me. You cannot serve the goddess unless your concentration is perfect."

"I understand," Julia said meekly.

"You may go," Livia said, not looking at her.

Julia rose and quickly exited the Chief Vestal's suite, her hands shaking so badly she had to clasp them in front of her to steady them.

Was it possible that Livia Versalia actually knew something? It was widely rumored that she had spies; her position was powerful and she obviously did what was necessary to protect it. Or maybe she really was in direct communication with the goddess, as others, more superstitious, suggested. Whatever the explanation, she seemed to have a lot more information

than her cloistered position would allow.
Preserving the integrity of her women was
paramount to her, and she would sacrifice
Julia without a second thought if Julia
threatened the reputation of the Vestals.

"Are you all right, Julia Rosalba?"
Danuta asked, and Julia jumped.

"Yes, of course, why do you ask?" Julia
said hastily, turning to face the servant.

"You were standing in the middle of
the hall staring into the air," Danuta said.

"I was just thinking," Julia replied. "I
have a lot on my mind. Don't you have
something to do?"

Danuta, who gave herself airs because
she was Livia's confidante, dropped her
eyes and walked away. Julia took a deep,
shuddering breath, resolving to maintain
better control of herself. Snapping at the
servants would only make her appear more
erratic than she already seemed.

She wished she could talk to Marcus.

The next market day seemed very far
away.

"It's very nice, Endymion," Larthia said,
examining the portrait he had done of her.

"I think so. I'm going to exhibit it in
front of my shop for a month before the
guild takes it." The artist glanced at Ver-

rix standing in the street and added in an undertone, "Are you sure he won't pose for me?"

Larthia sighed. "Go ahead. Ask him."

"With your permission?"

"With my permission."

Endymion walked out of his stall and had a very brief conversation with the Gaul. When he returned he was wearing a chastened expression.

"What did he say, Endymion?" Larthia inquired, in an amused tone.

"He said that there were easier ways of earning money," Endymion replied.

"So?"

"Apparently he thought my intentions exceeded just sculpting him."

"And didn't they?" Larthia asked, laughing.

"I'm not quite as lascivious as you seem to think," Endymion replied primly. "I would never dream of trying anything with someone of his size, anyway. If he took offense he would kill me. I just thought he would make an excellent model, but I will now officially abandon that idea."

Larthia giggled and rose, looping her *diploidion* over her arm. "I hope the portrait brings in some new business," she said to the artist.

"It should. When I exhibited my painting of Cytheris I had them lined up in the street."

"I'm hardly as popular as she is," Larthia said slyly, with a sidelong glance.

Endymion chuckled.

"Well, I must be off, I have to receive the manager of Sejanus' mines in Numidia later this morning and get his report on the business," Larthia added.

"That sounds like a fascinating encounter," Endymion said dryly.

Larthia nodded. "I'll be in next market day for those miniatures you're framing for me."

"They should be ready by then."

"Goodbye."

"Goodbye, Lady Sejana."

Larthia emerged to find Verrix waiting for her with folded arms and an expression of exaggerated patience on his face.

"So you found Endymion's suggestion unacceptable?" she said to him, smiling.

He made a disgusted face.

"He's very interested in you," Larthia added.

"I don't know why you waste your time with people like that," Verrix said darkly.

"What do you mean? He painted my portrait."

"You see him socially, too. He was at your party, I saw him there."

"I like his company, I find him amusing. And I'm not the only one who feels that way. He's invited to the best parties in Rome."

"He's a degenerate."

"You are such a prude! Why do you care about his private life? I don't."

"Back home we drove such people from the tribe."

"What an enlightened society that must have been! Though it hardly surprises me to find you come from a warren of narrow-minded bog trotters, since you are one yourself."

"And what are you? A bored and boring rich lady who idles away her days with flatterers and tradesmen who only want to use you for your money or your late husband's good name."

They were standing in front of a vegetable stall, bickering, Verrix glowering down at Larthia, whose balled fists were planted on her hips. When she realized that she was having a public argument with a slave she bit her lip, turned her back, and stalked away, ignoring the curious glances of several passersby. She moved rapidly through the pressing crowd, careless of her safety, desiring only to put as much distance between herself and Verrix as possible. He bolted after her, but since she was small and swift and angry, she succeeded in getting away from him. Verrix shoved a boy out of his path, and the child's tutor shouted after him, outraged. He bounded around a corner just in time to see the gilded hem of Larthia's azure gown disappear down an alley.

He broke into a full run, cursing her under his breath. What could she be thinking? The main thoroughfare during the day was fairly safe, but these side alleys were warrens where all sorts of ruffians lurked, passing the time until they could throng into the streets at night and claim them for their own. Verrix had panted to a stop and was looking around him wildly when he heard a woman's cry. He saw a teenage boy dash from what looked like a tent and take off headlong for the other end of the alley.

Verrix followed the direction of the sound he'd just heard and discovered Larthia sitting on the ground next to the canvas tent, clutching her face, in shock.

"He hit me," she said dazedly, when she saw Verrix. "He hit me in the face and snatched my coin purse."

"I feel like hitting you myself," Verrix said grimly, reaching down to help her. When she attempted to stand, her legs collapsed, and he scooped her up and carried her back toward the street, turning in when he saw what looked like a private home with a courtyard and small fountain. He set her on the fountain's edge and said, "Let me see your face."

She looked at him, but didn't move.

He reached up gently and pulled her hand away from her mouth. Her lower lip was already swelling, and there was a purpling bruise at the corner of it.

"Why did you run away from me!" he burst out angrily, when he saw the damage. "You brought this on yourself! What do you think happens when a lady dressed like you wanders around alone in this den of thieves? You're lucky all he took was your money!"

Larthia glared back at him mutinously. "Some bodyguard you are," she retorted, a trifle thickly through her puffed lip. "Before I met you I was fine. Since I met you I've been run over by a banana cart and attacked by an adolescent cutpurse! My grandfather would have done better to hire that criminal Spartacus to take care of me."

"He would have been welcome to the job. If you listened to him as much as you listen to me he would have crucified himself before the Romans got to him!"

A housewife walked out of the stone

cottage behind them and tossed the shells from a pan of peas into a pile of mulch by her door. She paused when she saw Larthia and Verrix sitting on the rim of her fountain.

"We'll be off shortly, madam," Verrix called to her. "We just paused to get a drink."

She stared at them curiously, not answering. Verrix waited until she had gone inside again before saying to Larthia, in a low tone while he struggled for calm, "Do you think you can come home with me now?"

She nodded and stood up, then put her hand out to him, to steady herself.

"All right?" he said.

She nodded again, but instantly her face crumpled and tears formed in her eyes.

"I was so scared," she whispered.

"Larthia, why won't you just let me do my job?" he asked quietly. He didn't even notice that he had called her by her given name, since he always thought of her that way. "Why do you run away from me and make it impossible for me to protect you?"

"I don't know. You make me so angry . . ."

"Why?"

She shrugged helplessly, biting her swollen lip, then wincing at the pain. She closed her eyes.

"I guess I can't forget that you're here only because my grandfather forced you into it," she finally said.

He felt a sharp stab of sympathy for her. She was her own worst enemy. Her iron will and childish impulsiveness disguised an intelligence and kindness that might come to the fore if only she would let them.

"Does the reason for my presence make a difference?" he asked her. "I'm supposed to watch out for you and make you feel safe. Don't you?"

"I feel . . . exasperated."

"You might not if you cooperated with me instead of fighting me every day."

She smiled thinly. "I thought I was cooperating—to the best of my ability, that is."

Verrix considered that, trying to see their situation from her point of view. How could she be anything but difficult? Her father had bartered her into a loveless marriage and her husband had preferred the sexual favors of children. She had plenty of reason to resent another man shoving his way into her life and ordering her around; although she was ostensibly the mistress and he the servant, his daily warnings and constant looming presence had the effect of making her feel trapped and dominated. He put his arm around her, and she turned her face into his shoulder.

"I'm just trying to make sure you don't come to harm," he said softly into her ear.

She stirred, and he pulled her closer, forgetting their circumstances for a moment in the heady sensation of having her in his arms. The softness of the body against his, the scent which clung to her clothes, the slight sound of her breathing intoxicated him. He was putting his hands on her shoulders to hold her off and look down into her face when the housewife came back outside and called loudly, "Be off now, the two of you! I don't want vagrants hanging around back here."

They sprang apart, and Verrix avoided Larthia's eyes as he said, "Madam, this lady is not a vagrant. Does she look like one to you?"

The woman snorted. "Then what is she doing down here? We don't exactly get the quality people visiting in the market district. Get lost."

Verrix took a step forward, but Larthia put a restraining hand on his arm.

"Don't argue with her, Verrix. What does it matter? Let's just go."

He subsided, glancing back at the woman menacingly. As they left, he took Larthia's arm and held her close to his side until they were back on the main street with the market crowds swirling around them. Then he released her and walked behind her until they reached the litter and she climbed into it. When the bearers lifted it he fell into step with them, trying not to think too much about the incident in the alley.

It didn't mean anything.

It couldn't.

When Larthia got home she put salve on her bruised lip and stretched out on her bed, telling Nestor not to disturb her unless it was absolutely necessary. Then she replayed the morning in her mind, wondering why she was behaving like such an idiot.

She could not seem to stop arguing with Verrix, taking offense at everything he said or did, disagreeing with even his most innocuous suggestions. She knew that Endymion was a sycophant and had many reservations about him herself, but when Verrix criticized him she leaped to his defense as if the artist were her best friend in the world. And dashing off into the back streets of the market district dressed like Palatine gentry was sheer folly; when she thought about it now she shuddered at her own stupidity. Instead of providing for her safety, Verrix was provoking her into behavior that was almost guaranteed to put her in danger.

Larthia touched the corner of her mouth gingerly and then put her arm over her eyes. She knew it wasn't his fault; it was hers. He was just doing his duty, and she was acting like a fractious child. If she continued in this way she would wind up bringing both of them to a bad end.

Larthia sighed restlessly. She should sell him, she knew that; if her grandfather insisted she would find another bodyguard. But already the thought of life without Verrix loomed as an empty prospect.

She would miss him.

She wished she had never met him.

"Mistress, may I have a word?" Nestor called softly, tapping at her door.

Larthia groaned. "Is it an emergency?" she called back to him testily.

Nestor cleared his throat. "Atticus Marsalius is here," he replied.

Larthia sat bolt upright. She had forgotten that the manager of her late hus-

band's mine was coming to the house!
She shot off the bed and began to change
her clothing rapidly, dropping the discarded items on the floor.

"Take him to the *tablinum* and give him
a drink," Larthia called through the door
to the servant. "The Samnian wine. Tell
him I'll be with him shortly."

"Yes, mistress." She heard Nestor's footsteps padding away down the hall and
dashed to her dressing table as she adjusted the folds of a fresh *palla*. When
she glanced into her mirror she moaned
aloud.

She looked as though she had been
punched in the mouth, which wasn't too
surprising since she *had* been. She reached
for her pot of costly Egyptian makeup, a
clay-based foundation intended to conceal
flaws, and dabbed some of it on the
bruised skin. She covered the damage as
well as she could and then paused to examine the result. That was better. The
swelling was still there, but you had to look
for it. She smiled at herself and saw that
her grin was lopsided. Oh, well. She would
have to make do as she was. Marsalius need
not become enamored of her, but she
didn't want him to report to her husband's
trustees that she was engaging in brawls. If
she was deemed at all unsuitable to man-

age the Sejanus estate they would surely replace her and then she would be completely at her grandfather's mercy.

Larthia rose, affecting a calm she did not feel, and left her bedroom to face her visitor.

"And when you're finished with that you can carry the trash down to the alley for the collectors. They're coming through tonight," Nestor said.

Verrix nodded.

"Then bring in the kindling for the kitchen stove. It's stacked by the well out back."

Verrix nodded again, wondering how many orders the old man was going to fire off before he ran out of ideas. Nestor glanced at him and then left the hall.

Verrix finished scouring the fish baskets with sand and then headed for the trash bins, which he began to transfer to a wagon standing on the cobbles behind the kitchen. He didn't mind the chores; keeping busy helped to stem the tide of longing which washed over him every time he thought of Larthia.

What would have happened if that harridan had not emerged from her house just as he had been about to kiss her?

Would Larthia have let him do it? Would she have been outraged and slapped his face? Would she have stormed off in high dudgeon and put him up for auction at her earliest opportunity? Just because she had let him hold her during a moment of weakness did not mean she would allow further liberties. Maybe the inhospitable housewife had actually saved his hide.

He had been thinking seriously of running again. After years of experience he knew how to hide himself in teeming Rome; the search for a runaway slave was perfunctory at best. There were simply too many of them.

But the thought of his emancipation papers stopped him. He would never be free if he let his feelings for Larthia drive him from her house. He would just have to continue with his job and keep his distance from her at the same time. No easy task, but the thought of a lifetime of slavery was worse.

The thought of a lifetime without Larthia was worse than that.

Verrix shifted the last of the bins into the wagon and then led the horse downhill to the collection point. He glanced back at the house above him, the limestone bits in the stucco sparkling in the sunlight, and wondered how long Larthia would be closeted with the mine manager.

Verrix had seen the man arrive and didn't like the look of him. Like many expatriate Romans, Marsalius affected a more Roman air than the natives and was dressed in a dazzlingly bleached, very broad toga of the finest wool, with heavy gold jewelry around his neck and on his fingers. A hooded cloak, adopted from the defeated Gauls and currently the rage of fashion, was draped over his arm. Seeing the clothing of his people appropriated by this company man offended Verrix, and he wondered, as he had before, about the mentality of conquerors who seemed to think the people they had vanquished were better dressed.

As he returned to the house he saw Marsalius leaving by the front door. The man bent over Larthia's white hand and kissed it lingeringly.

Rage rose in Verrix, and he had to look away.

He was a slave, the lowest of the low, hauling garbage, and that fawning manager could touch Larthia when he, Verrix, never could.

He would not endure it. The New Year's festival coming up in a few days on the

first of March would provide the perfect
cover for his escape.

He would run.

Six

It rained the next *nundina,* and canvas awnings went up over the stalls in the marketplace near the forum. The Campus Martius became a sea of mud, and the *apparitor* whose job it was to declare the exact time of noon could hardly determine the passage of the sun. The Tiber, gray and roiling, rose toward its banks, and the reeds standing in the Pontine Marsh sank closer to the surface of the water. The citizens, those brave enough to defy the weather, tried to remember if the augurs had predicted early flooding this year, wrapped their clothing closer around their bodies, and stepped over the deepening puddles.

Marcus had the afternoon watch, and he sat in the guardhouse, protected from the rain, watching the calibrated candle melt away to the point where he would be dismissed and the next man take over for him. Septimus sat cross-legged on a storage case next to him, sharpening the point of his *pilum* with a whetstone. He was not on duty, but keeping Marcus company.

"So you're seeing her again tonight?" Septimus said, holding the whetstone up to the candlelight.

Marcus nodded.

"What is she like?"

Marcus hesitated, then said, "Sweet."

"Is that all you have to say?"

Marcus shrugged. "She's not easy to describe. I've never met another woman like her." He sensed that Septimus was feeling shut out; previously they had discussed their conquests with one another and laughed about them. But Julia was not a barbarian whore whose finer points could become the subject of a ribald conversation.

His relationship with her was private.

"What are you going to do about her?" Septimus asked curiously.

Marcus stared out at the driving rain and sighed. "I don't know."

"Could you give her up?"

"Never."

Septimus' face became grave. "Then you will have some difficult decisions to make."

Tiberius Germanicus interrupted this sober exchange by barging into the guardhouse, pulling his cloak from his head and shaking himself like a drenched dog.

"What a torrent!" he said. "The merchants will be losing money this market day, the only creatures abroad are those with webbed feet."

"Juno's tears," Septimus commented, harking back to an old Etruscan proverb.

"More like Neptune's revenge," Tiberius replied, draping his cloak near the brazier and then holding his hands out to the warmth it gave. "How was the watch?" he asked Marcus.

"Quiet," Marcus said, standing. Septimus followed suit, storing his *pilum* in the chest where he had sat and then handing Marcus' cloak to him before donning his own. Both men wrapped up and headed for the door.

"Stay dry," Marcus called to Tiberius as they left.

"I'll try," he answered, and saluted them.

"Are you going straight to the Sejanus house?" Septimus asked, as they paused outside the wooden shack, squinting into the pelting rain.

"No, I have some time to kill. Julia sees the physician first, it's her excuse for getting away from the Atrium."

"Then come over to my house and have

a drink. Even I don't feel like trudging over to the baths today, I'll be drowned by the time I get there."

Marcus grinned. "Only a Persian monsoon could keep you away from the baths."

"So will you join me for a cup?"

Marcus nodded. "Why not?"

The two friends trotted off toward the Palatine, heads bent against the driving rain. When they reached the Gracchus house they were admitted by a servant who took their cloaks and led them into the *tablinum*, where a fire was burning and the Senator was already enjoying his pre *cena* libation.

"Well, Marcus, how good of my son to bring you! We don't see enough of you around here. Sit down and dry off, I'll get Castor to bring you a drink." He rang the silver bell at his elbow and a manservant appeared. The slave bowed and retreated as soon as his master had instructed him.

"You two look like survivors of a Cilician pirate raid," Gracchus observed, laughing. "Did you abandon ship and swim to shore?"

"I didn't see you venturing forth today," Septimus said, holding his damp tunic away from his body.

"That's because you slept until noon. I went to the Senate this morning. And if you used a litter like other civilized people you wouldn't get wet."

"Litters are pretentious," Septimus announced.

"Only for those who don't think they deserve them," the Senator snapped back.

"How was the Senate session today?" Marcus asked quickly, to defuse the tension between father and son.

"Oh, that old fool Lucius Cotta is still mumbling about the Sibylline Books," Gracchus replied, "and worse still, some people are listening to him."

"Caesar is probably paying him to bray about those prophecies," Septimus observed darkly. "Anything to get what he wants."

"Caesar wouldn't do such a thing," Marcus said flatly. "He doesn't want any trouble over the title of *'rex'*, much less the Senate being forced into giving it to him by the babblings of some senile *pontifex*."

"Well, Marcus Brutus and Gaius Cassius believe the prophecy about Parthia to be true," Gracchus said gloomily.

"How do you know?" Septimus asked.

"They kept quiet and looked worried," the Senator replied, and both younger men laughed.

"It isn't funny," Gracchus said. "Cotta

is calling for a vote on the measure to be demanded of the magistrates, and that puts Brutus and Cassius in an impossible position. If they dare to oppose it, they declare themselves open enemies of Caesar, and if they remain silent he becomes king."

"No wonder they're unhappy," Septimus chortled, and then grinned wider as Castor came into the room with a golden goblet on an inlaid tray.

"Ah, Marcus, here is your drink," he said.

The talk turned to the upcoming New Year's celebrations and Marcus passed the time until he was due to meet Julia, declining a dinner invitation from Senator Gracchus. By the time he left the Gracchus house the rain had stopped and the air was filled with a clean-swept freshness and the scent of early spring flowers. He walked the short distance to the Sejanus house and brushed the shrubs on the edge of the estate as he climbed the back wall. They flung droplets back at him, splashing his face. He vaulted over the hedge and then dropped back down to the wet ground when he saw a figure silhouetted against a window. Raising his head cautiously, he saw the old servant, Nestor, push open the shutters. Marcus waited until the slave had walked away and then dropped onto the portico, flattening himself against the outside wall of the house until he could see into the bedroom.

It was empty. Julia was not there.

He drew back, his heart beginning to pound. Had something gone wrong, had something happened to her? It was past time for her to be finished with the doctor. He closed his eyes, forcing himself to be calm, and then heard a slight sound inside. He looked in again and saw her entering the room; he almost sobbed with relief. Someone was standing behind her, and she turned for a final word. Marcus could hear the murmur of their voices, but could not understand what was being said. He waited until Julia had closed the door and then slipped into the room.

She looked up as he entered, and her features were suffused with a tenderness that pierced his heart.

"I was afraid you wouldn't come," she whispered, as he kissed her.

"Why?"

"Oh, I'm always afraid you won't come," she said, half laughing at herself as she slipped her arms around his waist. He closed his eyes and propped his chin on the top of her head, just holding her tightly, inhaling her unique fragrance and wishing that he never had to leave her.

"Did you have any trouble getting here?" he asked, as she led him by the hand to the bed.

"No, Livia has given me permission to see the doctor on a regular basis."

"For how long?"

She shrugged. "Until she objects, I guess."

Marcus looked worried.

"Marcus, what is it? We're alone, Larthia's servants think I have left the house. Let's not waste the time we have together." She ran her tongue enticingly over his lips, but he drew back, restraining himself from accepting her invitation. Instead he grasped her hands and held them together inside his own, covering her fingers with kisses.

"Julia, please listen to me. There's something I have to tell you."

She stared at him, her cheeks draining of color. "You don't want to see me anymore," she said dully.

"Oh, darling, no," he said, embracing her again, closing his eyes to blot out the look on her face. "It's just that I've been telling you I'll take you away—I know it's the only future for us—but I can't desert the army."

She said nothing; he was unable to tell what effect his words were having on her.

"I've thought about it," he went on, "and I want to take you out of Rome more than anything in the world. It's the only path to provide for your immediate safety, but I can't desert Caesar right now. I owe everything to him. If he hadn't picked me for his legion I would still be on the farm in Corsica, cursing my fate. He's in the midst of a crisis, his test of power is coming, and I'm the *pilus prior* of the first cohort. If he has to marshal the army for a civil war I'd be almost impossible to replace. And think of the humiliation, the *indignitas,* for him if someone he raised so high disappeared from his post. Caesar's enemies would make the most of it, saying his judgment was poor, to heap honors on a man unworthy of them, an officer who thought so little of his *sacramentum* that he abandoned his commission and his men just when he was needed most."

Julia looked up at him and put her finger to his lips. "Don't explain. I understand."

"Do you?" Marcus said anxiously, concerned that she would misinterpret his words and think that the army was more important to him than she was.

She nodded. "You have many reasons to be grateful to your commander, to feel loyalty to him and the institution which he represents. You chose your path freely, and it has richly rewarded you. My position with the Vestals was forced on me and therefore I feel very differently about it. I will have no regrets about leaving my present life behind."

Marcus sighed with relief. She did understand.

"When can we go?" she asked.

"After the Parthian campaign," he replied. "I don't have to reenlist this fall as I have every year in the past. The oath I took extends just through October. Then I will leave the army in good standing and take you away from here. We'll still have to keep our relationship a secret until then, of course, but it will only be for the summer months, until I come back."

"And what if you don't come back?" Julia said softly.

"I'll come back. I always do."

He bent his head to kiss her, and she submitted with a luxurious sigh. She twined her arms around his neck and kissed him back, then let him undress her, watching his face as he drew the silken garments from her limbs. His eyes moved over her avidly, his lips parted, his breathing harsh; it was clear that he found her exquisitely beautiful, and she was glad.

Marcus touched a smooth tan nipple and it rose into his palm, hardening as he cupped her breast. Her body glowed like a marble statue in the flickering candlelight, slender and white, perfect. He kissed her everywhere he could reach as he lifted her onto the bed, removing her shoes last and then gathering her, naked, into his arms. She hid her face against his shoulder, the rough wool of his garnet tunic caressing her cheek.

"Are you sure?" he said against her ear.

"Sure," she replied shakily, nudging aside his neckline and rubbing her nose on the satiny surface of his shoulder. She could feel his indrawn breath, the way he reacted to her slightest touch. It gave her a feeling of control she had never experienced before; this powerful man, who commanded a cohort, was now at *her* command. When she ran her hands down his lean back his muscles contracted under her fingers. She dragged her tongue along the line of his collarbone and he groaned, a soft sound indicative of his helplessness against the wave of desire engulfing him. When he eased her onto her back she wrapped her arms around his neck and accepted his weight.

He lay against her, heavy and ready, pressing her thighs, and the need to feel him inside her was overwhelming. Julia sighed with gratification as his mouth went from her lips to her neck, and she urged herself against him, sliding her hands up his arms inside the short sleeves of his tunic. She loved the feel of his skin under her hands; he looked his role, tough, work hardened and war weary, but his skin was smooth and warm, his hair like cornsilk. He was young, and she was young. Desire carried them like the tide.

"Take this off," she whispered, tugging on the hem of his tunic.

He obeyed, standing, and Julia felt the loss of connection with him like a pain. He stripped rapidly, revealing a hard, sculpted torso, brown and crosshatched with scars, sprayed with a thatch of black hair that narrowed to a line bisecting his belly. Julia could not look lower; she focused on his face, his dark features intense with passion, and then closed her eyes as he rejoined her.

"Shh," he said against her mouth, as she stiffened in his arms at the contact. He kissed her to relax her again. She was soon responding, sinking her fingers into

his hair and wrapping her legs around
him, unconsciously seeking fulfillment.
When he was sure her resistance had
passed he took his lips from her mouth
to kiss her body, his movements growing
wilder as his lips moved from her breasts
to her stomach to her thighs. When he
was sure she had passed the point of ob-
jection he slipped his hand between her
legs. She turned her head aside and
moaned deeply, her face flushing, her
whole body dewed with perspiration.

Marcus lost control and bent to tongue
her navel, lifting her to his mouth. He
was almost rough; he couldn't get enough
of her as she wound her arms and legs
around him, imprisoning him within her
limbs. Passion made her reckless; she
could not resist him as he did things she
had only imagined, and some she had
never imagined, leaving her weak and en-
ervated, desperate for more. She clutched
his shoulders and stroked his hair, both
now damp with sweat.

"I want . . ." he said thickly, lifting his
head.

"Yes," she replied. "Yes, yes."

He poised to position her under him,
resisting the urge to drive into her, as he
would a more experienced woman. In-

stead he entered her slowly, pausing when she gasped and went rigid.

"Do you want me to stop?" he asked between clenched teeth, sweat breaking out anew on his forehead.

"No," she whispered. "Just . . . wait."

He waited, his arms trembling as they supported the weight of his body, the need to plunge deeper so strong he had to bite his lip to overcome it.

"Now," she said softly, stroking his back.

He sank into her a little further, hesitating as she moaned, then continuing as he realized that the sound was one of pleasure. He closed his eyes when he felt her legs come around his hips, her heels digging into him.

"More," she said.

He gave her more.

"I think it's going to rain again," Julia said dreamily, listening to the rising wind whipping the trees along the edge of Larthia's back garden.

Marcus grunted, almost asleep.

She stirred, touching herself gingerly to see if she was still bleeding. She was not. Larthia had thoughtfully provided a *lavabum*, a water bowl and pitcher, and clean cloths. Julia had washed, but she still felt marked, as if everyone could read on her forehead that she now belonged to Marcus.

"Tell me about yourself," she said to him, snuggling closer to his warmth, her head on his bare chest.

"You just learned all you need to know about me."

"You know what I mean."

"What do you want to hear?"

"Everything."

He smiled, his mouth moving in her hair. "For the last thirty years?"

"Well, why did you join the Roman army?"

"To get off the farm," he said promptly.

"Did you hate it so much?"

"I was a very bad farmer," he said shortly.

"And your father?"

"He was a good farmer."

"He must have been sorry to lose you."

"I have a younger brother who stayed in Corsica."

"And how did you join the army?" Julia asked, running her fingers lightly down his sinewy arm.

"I came to the Capitol and the Consuls with the help of the military tribunes selected four thousand of the applicants to form a legion. Caesar saw me and personally picked me from a crowd to be in his."

"Picked you?"

"For obvious physical attributes: size, stamina, general health."

"And that was all?"

"That was all. Rome has many enemies. The army needs men to fight them."

"And you have lived the army life for eleven long years," Julia said.

"The time passed quickly."

"Because you were always fighting?"

"Or preparing to fight."

Julia sat up and touched the livid scar which bisected his chest just above the left nipple.

"Where did you get this?" she asked.

"In Gaul."

"How?"

"A naked barbarian with his face painted blue tried to thrust his dagger into my heart."

"And all these others?" she asked, trailing her forefinger down his chest to his belly.

"Different places. The Roman style of warfare is mainly hand-to-hand combat, you get carved up fighting in close quarters."

She kissed his shoulder lingeringly. "I'm

so afraid you'll go to Parthia and I'll never see you again."

He put his hand under her chin and turned her face up to his.

"As long as I'm alive you'll see me again."

"That's what worries me. Will you be alive?"

"I've survived eleven years against all manner of men, and now I have a better reason than ever to go on living."

"You must have had a lot of lovers in that amount of time," she observed.

Marcus knew better than to discuss this subject with any woman, much less Julia, who was already insecure about her lack of experience.

"Not so many," he said.

She snorted. "I've heard about soldiers."

He laughed aloud at her worldly-wise tone. "What have you heard?"

"That they'll mount anything that moves," she replied, and he stared at her, amazed that she had ever been exposed to such vulgar language.

"Who told you that?" he said.

"Margo, my slave. She was a Helvetian captive, and she said when the Romans took over her village the soldiers raped all the women and stole everything."

Marcus shrugged dismissively. "Warfare

is different, though I confess I have never taken pleasure in forcing myself on an un-willing woman. Mutual yearning is much more satisfying to the soul."

"Mutual yearning?" she said, running her hand down his middle and encircling him with her fingers.

He closed his eyes.

She stroked him as he rose to fullness in her hand. "Like this?" she breathed.

He seized her and rolled her onto her back. "You learn fast, white rose," he murmured, as she surged against him.

"Make love to me again," she whis-pered, and he did.

Verrix knelt outside Larthia's bedroom door, scouring the grout in the tiled floor. She had chosen this task for him because it would put him in the right place and take a lot of time, so he could protect the people inside the room. The irony of his making sure that the officer who had turned him in to the Roman magistrates was able to enjoy a lover in peace was not lost on him.

But if Larthia wanted him to do it, he would.

He had been at his task for some time

when Larthia rushed up to him, her face as white as her *stola*.

"What is it?" he said in an undertone, rising from his crouching position.

"My grandfather has just appeared at the front door," she said, her expression indicating what she thought of this development. "I must keep him busy in the *tablinum* so he doesn't wander around the house."

"What does he want?"

"I have no idea, but if he finds out that Julia is in my bedroom at this very moment, entertaining her soldier lover, we are all in big trouble."

"What do you want me to do?"

"The same as before, make sure nobody gets past you until I'm able to send him on his way."

Verrix nodded.

"I'm counting on you," Larthia said.

"I understand."

She fled, rounding the corner outside the *tablinum* just as Nestor arrived with the wine she had ordered.

"Grandfather," she said as she entered, flashing her widest smile, "I'm sorry about the interruption, just a domestic matter I had to settle. Would you care for some wine? It's the best Lesbian, your favorite."

Casca nodded distractedly, and Larthia gestured for Nestor to pour the drinks. When he had done so she told him he might go, adding, "Do not disturb us for any reason."

Nestor bowed his head and left.

"Now what can I do for you?" Larthia asked, sitting across from her grandfather.

"I've come to give you some advice."

As Casca draped his elaborate toga over his knees, Larthia noticed that the hem of it was stained with mud, and reflected that he must have been in a hurry to get to her.

"What a surprise," she said, smiling again to take the sting out of her words.

"I'm serious, Larthia. The political situation is worsening, the Senate was almost in chaos this morning. I think you should take your money out of the banks and put it into gold, plate and coins and jewelry. Do it discreetly, in small lots, but turn it into transportable goods."

Larthia stared at him. "Are you doing this?"

He nodded. "Yes."

"Won't word of it get out to the rest of the people? There will be a run on the banks."

"We're keeping it quiet."

"Are things that bad?"

He sighed. "If it comes to civil war, who knows who will wind up controlling the government-backed banks? If Caesar prevails those of us who opposed him will be removed from our positions at the very least, bankrupted at worst. The last time it reached this point, under Sulla, his enemies found their homes razed and all of their personal property confiscated."

Larthia was listening now. "Tell me exactly what to do," she said.

Casca outlined his plan, and Larthia was closeted with him for a good while. There was no need to prevent him from going through the house; he accomplished his mission and then left. When Larthia returned from seeing him out she noticed that Verrix was absent from his post in the back hall. She sought out Nestor immediately, trying not to panic for the second time that night.

"Where is Verrix?" she demanded. "I see that his task here has been abandoned, and I specifically asked him to finish it tonight."

"I'm afraid there was an incident with him, mistress, while you were closeted with Consular Casca and had asked not to be disturbed."

"An incident?" Larthia said. She did

not like the way Nestor was avoiding her
eyes.

"He refused to obey a direct order I
gave him," Nestor replied uneasily.

"What was that?"

"I wished to enter your room because
it had begun to rain again. I had left the
windows open, and I was sure the floor
would be flooded."

"I told you not to go in there for any
reason," Larthia said sharply, beginning to
see where this was leading.

"Yes, but—" the servant began.

Larthia cut him off. "No buts. The
bedroom floor is my concern, not yours.
Now what happened with Verrix?"

"He tried to prevent me from going
into your bedchamber, I have no idea
why. I knew you were not in there and
could not understand his behavior, except
to say that he always seems to take great
pleasure in thwarting my objectives. When
he would not stand aside I ordered Cammius and Menander to lay hold of him
and force him back to his room. He re-
sisted violently, injuring Cammius and
breaking the valuable Etruscan vase that
stands in the hallway outside your room.
He made so much noise, I was afraid
Consular Casca was going to hear it at
the other end of the house."

Verrix had created a disturbance to warn
Julia and Marcus, Larthia thought.

"And what happened then?" she asked
fearfully, holding her breath.

"Nothing. I went into the bedroom and
closed all of the windows."

"Was anything wrong in there?"

"No, mistress, what could have been
wrong? The bed was disturbed, but I
straightened it."

"I took a nap earlier. So where is Verrix?" Larthia asked, relieved.

"Well, naturally I had to punish him,"
Nestor replied.

"Punish him?" Larthia said softly.

"Yes, of course. How can I possibly
maintain discipline among the slaves if
they see Verrix refusing to take direction?
There must be consequences for such behavior." Nestor paused. "In my opinion,
he should be sold."

"What 'consequences' did you arrange?"
Larthia said impatiently, ignoring the advice.

"I had him flogged," Nestor replied.
"Ten strokes."

Larthia stared at the old man, stunned,
unable to find her voice.

He looked back at her unblinkingly.

"What?" she finally managed to whisper.

"It's the usual punishment for—"

"It's not the usual punishment in this house, and well you know it!" Larthia said in a deadly tone. "How dare you take such a step without consulting me!"

"You said not to disturb you," Nestor replied, his voice beginning to quaver.

"Don't try to use my words to defend yourself!" Larthia shouted, livid with rage. "You seized the opportunity when I was preoccupied to do something you've wanted to do since Verrix first arrived here! Where is he?"

"In his room," Nestor answered in a subdued tone.

"Send Menander to fetch Paris immediately. I don't care what that doctor is doing; tell him I'll pay him whatever he requires to come here right now and tend to Verrix."

"His wounds are not serious," Nestor started to say. "He is just—"

"I will be the judge of that!" Larthia shouted, cutting him off. "And take yourself out of my sight. If I deal with you now I may regret my actions, I'm too angry to make any decisions. I'll summon you later."

Nestor bowed and withdrew without a word. As soon as he left Larthia ran down the corridor to the servants' quarters, her skirts gathered into her hands. The slaves who had heard her voice raised in the *tablinum* scurried out of her way, each anxious not to be the next victim of her wrath.

Larthia burst into the cell next to the kitchen, raising her hand to her mouth when she saw Verrix sprawled face down on the bed. His tunic had been ripped open to the waist to expose his broad back, which was now striped with ugly red welts, the skin flayed open and oozing blood. The tunic still hung down in shreds over his homespun trousers, which he insisted on wearing in spite of the fact that they marked him as an outsider, a non-Roman, as much as his torque. His blond hair was dark with perspiration, the valley between his shoulder blades damp and glistening. His eyes were closed and his breathing labored.

Larthia went over to his bed and sat on its edge next to him, putting her hand gently on the back of his neck.

How often she had longed to touch him like this, longed to see him stripped to the waist, his beautiful torso bare, but it had taken this awful accident to make her wishes reality. He had suffered this painful punishment, and said nothing to stop it, because he wanted to keep close the secret she had entrusted to him.

Larthia's throat constricted and she forced back tears. Crying now would not help Verrix; she had to be strong in this situation. She dug her fingers into the golden curls at the nape of his neck and then caressed his arms, the well-developed biceps, the tanned skin covering them warm and dry. She tried not to look lower, but eventually had to see each individual stroke of the lash, the skin ripped at the edge of each welt indicating that the flogger had used the metal tipped *flagellum*, the leather whip, not the less abrasive rope favored for servants.

Nestor had not done this himself, she thought; he didn't have the strength to cut so deep. He must have assigned one of the younger men to the job.

"Oh, my poor darling," she whispered, her voice breaking. "This is all my fault. I was so flustered at my grandfather's sudden arrival that I didn't think—" She broke off despairingly. "I told Nestor not to go into my room but he just wanders the house at will, no matter what I say to him. He seems to think the place is his. He's old and getting senile, but I can't put him out on the street; he was with my family before my father was born." She stopped, realizing that her distress was making her ramble. "What does it matter now how it happened? It did, and I am so sorry."

Verrix stirred, and she withdrew her hand as if she had been burned. He rolled to one side, wincing as the edge of his back came into contact with the bedding, and looked up at her.

"Larthia," he said hoarsely, reaching out with one hand as he propped himself up with the other.

"Yes," she said soothingly. "Yes, it's me. Just lie still, don't try to get up. The doctor is on his way."

"Don't need . . . doctor."

"Yes, you do." She pushed him firmly back into position, face down on the bed, as he murmured, "Nestor . . . going . . . your room . . . had to . . . stop . . ."

"Shh, shh, no talking. Don't waste your strength. I know all about it. He saw nothing, they must have gotten away safely. I will deal with Nestor in my own good time."

His eyes drifted closed, but as she slipped her hand into his open one on the bed his fingers coiled around hers.

"I am so sorry," Larthia whispered again, biting her lip to stem the tears that threatened once more. "This should never have happened. I shouldn't have drawn you into my sister's intrigue, just look at the price you've paid."

His breathing slowed, became deep and even. He was either sleeping or unconscious; in either event the doctor would be with him soon.

Larthia crawled up onto the bed and put her head on his bare shoulder, taking care not to touch the abraded skin below it.

She would stay with him until the doctor came.

The Gracchus house was dark except for the torchlight blazing in the *tablinum* windows. Marcus hoped that the Senator and Septimus were sitting up talking (fighting), which meant he could slip Julia into his friend's bedroom unnoticed. He carried her across the portico and then set her down, barefoot, on the flagstones outside Septimus' window. When he tried the shutters he found that they were locked. Quietly, carefully, he took his knife from the sheath at his waist and sliced through the latch, then removed the bar from the inside. He lifted Julia over the sill before vaulting into the darkened room after her.

"Just wait right here," he said softly. "I'll go and get Septimus."

"What if someone comes in here while you're gone?" Julia whispered. She was pale, damp, terrified; he felt like a brute, hauling her around in the night like a sack of grain. He knew she felt humiliated. They had fled the Sejanus house like a pair of thieves when they had heard Verrix making a commotion in the hall, and now they were entering the Gracchus house in the same surreptitious manner, through a window.

"Get into the bed. Any servant who comes in will think you're Septimus' . . . companion. He often brings women home, his parents prefer that to his risking his life in the Suburra."

He could see from the expression on her face that the whole episode was distasteful; their romantic interlude had deteriorated into a farce by Plautus. But he didn't have time to worry about that now. He had to find Septimus and get Julia back to the Atrium before Livia Versalia began to wonder where her charge was.

He kissed her forehead. She was shivering uncontrollably, even while wearing his heavy cloak. He put his arms around her and held her tightly until her tremors subsided.

"Better?" he said.

She nodded.

"I'll be back as quickly as possible."

He left her standing in the middle of the room, a dim outline of light clothing as he vaulted back over the sill and onto the portico. He raced through the garden and sprinted around to the front of the house, pausing to smooth his hair with his palms and straighten his clothes. Then he knocked on the door, hoping nobody would notice that he was missing his cloak.

A servant admitted him and went to summon Septimus. When the latter appeared it was immediately apparent to Marcus that he was drunk.

"Marcus! Did you decide to take us up on our offer anyway? Better late than absent is my motto. Come into the parlor and have a drink."

Marcus waited until the servant had left and then grabbed his friend's arm.

"Septimus, sober up. I need your help."

Septimus tried to focus on him.

"What is it?"

"I had to get Julia out of her sister's house in a hurry, and I brought her here. She's in your bedroom."

That seemed to get through; Septimus blinked rapidly several times and said, "Here?" as his father walked into the atrium behind them.

"We came in through your window,"

Marcus added in a low tone, then looked up and smiled warmly at Senator Gracchus. "Good evening again, sir."

"Come to us for a nightcap, son? Why don't you join me inside?"

"Sorry, sir, I can't. There was just something I forgot to tell Septimus. I'll be brief."

The Senator nodded and left the hall. Septimus shot Marcus a look which indicated that he was fully sober now.

"Are you telling me she's in my bedroom?" he hissed, drawing Marcus to one side.

"Yes."

Septimus closed his eyes. "If my father knew he would have apoplexy."

"Would he recognize her?"

"Let's not test his memory. Even when dead drunk he has an eye for a pretty girl. Come on." The two men hurried down the side passage which led to Septimus' bedroom as he said, "I can't believe you brought her here, Marcus. Do you want to get us all arrested for *sacreligium*?"

"What else was I supposed to do? That old servant at the Sejanus house was about to barge into the bedroom when we were in there. I had to get her out, and your house was next door."

"What do you plan to do with her?"

"Julia's litter is waiting in the street by the Sejanus estate. I have to get her down there and make it seem as though she just left her sister's house."

"Why didn't you just bring her to the litter when you left Larthia's house?"

"She has no shoes."

Septimus stopped short in front of his bedroom door. "What did you say?"

"We left in a hurry, there wasn't time to get her sandals. They're under the bed in her sister's room."

"So now I have to find her shoes, too?"

"The Vestals are closely watched, Septimus. Someone will notice if she returns to the Atrium barefoot. Livia Versala doesn't miss anything."

Septimus opened the door to his room, and his expression changed from annoyance to compassion when he saw the small form huddled on his bed. Julia started up in alarm, then relaxed as she recognized her visitors.

Septimus went to the table near the window and got a candle, lighting it from a torch on the portico. He came back in and sat by Julia on the bed and said, "So how are you, little lady?"

Julia smiled wanly. "All right."

Septimus looked at Marcus, standing

next to them. "I'll have to give this friend
of mine some lessons concerning how to
treat a lady. Dragging you around barefoot in the rain doesn't seem very gentle-
manly to me."

"It wasn't Marcus' fault."

"Dulcetta, you must be in love," Septimus said dryly, patting her hand with his
free one. "Now let me see what I can do
about lifting a pair of sandals from my
mother's room."

Marcus embraced Julia as Septimus left.
"Are you really all right?" he asked. She
felt chilled, as if the close call had pene-
trated to her very bones.

"Yes."

"Septimus will be back shortly, and then
I'll take you down to your litter."

She nodded.

He stroked her hair. "It will all be different in the future," he said soothingly.
"We'll go to some place where we can be
together without having to hide."

She clutched him desperately, silently, as
if she wanted to believe him but couldn't
quite manage the feat.

Septimus returned, a pair of leather
sandals dangling from his hand.

"My mother was sleeping, she has so
many shoes I don't think she'll miss these.
Terentia's would probably fit better, but

she's staying in Herculaneum and I'm afraid she took all of her clothes with her."

Julia accepted the shoes and put them on, tying the laces around her ankles.

"They're very like the ones I had. No one should notice the difference," she said. She stood and shook out her *stola,* rearranging her *palla* and then her *diploidion* over it. "Do I look acceptable?" she asked.

"You look beautiful," Marcus replied. He held out his hand, and she took it. They went to the window, where he lifted her over the sill. "I'll leave by the door and come around and get you," he said. "Just wait here."

Julia flattened herself against the wall of the portico, glancing up at the clouds scudding across the barely visible moon, then back at the man inside the house.

"Hurry," she said.

"Do you think I can leave without saying goodbye to your father?" Marcus asked Septimus as they went into the hall. "I don't want to leave her there long."

"I'll make your excuses. He's too far gone in wine to care much about anything," Septimus replied, as they walked into the atrium and stopped by the front door.

Marcus put a hand on his friend's shoulder. "Thank you, Septimus. I don't know what else to say."

Septimus shook his head. "Be careful. You're playing a dangerous game."

Marcus took a step, and Septimus added, "She's lovely, Marcus. As I've said before, in a way I envy you."

Marcus glanced back at him gratefully, and then went out the door.

Septimus turned to the servant who had just appeared and said, "Castor, another cup of wine. I'll be rejoining the Senator in the *tablinum.*"

Septimus mentally sent good wishes to the fugitive pair as he went back inside to his father.

"He'll be all right," Paris said to Larthia. "He's young and healthy; he'll be up and around in two days. There will be some scarring on his back, though."

"But no permanent damage?" Larthia said anxiously.

"Except to his beauty," Paris replied dryly. "I've given him some extract of fox-glove for the pain, and I'll leave you more to be administered twice a day."

"You're very free with that potion, Doctor, you gave some to my sister, too. Isn't it poison?" Larthia asked, looking at the vial suspiciously.

"Only in higher doses, then it can stop the heart. Just make sure he doesn't drink all of it at once." Paris stoppered the large bottle of the liquid and slipped it back into his pouch, taking out a small clay pot and setting it on the bed.

"And what is that?" Larthia asked.

"Crushed oak leaves. The green sap prevents infection. Tell the person tending him to wash the wounds thoroughly with Nestor's soap and clear water three times a day, and then apply this salve to the cuts."

"I'll be tending him," Larthia said.

Paris raised his brows. "I see. Well, then, listen carefully. Once the scabs start to form discontinue the use of this salve and apply butter to the wounds, keeping them moist at all times. That will minimize the scarring, but as I said, he will have some, it can't be avoided."

"Butter?"

"Yes, you know, skim the cream off cow's milk and then churn it."

"I know what butter is, Doctor, I don't think I have any. I'll have to send Menander to the market."

"Send him to the Parthian section.

They're sure to have it, they eat it in Persia."

"Eat it?" Larthia said, gagging.

"Yes, as a condiment, and they heat it to clarify it and then use it in cooking."

Larthia made a disgusted face. "Can he be moved?" she inquired, nodding at Verrix.

"Where?"

"To my room. There's a cross breeze there, I thought the fresh air would be better for him."

"Tomorrow or the next day, as soon as he can walk, I don't see why not." Paris stood back from the bed and surveyed Larthia curiously.

"Lady Sejana, there's something I don't understand," he said. "You seem very concerned about this slave's welfare, but didn't you give the order to have him flogged?"

"It was a misunderstanding, Doctor. My orders were not interpreted correctly."

Paris nodded. "I was very surprised to hear that I was to be tending a man who had been flogged. I didn't think it was the practice in your house to flog the servants."

"It is not," Larthia said shortly. "Is there anything else I should know in order to take care of him?"

"Just watch him for signs of infection: fever, suppuration of the wounds. If he seems hot to the touch, confused in his mind, or if the flesh around the abrasions becomes raised and purpled, swollen, call me back. Otherwise, just let him sleep as much as he wants and proceed as I have already directed."

Larthia nodded.

"I doubt you will have any problems with him, he looks like a very hale specimen. How old is he?"

Larthia shrugged. "Twenty-six, twenty-eight."

"From Gaul?"

She nodded.

"They're very sturdy," the doctor said reassuringly, closing the flap of his pouch.

"How much do I owe you?" Larthia asked.

Paris thought about it. "Six sesterces," he said.

Larthia took a gold denarius out of the coin purse at her waist and pressed it into his hand.

Paris looked down at it in shock. She had given him more than twelve times the sum he'd requested. He was well known for his keen interest in money, but even he had to protest this largesse.

"It's too much," he said. "I did very little . . ."

"Keep it," Larthia said. "What you did was very important to me."

Paris closed his fingers around the coin.

"One more thing," Larthia continued. "Please keep this incident to yourself. I wouldn't want anyone to think—"

Paris held up his hand. "Say no more, Lady Sejana. In my profession, I have seen and heard everything. I will tell no one how you feel about this man."

Larthia felt the hot color come up in her face, but made no reply.

"Good evening, Lady Sejana. Call me again if you need me, anytime."

Larthia didn't walk him to the door.

She sat in a chair next to the bed on which Verrix lay and stayed there for the rest of the night.

"I don't want any more of that," Verrix said crossly, as Larthia held another dose of medicine to his lips.

"The doctor said—" Larthia began.

Verrix turned his head. "I don't care what the doctor said. It's making me sleep all the time, and I want to talk to you."

"You'll feel better if you take it."

"I feel fine. Sit down."

Larthia sat in the chair next to his bed. He had been recovering for three days, and during that time had refused to move to her room, refused to stay in bed, and was now refusing to take his medicine. The wounds on his back had healed to a mass of scabs. They itched furiously and were coated with a rancid grease which seeped through his clothing and stained the bed.

Not surprisingly, he was in a bad mood.

"When this first happened, were you here in the room with me?" he demanded.

"Of course. I called Paris."

"Before that. I remember your being here, but I'm not sure whether I was dreaming." He was watching her closely.

Larthia shifted uncomfortably.

"Maybe you were," she said.

"Did you say anything to me?"

"I told you not to talk, that I knew what had happened, and that I was getting the doctor."

"Did you touch me?"

She knew what he wanted her to say. But now that he was awake and kicking and back to his formidable self she couldn't admit what had occurred when he was half-conscious and she was worried, her guard down.

"You were trying to get up, I held you back," Larthia replied obliquely.

"I remember . . ."

His voice trailed off as Menander appeared in the doorway and said, "I have summoned Nestor to the *tablinum* as you requested, mistress."

Larthia rose immediately, glad of the excuse to escape the interrogation.

"I'll check in on you later," she said to Verrix, leaving him to look after her as she swept out of the room.

Nestor was staring at the floor as she entered the parlor. Even when she stood before him he was unable to meet her eyes.

"You overstepped your authority in an inexcusable fashion with Verrix," Larthia said to him sternly. "I would never have authorized such a punishment. You know I am not in favor of brutal methods to extract obedience from servants. Since my husband died and left me in charge of his affairs, there has never been a flogging of a slave in this house."

"But, mistress—"

Larthia held up her hand. "I have left you alone for several days to think about what you did, and I see you are unrepentant. You have been suspicious of Verrix since he came, and ordering his beating was your way of dealing with your resentment."

"He seems to have an undue influence over you," Nestor said primly. "I am not the only one who has noticed it. Many of the servants have remarked on your partiality toward him."

"That is my concern, Nestor, not yours! You are relieved of all duties and confined to your room in the dormitory. Menander will take over for you in the house until I have decided what to do with you. That is all."

The old man didn't move; he seemed frozen to the spot. Larthia saw that he was shaking, and she took pity on him. Old servants were often discarded by heartless masters when they could no longer perform up to standard; the fate they met when passed on to lesser houses, or even the streets, was not kind. Perhaps that was why Nestor had been so threatened by Verrix from the day he'd arrived. Verrix was obviously intelligent and capable; his job kept him close to their mutual mistress. Nestor feared replacement by a younger, more able man.

"It's all right," Larthia added in a gentler tone. "Nothing will happen to you,

Nestor. I just need time to think about all of this. I must be mismanaging this house if such a thing could happen under my roof. I will talk with you and share my thoughts when I have formulated them."

Nestor bowed his head and fled, clearly relieved.

Larthia sat on her couch and wondered what she was going to do about him, Verrix, Julia's forbidden liaison, and the shambles her own life had become.

Julia knelt before her clothes chest and rummaged inside it, finally extracting the garment she sought.

"Here it is," she said to Margo. "I knew it was in here." She handed the servant the gold-bordered *suffibulum*, used only once a year on the first of March.

Margo examined it closely. "It should be steamed, I'll give it to the wardrober." She folded the veil on a side table and said, "You'll need the purple-embroidered *stola*, too. Where is it?"

Julia pointed to the tunic on a chair. The two women were preparing for the New Year's celebration to take place the next day. The ceremony involved the annual ritual of extinguishing and relighting the sacred fire of Vesta. In the time of the Etruscan kings, the fire was rekindled by the friction of dry sticks; now it was rekindled by the suns ray's brought to a focus by a concave mirror. If the fire went out long ago, when it was the focal point of village life and needed to start the home fires of the locals, the negligent Vestal was scourged. But in Julia's time, when the fire was symbolic and supervised constantly, it failed only when doused on the sacred hearth by the Chief Vestal and rekindled before the watchful eyes of the Roman people on New Year's Day.

Julia's special clothes were part of the tradition. Livia Versalia performed the kindling by herself, but the rest of the Vestals dressed in the ancient robes and looked on as witnesses. The ceremony's humble origins were seldom remembered by the average citizen who saw it, but it was a beloved passage into each year, the unifying ritual of the Roman state.

"Whose sandals are these?" Margo asked, turning to Julia with Lady Gracchus' shoes in her hand.

"My sister Larthia's," Julia lied smoothly. "It was raining when I went to her house and I ruined my own. She gave me those to wear."

"You should have brought yours back," Margo said, scowling. "They might have been salvageable. The Roman people bear the cost of your wardrobe, you must not be wasteful."

Julia smiled to herself. Margo had lived in the Atrium so long she was beginning to sound like Livia Versalia, Margo's Swiss origins obscured by long years of Roman service.

"Why were you so late the other night?" Margo asked. "Livia was inquiring about you."

"The doctor took a long time."

"Does he think you're improving?"

"He seems to find me better."

"Do you feel better?"

Julia nodded.

"Good. Then the physician's visits won't have to last much longer. I've always thought I should go along on them anyway, but you know Livia, she finds some busy work for me to do here when you're gone."

Julia did know Livia; the Chief Vestal regarded Margo's time as hers. Livia preferred to see the slave occupied with domestic chores rather than exchanging gossip with the Sejanus servants while Julia visited her sister. Julia thanked fate that this was so; if Margo had received

permission to go with Julia the ruse of
consulting the doctor would have been
rendered useless. Margo would not be
content to remain in the street with the
litter, like the bearers. She would want to
lounge inside the house, watching every
move Julia made, just like the nosy
mother she was to her in all but nature.

Seeing Marcus would have been impossible, and seeing Marcus was all Julia
lived for these days.

The next *nundina* seemed an age away.
Julia longed for her lover. She lay awake
at night and remembered the strength of
his body, the tenderness of his touch; then
the hunger would begin again, a hunger
which knew no outlet but Marcus. She
was restless, sleepless, thinner; Margo,
who watched her the way a timekeeper
watched a sundial, knew that something
had altered, but couldn't imagine what it
was. Julia saw this, and tried to make the
servant think it was her "illness" which
had caused the sea change. That was why
Margo questioned her so closely about
her visits to Paris. The slave was looking
for signs of improvement in her mistress'
condition and could find none.

For Julia's condition was the result of
love.

Danuta, Livia's slave, appeared in the

doorway of Julia's suite and said, "Please come to the Aedes, Julia Rosalba. The cleansing is about to begin."

Julia rose from her knees and shook out her skirt, following the slave into the hall. On New Year's Eve all the Vestals swept the shrine with water from the sacred spring in preparation for the rekindling of the fire the next day. It was forbidden to use water brought in a pipe or other conduit for this purpose, or any other ritual cleansing of the temple; hence the trips to the spring of Egeria which had enabled Marcus to first speak to Julia.

"The others are waiting for you," Danuta added, in a tone which suggested that Julia was late.

Julia sighed. She no longer had any patience for the Vestal duties which claimed so much of her time and which now seemed so unimportant.

She wanted only to go away with Marcus.

But until that happened, she had to keep on with the daily charade.

She walked behind Danuta into the temple.

Verrix sat up on the edge of his bed and pulled on his tunic, wincing with the act; his back was so stiff he could hardly move his arms. He stood and stretched gingerly, combing his hair with his fingers, then went to his door and out into the hall.

It was the middle of the night, and everyone was asleep.

He was going to have it out with Larthia right now.

He was tired of her mercurial behavior. She could lie to herself but no longer to him. He remembered her coming into his room when he was hurt, he *knew* he had not been dreaming. She had spoken to him lovingly, caressed him; but now that he was recovered she had withdrawn again, trying to pretend that her concern for him was no more than what she would show for any injured servant.

That was going to stop.

The house was very still as he walked through it, the torches burning low, his shadow looming on the polished floors. He paused outside Larthia's room, saw that her door was ajar, and pushed it open all the way.

She was not in her bed. He looked toward the portico and saw her slender figure outlined by the light of the full moon.

She was sitting on a bench under the stars, obviously as sleepless as he was.

He crossed the bedroom and went out to the back. When she looked up and saw him she went very still.

"What are you doing here?" she said. "You're supposed to be sleeping."

"So are you."

Larthia rose, and he saw that she was wearing a diaphanous night robe of ribbed silk, almost transparent when the moonlight shone through it. She gathered it around her quickly and folded her arms, facing him.

"Go back to bed, Verrix. You haven't recovered completely yet, and what if someone saw you out here with me?"

"I don't care. It's the fifth watch, anyway. Everyone else is asleep."

Larthia turned her back on him.

He strode across the portico and seized her by the shoulders. When she tried to dash away from him he grabbed her wrist and spun her around to face him.

"I remember what you said to me after the flogging, Larthia. I know I wasn't dreaming. I remember what you did, how you touched me, exactly what you said."

She stared up at him, her pale eyes wide, her slender throat working.

"Do you love me, Larthia?" he demanded. "Do you?"

He saw the answer in her face, but she

made no reply, refusing to admit the truth.

"If you do, say so now, because if you don't, I am leaving this house tonight and you will never see me again. I don't care if I never attain freedom or if you send every bounty hunter in Rome after me. I can't stay here any longer and not have you."

She was trembling; he could feel her shaking like a leaf in the wind.

"Do you think you'd be lowering yourself with me?" he said. "Is that it? Are you worried about what people will say? How can you help your sister with what she is doing and still be so cowardly yourself?"

Larthia tried to pull away from him; he held her fast, her face inches from his.

"Or is it that you're afraid all this," he nodded back at the house, "will be taken away from you if your husband's trustees discover you're sleeping with a slave?"

She closed her eyes.

Disgusted, he flung her away from him, so rudely that she stumbled.

"I'm going," he said, the slight catch in his voice the only indication of the emotions raging within him. "If I mean anything to you, don't send the dogs after me. If you cover my absence for a few days it will give me a clean head start."

He was halfway across the portico when she ran ahead of him and blocked his path.

"Please don't go," she whispered, tears streaming down her face.

He stopped short, his heart pounding.

"You don't know what they would do to you," she added, wiping her eyes with the back of her hand.

"Who?" he said softly.

"The magistrates. If we were discovered it would be *stuprum*, a sex crime, illegal carnal relations with a noblewoman. You would be sentenced to death," she said.

"Do you think I care about that? I've been sentenced to death before, it's a dull day for me when I'm not."

She smiled through her tears, shaking her head at the absurdity of his reply.

"Larthia, give in. Give in to what you feel. It's very late, there's no one else here, no one to see you do what you want instead of what you're supposed to do."

She closed her eyes, and when she opened them again her expression was resigned, but at the same time incandescent.

He held out his arms, and she ran into them.

Seven

"I'll be awkward," Larthia whispered. "It's been so long and I was never very good at it in the first place."

"You'll be good at it with me," he promised. He picked her up and carried her into the house.

Larthia lay back in his arms, content to let fate overwhelm her. She was tired of worrying about her love for him, tired of debating what to do and how to keep all the conflicting elements of her life from running into one another. This was what she really needed; it was like a miracle to touch him after wanting it for so long. He was so warm and secure, he enveloped her slight form with his larger one as he set her on the bed; his kisses drove everything but the hunger of the moment from her mind. When she opened her mouth under his she felt the response of his body in a single fluid movement.

Verrix took the initiative masterfully, reversing their traditional roles, and Larthia reveled in her submission as he enclosed her in a muscular grip, binding her to him. One large hand moved up her back caressingly, his fingers tangling in her loosened hair, the silken strands clinging to his palm. He held her motionless as his mouth took hers greedily, with such total abandon, that Larthia clung to him desperately. He was the only stable object in a reeling world. Verrix made a sound, half-sigh, half-groan, and dropped his hands to her hips, pressing her into him forcefully. Larthia gasped against his mouth as she felt his fierce arousal.

He was a complex of contrasts: the lean strength of his limbs, the surprising softness of his mouth, the clean scent of his skin and hair, the dry woolen smell of his homespun tunic. Her fingers slid luxuriously into the wealth of golden curls at the nape of his neck as she responded to him helplessly, powerless to resist. She forgot that he was a slave and she a great lady with a name to protect; she forgot that he was Gaul who wore a torque and trousers and she a Roman matron with a house and staff on the Palatine hill. He was a man, and she was a woman. That was all.

He kissed her over and over again, with

the deep avidity of long denial. When he stepped back to remove his tunic she waited breathlessly, then embraced him once more as soon as he had pulled the shift over his head. Her fingers encountered the scabs on his bare back, and she paused, unsure, unwilling to hurt him. He felt her hesitation and said hoarsely, "Touch me, Larthia, I've wanted you to touch me so badly."

She took him at his word. He inhaled sharply as she bent to kiss his chest, running her tongue over his pectoral muscles, the flat hard nipples nested in soft golden hair. She didn't know what she was doing, she was acting on instinct, but his reaction told her that her instinct was correct. He gripped her tightly, holding her head against him, his eyes closed, his lips parted, his breathing harsh. Then his fingers curled around her slender shoulders and he raised her up to his level, seeking her mouth again with his.

Larthia kissed him back with reckless intensity. She had never felt like this in her life, and she wanted more of it, much more. Verrix seemed so sure, so confident, and she followed where he led; but when he reached for the sash of her robe his fingers were shaking and he fumbled

with the gauzy material. Larthia caught
his hand and raised it to her lips.

"Let me do it," she whispered, and he
watched avidly, his eyes luminous in the
candlelight, as she removed her robe and
dropped it on the floor. He saw the delicate, ivory skin, the small, perfect breasts
tipped with rosy nipples, and he was lost.
He grabbed her and pushed her down on
the bed, taking one raised nipple into his
mouth, where it swelled more, hardening
between his lips. His callused fingers
closed around Larthia's other breast, engulfing it, his thumb brushing the sensitive tip until she arched her back and
moaned aloud, drowning in the twin sen-
sations.

Verrix murmured something in his native language as his mouth left her breast
and traveled to her navel. Larthia didn't
understand what he was saying, but his
loving tone told her everything she
needed to know. He pressed his face to
her bare thigh, closing his eyes, and
Larthia looked down breathlessly, watching
him as the golden brown lashes rested on
his cheeks. His face was hot, his tanned
skin flushed, the muscles in his arms and
back rigid with tension as he held her.
He moved suddenly and buried his face

in the mound of dark hair at the apex of her thighs.

Larthia froze, suddenly shy. Her husband had never done such a thing; it thrilled her and yet unnerved her at the same time.

Verrix felt her withdrawal and moved up next to her on the bed, enfolding her tenderly.

"I'm sorry," he said thickly, stroking the satiny curve of her back. "I got carried away, I'm sorry. I don't mean to scare you, but you're so beautiful, you've been driving me crazy. It's hard to hold back . . ."

Larthia put a finger to his lips to silence him. "I feel the same," she whispered. "But this is new to me. My husband didn't make love, he just got it over with fast, and even that didn't happen very often. He just wanted children, he didn't care—"

"Shh, shh, don't remember that now," Verrix said soothingly. "Think of me, only of me." He eased her onto her back, letting her take his weight. She felt him again through his thin woolen pants and moaned.

"What?" he said against her mouth, pulling her bare legs around him. "Do you like that?"

She whimpered helplessly.

He pressed into her, rotating his hips, and her breath escaped her parted lips in a silent exhalation.

"Do you see what you do to me?" he said huskily.

Larthia tried to answer, but couldn't. He laced his fingers with hers and stretched her arms out, pinning her to the bed and moving down over her, kissing her prone body everywhere. Larthia was still unable to make a sound, gliding her nails across his scalp as he encircled her waist with his big hands. When he bent to caress her again she didn't stop him.

Verrix knew what he was doing. He had lost his virginity when he was twelve. But he had never been with a woman like Larthia and didn't know how she would respond, especially after her sorry history with Sejanus, an experience that might have killed desire in a lesser woman. But he needn't have worried. Larthia gasped, then slowly relaxed under his touch, tossing her head on the bed restlessly. When she could take no more she tugged on him urgently, her hands sliding over his broad shoulders, now slick with sweat.

"Please," she begged. "Now. Take me now."

He obeyed. He stood and stripped, then moved next to her and turned her to face him, taking her hand and placing it on him. She sighed and closed her eyes, pressing her face to his shoulder, her fingers busy, exploring, driving him to the edge.

"Stop," he gasped, rolling away from her.

"Did I hurt you?" she said, worried.

He threw one arm over his eyes, holding up his free hand. She waited until he said, "You didn't hurt me," then took her arms and wound them around his neck. He eased her under him, and she twined her limbs with his, suspended in time, waiting for penetration. That much she knew. But when it came she turned her head and made a sound of gratification deep in her throat, unable to believe the exquisite bliss of the sensation. Verrix was so full, and into her so deep; her husband had barely managed to complete the act before rolling off her, leaving her feeling dry, incomplete, and inadequate. That experience had not prepared her for this. She clung to Verrix like a limpet, afraid to change position and disturb her pleasure, yet waiting breathlessly for more.

When he began to move she caught his rhythm and joined in with it, learning the lesson only he could teach her.

* * *

"I love you," Larthia said, curled against him in the bed, as a stiff spring breeze from the portico dried the perspiration on their skin.

Verrix drew the blanket from the bottom of the bed and spread it over them.

"Are you sure?" he said, his arm tight around her. "I satisfied you in bed, that's not the same thing as love."

"I loved you long before you bedded me, Verrix. You know that. You never would have pushed things to this point if you weren't sure about it."

"I wasn't sure you would admit it."

He got up abruptly and crossed the room to jam her straight chair under the latch on her door.

"If Nestor tries to get in here tonight I'll kill him," he said grimly.

Larthia bit her lip. "You said everyone was sleeping."

"I don't think he sleeps, he's like a shade who haunts the place at all hours," Verrix replied, getting back in with her. She turned to him immediately, embracing him again. She couldn't seem to get enough of him: the feel of his hard body, the scent and texture of his skin, his hair. Just the size of him intoxicated her; she was drunk on the way his body engulfed hers, making her feel small and female and protected. He was like a banquet after a fast, and she would soon be hungry again.

"Would you really have left me tonight?" she asked, trailing her hand across his chest.

"I knew I had to. You cannot imagine what it was like to see you every day, be so close to you, and know that you were forbidden to me."

"I can imagine it very well," she said with real feeling, and he smiled.

"You are the last person I ever thought . . ." he began, and stopped.

"Yes, I know," she said, sighing deeply. "I hated you at first, too. I thought you were the most arrogant man I had ever met." She leaned over him and kissed the hollow in his throat, just above his torque. "But even then it was not entirely lost on me that you were very handsome."

He snorted. "Not by Roman standards. They think the Gauls are barely human."

"That's not what they think. That's what they *say*. They're afraid of you."

"They conquered us, Larthia. Haven't you heard?"

"Not without the toughest fight they ever had. If you had had half the manpower and weaponry we possessed you would have won, and everybody knows that."

He stared at her. "Who told you so?"

"My grandfather."

Verrix snorted. "Casca is Caesar's enemy. He would say anything to minimize your dictator's victory in Gaul."

"That's not all Casca said. He told me to take my money out of the banks and convert it into gold plate and coins in case it has to be transported."

"Transported?" Verrix said, looking at her.

"He's expecting trouble."

"What kind?"

"Political trouble."

"He already has that."

Larthia shrugged, her rippling light brown hair cascading over one pale shoulder. "I don't know, he seemed . . . nervous. Scared, almost. Something must be coming." She put her head on his chest, and his arm came around her tightly.

"May I ask you something?" she said.

"Anything," he replied agreeably, and kissed the top of her head.

"When you first came to this house you said you had been betrayed to the authorities after your second escape by a woman. Who was she?"

"Another Gaul I met here."

"Your lover?"

He glanced down at her, drawing in his chin. "No, just a fellow colonial I thought might hide me for a night. I was wrong. She turned me over to the Romans for the price of a meal."

"How awful."

He shrugged. "She was poor, and afraid. I can understand why she did it."

"l thought . . . Well, it sounded like a lover's quarrel, and I was curious."

He smiled roguishly. "Maybe I made it sound that way deliberately."

"Why?"

"It certainly makes a better story for the ears of a pretty young woman," he answered, and she sat up, gazing at him through narrowed eyes.

"You were already trying to make me jealous that first day?" she asked incredulously.

"I don't know. Maybe. It worked, didn't it?"

She flung her arms around his neck. "You're a devil. Nestor says that all Gauls are possessed by spirits from Hades, that's why they're so fierce."

"Do we have to talk about Nestor? My aching back reminds me of him every day."

"Please don't speak of that. I didn't

trust myself to deal with Nestor when I first heard what he had done to you, I had to wait until my rage had subsided." She fingered his hair lovingly. "Did it hurt very much?"

He grunted.

"What does that mean?" she asked.

"It was only ten strokes."

"But it must have been painful."

"I think Menander took it easy on me. He huffed and puffed so it would sound as though he was putting his back into it, but he stiffened his wrist so the whip wouldn't crack."

"You must have been furious with me for putting you into that position."

He was silent, stroking her slender arm.

"Were you?" Larthia asked.

"I knew you were just trying to help your sister. The rest of it was an accident," he said shortly. He looked down at her soberly. "Larthia, we have to talk about what we're going to do."

Her face fell. "At this moment? I'm so happy."

"We have to."

"All right."

"We can't stay here, you know that. I won't live as your kept man, and we'd be discovered sooner or later anyway. Does old Sejanus have any children you could leave this place to if you went off with me?"

Larthia shook her head. "His son from his first wife died years ago. A large part of the reason he married me was to give him an heir, but I failed."

"Maybe if he had paid a little more attention to you that could have gone better."

Larthia shuddered. "I doubt it. I really hated to be touched by him."

"So are there any relatives?" Verrix asked.

"Some cousins. The will provides that if anything happens to me they get the estate."

"Good. Then we can just walk out."

"And take nothing?"

"And take nothing," Verrix confirmed.

"The magistrates will have to declare me *nulla in absentia*, legally dead as a result of desertion, for the cousins to inherit the lot. They're an avaricious bunch; once it's obvious that I'm gone they'll be in the courts to settle the estate immediately."

"How is that done?"

"They'll hire someone to plead their case, probably Cicero, and he'll bring in witnesses to swear before the public in the forum that I'm gone. It should be pretty obvious that I've taken off with you; if nothing else the doctor, Paris, and old Nestor will be certain to testify about my feelings for you."

"Why the doctor?"

"It was plain to him from my concern about you that I was in love with you," Larthia said.

"Was it?" He kissed the tip of her nose.

"Yes, and although he promised to be discreet about it, once it's clear that we've absconded I'm sure he will not be averse to taking a bribe to appear in the courts."

"I think we should go in the middle of the night when we're least likely to be spotted."

"That seems to be when we do our best work," she replied dryly, and he laughed.

"When?" he said.

"I'd go with you right now, but I'm worried about Julia. If I leave she has no place to meet Marcus, and that will certainly devastate her. I must talk to her first."

"They'll just have to make other arrangements, Larthia. And if they're smart they'll get out of Rome, too."

"Marcus is a centurion in the army!" Larthia said to him, shocked.

"So? That hasn't stopped him from having an affair with a Vestal, not to mention that she's hardly taking her vows very seriously either."

"Julia never wanted to take those vows, and she certainly doesn't feel bound by them," Larthia said quietly. "She was a political pawn. She regards her Vestal service in the same way you do your slavery, Verrix. It was forced upon her, and it is preventing her from having a free life."

Verrix shrugged. "Maybe so. But if your sister and her lover can break such cardinal rules there are few others that should intimidate them." He took her hand. "We have to move fast, Larthia. Rumors fly. The doctor already knows about us, and you're right, I'm sure Nestor suspects. Get to your sister Julia as soon as you can and tell her to make other plans."

Larthia nodded unhappily. She felt she was deserting Julia, but she knew that Verrix was right.

They could not afford to waste time.

"Should I try to free you?" she suggested. "Technically I own you now, I could emancipate you. Of course my grandfather might object, but . . ."

She stopped. Verrix was shaking his head.

"You can't free me," he said. "You didn't read the document Casca filed with

the Vestals. I did. Your grandfather transferred ownership to you but retained *do-
natus libertatis* for himself. I can only be
freed by him personally or through his
will."

Larthia called Casca a name under her
breath. "You don't think he foresaw—"

"No. I think he just wanted to maintain
control of the situation."

"So you knew this all along?" Larthia
said.

"Yes."

She sighed with a relief Verrix did not
miss.

"Did you think I pursued you because
you could free me?" he demanded, looking down at her.

"The thought had occurred to me," she
admitted.

"No wonder it was so hard for you to
give in," he said softly. "I always knew
that wasn't possible, Larthia. I don't want
the mansion or the money or the title, or
the Lady Sejana, whoever that is. I want
you."

Larthia snuggled into his shoulder. "The
sky is getting light," she said regretfully.
"The servants will be up soon. You have
to go back to your room."

He sat up and retrieved his clothing
from the foot of the bed, pulling on his

trousers and yanking his tunic over his head. Then he stood upright and offered her his hand.

She took it, allowing him to pull her, naked, into his arms. She pressed herself to him when he kissed her, and soon he was dragging her back to the bed.

"No," Larthia said, forcing herself to say it even as she responded hungrily. "You can't stay, you'll be discovered. Tonight. Come back to me tonight."

He let her go reluctantly, with a final, lingering kiss.

"Tonight," he said, and went out to the portico.

Larthia fell back on the bed and stretched like a cat, then ran her hands down her body, still singing from his touch.

They would get away together. Life, which had denied her so much, a careful father, a loving husband, a child, would surely not deny her this, too.

She drew her blanket up to her chin and closed her eyes.

Julia stood in a ring with the other Vestals and watched as Livia Versalia poured water on the sacred flame. It sputtered and died out, a cloud of steam rising from the altar as the Chief Vestal bowed and the onlookers sighed in unison. Then Livia held out her hand to Junia Distania. The latter gave her the mirror Caesar had sent to Livia at her anniversary party. Two other Vestals swept the hearth clean and Julia stepped forward with a bundle of kindling in her hands. Once the altar was ready Julia set it down and Livia held the mirror over it, waiting for the sun's rays streaming through the window above the altar to ignite the pile. The audience in the temple watched breathlessly, looking for the thin trail of smoke that would indicate the wood had caught fire. When it became visible they shouted and broke into applause. Livia waited for the noise to die down before prostrating herself in front of the altar and beginning the prayers for the new year.

Julia scanned the crowd for Marcus; she saw him standing at the front of it with Caesar and Mark Antony, Septimus Gracchus and Tiberius Germanicus right behind them. Marcus was watching her. Every time she looked back at him his eyes were fixed on her face. It was almost a shock to Julia to see him in his official capacity, dressed in full uniform and at Caesar's right hand. She thought of Marcus as her lover, the man who came to her by stealth and took her with such passion that its force had transformed her lonely life. But he was also this man, the career soldier and companion of the powerful whose presence here confirmed his position as a war hero and an idol of the people.

Livia finished her supplication to the goddess and rose, turning to face the crowd. She raised her arms and addressed the gathering in a carrying voice.

"Introibo ad altare Vestae . . ." She recited the words familiar to her listeners: "I will go in to the altar of Vesta . . ." They listened to her go through the whole ritual, some moving their lips along with her, waiting for her time-honored conclusion: *"Semper vale et salve, pax et prosperitas per novum annum."*

"All best wishes for peace and prosperity in the new year!" they shouted back at her, repeating it, and Livia smiled. They cheered wildly and then turned to go, flooding out the doors of the temple and down the steps. Julia watched them leave, Marcus among them; the thought that they had both participated in this ceremony the previous year, and had not known each other, was amazing to her.

When the temple had emptied the Vestals walked to the open doors and took

their places at the top of the steps, where
they could be seen by the people gathered
below them. Caesar moved to the center
of the speaker's platform, assembled just
that morning, and raised his arms to get
the attention of the crowd. They fell silent
immediately, gazing up at him raptly, their
king in all but name.

"Good citizens of Rome," he began, as
he always did, addressing them in his familiar manner, using what Cicero sarcastically called his *vox populi,* or "voice of the
people." Julia listened distantly as he went
on to describe all they had to celebrate,
referring to the past triumphs which had
led to this day and the future ones which
would make Rome even greater. It was a
skillful speech, reminding the listeners that
their current prosperity was mainly his
work and yet at the same time appealing
to the civic pride which was the Republic's
keystone. Caesar's eloquence was lost on
Julia, however; her mind drifted to other
matters. She saw her grandfather, Marcus
Brutus, and Gaius Cassius standing together. The three of them were listening
too, but not with admiration. The speaker
was their bitter rival, and the obvious thrall
in which he held his audience was a source
of continuing dismay to them. Julia looked
away from Casca, tired of the political in-

trigues which enmeshed these men in such a tangled web. Her world had recently become very small; it now contained only herself and Marcus.

Caesar finished his speech to enthusiastic cheering. Then he and Marcus and several of the other military leaders walked down the steps to the street as the crowd parted for them. Waiting in the temple square were the *Salii*, priests dressed as ancient warriors, symbolic of Rome's attacking army. March first, in addition to being New Year's Day, was also the *kalends*, or beginning, of the month dedicated to Mars, the god of war. In celebration of this event, the Salii danced through the town brandishing shields purified by their chief priest. The ceremony officially began the war season and the shields would not be returned to the *regia*, or priest's house, until October, when warfare ceased.

Caesar and his men fell into step behind the capering Salii, waving and gesturing to the crowd, forming a procession that wound through the city streets and would end at the *regia*. There the wife of the chief priest would sacrifice a sow to Juno, goddess of fortunate beginnings. Then the people would feast and relax for the rest of the day, since feast days

were considered *nefasti*, unlucky for work.
It was wise to take the time off and celebrate with the majority; if you did anything servile on such a day it would
surely come back to haunt you. If you
planted a tree it would later be struck by
lightning and cave in the roof of your
house. If you butchered a pig the meat
would turn rancid and poison you. The
gods demanded your attention during
ceremonial times, and if you turned your
face away from them you paid the price
for your impiety.

Livia Versalia gave the signal, and the
Vestals filed back into the Aedes. The
sound of music and cheering diminished
behind them as the parade moved out of
the square.

Rome recovered from the New Year's festivities and looked forward to the Ides, or
middle, of March on the fifteenth. Then
the city would celebrate the feast of Anna
Perenna, goddess of the returning year,
and the guild festival of Minerva. March
was the most festive month in the calendar
and usually by the time of the rustic *nefasti*
in April, which celebrated the goddess of
grain and the rites of spring, the citizens
were already exhausted. Nothing stopped

the Romans from observing these feast days, however; a deity ignored was one likely to exact revenge in the future.

The next market day fell in between the first of March and the Ides. As Marcus watched the Sejanus house, waiting for Paris to leave, he wondered how Caesar's opposition would respond to the news that the Imperator was leaving for Parthia with the advance guard on the eighteenth. Casca and his cohorts would certainly sniff something in the change of plan, but Marcus could not anticipate what they would do. Because of Caesar's popularity, open opposition was dangerous, but Marcus doubted they would let the dictator get away without trying something.

He sat up, peering at the Sejanus door as it was opened by a slave. The doctor emerged, followed closely by his own servant. Marcus waited until the men had departed before he walked up the hill, skirting the Gracchus estate and cutting through the back alleys until he could see the Sejanus garden and portico. His heart began to pound as he approached the house; it always did when he anticipated seeing Julia.

She had looked so beautiful at the kindling of the Vestal fire. For all the notice

Marcus took of the other participants, he and Julia might have been alone.

He had to take her away with him.

He was a practical man, and wasted no time lamenting the bitter fate that had put them in such an impossible position. The situation was what it was. As Caesar himself had once said, _"Alea jacta est"_: the die is cast. Irreversible decisions had already been made. Marcus had to figure out a way to deal with the present circumstances, not wish that they were different.

Julia was waiting for him in Larthia's room. When he saw her he didn't indulge in preliminaries. He picked her up and carried her to the bed.

He set her down gently and then settled next to her, cradling her against him. Julia watched his hands as he untied her _zona_ and pulled off her _stola_, his mouth immediately positioned to kiss and caress her breasts. She sighed and closed her eyes.

When he could wait no longer, Marcus sat up and pulled off his clothes, then was back with her almost instantly. Julia held up her arms to welcome him.

Their movements were sure, purposeful, carrying them swiftly to an exhausted but satiated conclusion. It was only when Julia was lying in his arms afterward that she realized they hadn't yet spoken a word.

"Marcus?" she said softly.

He looked down at her, the uncertain candlelight casting shadows along the planes of his face and emphasizing his high cheekbones. His black hair, longer now than when she first met him, curled over his forehead and down the nape of his neck. His dense eyelashes swept his lower lids, the same midnight color as the hair on his body. He was smiling slightly, and his teeth shone white against his dusky skin.

Julia swallowed, momentarily speechless. She loved him so much.

"What is it?" he said.

She sat up a little, to face him. "We have to change our plans. I don't think I can use seeing the doctor as an excuse anymore."

"Why not?"

"Livia Versalia is suspicious of the whole thing, and also . . ." She stopped.

He watched her curiously. She was blushing.

"I asked Larthia to interrupt us tonight before Paris could examine me too closely. I'm afraid that if I continue with him he will be able to tell I'm no longer a virgin."

Marcus considered that. She was right.

"Did he check—?" he began, but she interrupted him.

"No, I made sure he didn't this time, but I don't think I'll be able to avoid it in the future. He thinks I have a female complaint, after all."

Marcus shrugged. "That's fine, it's dangerous to keep meeting in the same place anyway. It would be wiser to change."

"Where?"

"I don't know. I'll think of something."

"Would Septimus help us?"

Marcus thought about it. "Maybe."

"Is he a good friend?" Julia asked.

"Yes, he always has been, but—"

"But what?"

"We're not asking him to lend us a plowing horse, Julia, the consequences for getting involved with this could be very serious for him."

"He's already involved with it. He hid me when I lost my shoes."

"That's not the same as acting as regular host to a pair of clandestine lovers."

"That's what Larthia is doing."

"Septimus is not Larthia," he replied dryly.

"What does that mean?" Julia said defensively.

Marcus squeezed her shoulder. "Relax, it's a compliment. Your sister is a woman of rare courage. But then, so are you. I can't believe that weasel Casca is your grandfather, and from what I've heard, his son was just as bad."

"You never knew my mother," Julia said quietly.

He smiled. "It would have been my privilege to know her. What was she like?"

"Like Larthia. She really stood up to my father. I think he would have divorced her for someone more compliant except that she was from a noble family, too, and he had used her dowry to invest in his businesses. He would have had to repay the money to her father if he'd repudiated her. Also he wanted a son badly. She died giving birth to the boy."

"And the baby?"

"He died too."

"I'm sorry."

"I never would have been forced into the Vestals if she had been alive."

"Really? She had that much influence?"

"Well, maybe I'm exaggerating. My father still would have made the decision, and Casca always ran him. But my mother would have had a lot to say on the subject, and my father might have listened. He sometimes did."

"He loved her, then?"

"Yes, he loved her. I don't think he realized how much until she was gone."

They both heard a sound in the hall, and Marcus stiffened, sitting up quickly.

"Someone is out there," he said. "I hope it's Larthia."

"It's probably Verrix."

"Verrix?"

"The Gallic slave who killed your friend Antoninus and who now works as Larthia's bodyguard. Larthia told me all about his history."

Marcus stared at her.

"He knows we're in here?" Marcus said incredulously.

"Yes."

"Julia, have you lost your mind? That man is a Gaul, with more reason to hate me than the average barbarian. I turned him in to the magistrates for killing a Roman officer!"

Julia nodded.

"How can you trust him?" Marcus demanded.

"Larthia trusts him. He gets his freedom in three years if he keeps her in good health until then. She says nothing is more important to him than his emancipation, and he'll do what she tells him until he's freed."

Marcus shook his head. "I don't like it," he said darkly, his expression grim.

"I knew you wouldn't like it. That's why I didn't tell you about it."

"He could turn us in at any time!"

"Not if he ever wants to be free."

"Julia, I am Caesar's man. I have many enemies through my association with him. Didn't it ever occur to you that this Gaul could be bribed by one of the people who would like to see me exiled to Illyria or sentenced to the galleys?"

"Marcus, servants were barging in here when you came to me. Did you want that to continue? We needed a watchdog, a lookout, and now we have one."

"But this Gaul, Julia, what a choice! He's the nephew of Vercingetorix!"

"There's another reason he won't turn us in," Julia said decisively.

"And what is that?"

"He's in love with Larthia."

Once again she had his full attention. "Are you certain of that?"

"I am."

"How do you know?"

"I've seen the way he looks at her."

"And your sister?"

"I think she feels the same."

"Is she doing anything about it?"

"I don't know."

Marcus closed his eyes and rubbed the bridge of his nose between his thumb and forefinger. "If they do get together they'll be committing a crime and no better off than we are. I must say that you and your sister are quite a pair."

"I hope she does act on her feelings. She was miserable with her husband. I want her to be as happy as we are."

"With a barbarian?"

"How can I condemn her? Look what I'm doing!"

"But he's a slave!"

"He wasn't a slave in Gaul, Marcus," Julia said quietly. "He was as noble as Larthia when he was at home in Vienne. His grandfather was Celtillus, the high king of the Arverni. But his side lost."

Marcus said nothing.

Julia turned to him and draped her arms around his neck. "Do you want to spend the rest of our time together talking about Larthia's slave?" she asked.

"No," he replied, and proved it.

The Ides of March approached, and with it the feast of Anna Perenna, when the Romans crossed the Tiber, symbolically going "abroad into the Etruscan countryside." The custom was to picnic on the opposite bank of the river, building huts of wattles or erecting canvas tents in which to eat *frigididati*, cold food, and drink wine. The citizens generally indulged to the point where they could barely stagger back across the bridge at sundown. They besieged the goddess with prayers to avert the bad luck of the Ides the next day, some actually remaining sober enough to worry about it.

Larthia was sober. She sat in the tent Verrix had erected and watched the procession of Vestals coming across the bridge, picking out her sister in the rear. March featured four of the seven public occasions throughout the year when the Vestals went out as a group, and as soon as Julia was close enough for Larthia to see her face it was evident that something was wrong with her sister.

Larthia gestured to Verrix. He was standing a few feet away and watching the crowd, which was already beginning to get loud and ornery. He came to her immediately.

"Can you leave all this revelry and come away with me, Lady Sejana?" Verrix said dryly in an undertone, his blue eyes smiling into hers.

"Where?" she said, playing along.

"Someplace where the differences between us won't matter," he said, his expression turning serious.

"And where is that?" she said despairingly, looking away from him, suddenly blinded by tears.

"Out of the Republic, to one of the colonies or even beyond the reach of Rome entirely. Rome is not the world, Larthia."

"It is my world."

"Then we'll find a new one. I can work in the building trade, I learned everything there is to know under Paulinus. You won't be Lady Sejana outside of Rome, but you can be with me without worrying that I'll be arrested at any moment."

She needed to touch him so badly that she folded her hands inside her *diploidion.* "That's all I want," she whispered.

"What are you looking at?" he asked, following the direction of her glance.

"My sister. I want to talk to her. Go over to the Vestals' hut and give Livia my compliments. Ask permission for Julia to come and visit me."

He nodded, and Larthia watched him walk away, finally fixing her gaze on something else lest her expression betray her feelings. When she looked back Julia was coming toward her.

She was as pale as the new moon.

"What is it?" Larthia muttered, taking her sister's hands and leading her inside the tent. "You look like death."

Julia glanced outside, making sure they were alone, before she replied.

"l think I'm pregnant," she said.

Larthia's eyes widened, and then she moved in closer to her sister, her voice barely audible. "Are you sure?" she whispered. "You've been upset . . ."

Julia shrugged miserably, not waiting for her to finish. "I've never been late with the issue of blood before, not even once. I'm like the Greek water clock, as regular as the sunrise."

"Anything else?"

"I had a dizzy spell this morning. My nipples are turning darker in color, and they're sensitive to the touch."

Larthia closed her eyes. She had been pregnant, and she knew the signs.

"It must have happened the first time I was with Marcus. Is that possible?"

"It's possible," Larthia said.

Julia looked as if she was going to faint. Larthia put her hand on her shoulder, to steady her.

"Don't panic. Does Marcus know?"

Julia shook her head. "I wasn't sure until a couple of days ago. I haven't seen him since."

"We'll find a way to get word to him."

"How? I dismissed the doctor, I didn't want to risk any more examinations. I have no reason to come to your house."

"We'll think of something. Just try to behave normally or Livia will wonder what is happening with you."

Julia nodded, taking a deep breath, and then both women groaned aloud as Livia emerged from the Vestal hut and waved to them gaily.

"You'd better get back over there," Larthia said. "I'll send Verrix to the Atrium with a message. You can trust him." She hesitated, then added, "Julia, there's something I must tell you about him . . ."

Julia shook her head. "No need. I already know."

"You know what?"

"That he's more to you than just a loyal slave," Julia said simply.

Livia looked over at them again, inquiringly.

"Go," Larthia said, relieved that she didn't have to go into a long explanation. "I'll send Verrix to you within two days."

Julia sailed forth from the tent, a forced smile on her face, and Larthia wondered if her little sister was equal to the challenge she was about to face.

She had to be.

* * *

In the morning, when Julia awoke and nothing had changed, she knew her suspicion was correct. And when she turned away from her breakfast in disgust, making an excuse to Margo that she was still full from the festival the previous day, she wondered how long she would be able to conceal her condition.

Margo did all her laundry. Any change in that custom would bring questions, and it wouldn't be long before she noticed that Julia wasn't bleeding. Excuses about her "female complaint" might put Margo off for a while, but she was far from stupid. She would report the news to Livia or summon a doctor; either event would bring disaster.

Julia was sitting at her table, staring sightlessly at the crumbs of bread on her plate, when Margo ran in from the hall, wearing an expression Julia had never seen in all the years she had known her.

"What is it?" Julia demanded in alarm, rising.

"Caesar has been murdered!" Margo cried, wringing her hands. "He was stabbed to death by a group of conspirators in the hall of the Senate this morn-

ing. He died at the foot of Pompey's
statue." Her anguished eyes sought Julia's.
"Your grandfather Casca struck the first
blow."

Eight

"Are you sure it's not a rumor? Caesar has been reported dead before."

Margo shook her head. "The body has already been removed to his house by his slaves. There are mobs in the streets, no one knows what the outcome will be . . ."

Julia's first thought was of Marcus. "Was anyone with Caesar when it happened?" she asked quickly.

"No. No, he was alone, as if tempting fate! He had dismissed the Spanish guard the Senate voted for him. Not even the Consul Marcus Antonius or that centurion Demeter were by his side."

Julia sighed soundlessly with relief.

"Oh, this is a calamity!" Margo moaned. "What will become of us?"

"My grandfather was one of the assassins?" Julia asked with a sinking heart. Where had Casca's jealousy led him?

Margo closed her eyes and nodded. "Along with Marcus Brutus and Gaius

Cassius, and others, some ten or twelve in all."

"Who told you this?" Julia asked, wondering how long Marcus would be safe. If the conspirators came out on top of this conflict his life would surely be in danger.

"A runner came to Livia Versalia from Mark Antony while I was helping Danuta air the linen. Livia is already in the temple, praying for the safety of the state. She was in tears; you know that she was a great favorite of Caesar's. The messenger warned us all to stay within the temple precincts. Since Caesar sponsored the Vestals so particularly Antony fears that we may be targeted next by the assassins."

"Where are Caesar's friends? Who is running the government?"

Margo threw up her hands. "Mark Antony and Lepidus and the others have gone underground. No one knows where they are or what they will do."

Julia suspected they would not be underground for very long; they would take action. "What about the Senate?" she asked.

"The runner was questioned closely by Livia about that when he was here," Margo replied. "He said that the conspirators planned to throw Caesar's body into the Tiber, confiscate his property, and revoke

all his edicts. But when they saw the pan-
icked response of the Senators, who dis-
persed in confusion when they heard that
Caesar was dead, the assassins fled themselves, using a party of gladiators supplied
by Decimus Brutus as a guard and taking
refuge in the Capitol."

"So they are not in charge?" Julia
asked.

Margo shrugged. "It seems no one is
in charge. The murderers had hoped the
Senate would be relieved by their decisive
move and happy that Caesar was dead,
not terrified and unable to act."

"The thinking of the assassins is under-
standable," Julia said reasonably. "Caesar
was always more popular with the average
citizen than with the Senate. The Senators
resented what they saw as his airs: a golden
throne in Senate house, the new calendar
with the seventh month named after himself, the dictatorship with the title of Imperator and Father of his Country on all
his statues and correspondence."

"The calendar finished him," Margo interrupted darkly. "March is the first
month and always will be; it's still celebrated that way. And calling the summer
month July after himself, well . . ." She
shook her head. "It was too much, it de-
fied the gods."

"You think he was impious?" Julia asked.

"I think he was arrogant. He ignored all the signs and portents or he would still be alive."

"What signs?" Julia asked.

Margo drew her chair closer to Julia's and leaned in to whisper conspiratorially.

"He was warned by his wife Calpurnia to stay at home until the Ides of March had passed, to dismiss the Senate until then. She had seen Caesar in dreams several times recently, his body streaming with blood."

"Who told you that?"

"Danuta. Calpurnia confided in Livia Versalia and asked Livia to pray for him. And that's not all."

Julia was too worried about Marcus to be much interested in gossip, but she knew there might be something valuable in what Margo had to say. "What else?" she asked.

"When Caesar took auspices this morning they were unfavorable, but Brutus persuaded him to come to the Senate anyway, saying that he could talk to the Senators but postpone the business until a better day."

"Such treachery," Julia murmured. Brutus had been Caesar's dear friend, like a son to him. Like Marcus.

"When Brutus struck his blow Caesar looked at him and said, 'You, too, my child?'"

Julia said nothing. It was too sad.

"Caesar dismissed Spurinna, the soothsayer who warned him, by saying that the Ides of March had come and he was fine," Margo added. "Spurinna replied meaningfully that they 'had come but not yet gone.'"

"Where did you get all of this, Margo?" Julia demanded, staring at the servant. "Surely the messenger didn't share this lurid chatter with Livia."

"No, I got it from the laundress, Costia, who also works mornings for Calpurnia. Costia was working in Caesar's house when Calpurnia received word of the murder. The laundress heard all that was said."

"And is now spreading it to anyone who will listen to her," Julia said with a grimace of distaste.

"It will be common knowledge soon," Margo said. "Everyone wants to know the details of the passing of a great man." She studied Julia thoughtfully. "Do you think these murderers will triumph in the end?" she asked.

Julia shook her head slowly. "I don't

know. I hope not; such a crime should not be rewarded."

"The rout of the Senate gives Caesar's allies time to plan their strategy," Margo said. "Antony is an influential consul, and Lepidus, the Master of Horse, is powerful too, not to mention Demeter and the home legions, all Caesar's men."

"But Brutus has a large army at his command as governor of Cisalpine Gaul," Julia pointed out, thinking about the balance of power distributed between the two sides. Who could possibly predict the outcome?

And where was Marcus? What was he doing? He was so closely identified with Caesar that Julia was sure if he had been with the dictator that morning he would now be dead.

How much longer could he remain alive if the conspirators gained permanent control?

Danuta came into Julia's anteroom, tears standing in her eyes. "Livia is summoning all the Vestals to the temple for the prayers to be offered in time of danger."

Julia nodded and rose.

"She is placing the seven sacred objects on the altar of Vesta right now," Danuta added.

Julia and Margo exchanged glances. This was serious indeed. The stability of

Roman power depended on the security of these icons; chief among them was the Palladium, a crudely carved, archaic statue of the goddess Pallas Áthena, said to have been brought by Aeneas from Troy as it burned. The Palladium was only displayed in times of peril, to provide for the preservation of the republic and the protection of its people.

If Livia was bringing it out at this time, she considered the situation to be extremely grave.

"I'm coming," Julia said to Danuta, putting aside her personal concerns for the moment. Caesar was dead, Marcus was in danger, and she might be pregnant, but if Livia was displaying the Palladium she needed all of the Vestals to join her in a show of unity.

Julia left her suite and walked toward the temple.

The granary on the edge of the Suburra was old and in disrepair, used mainly as a warehouse for storing corn in times of bountiful harvest. Marcus, dressed in a plain woolen tunic with a gallic cloak and hood to disguise himself, slipped along the street toward it, moving unobtrusively, taking shelter in overhanging porches and recessed doorways. He used great care to evade the rampaging crowd that thronged the street, screaming epithets and brandishing torches. It was impossible to tell if they were pro- or anti-Caesar, or a contentious mixture of both. He only knew if he was recognized he would be attacked or drawn into the fray, and he had an important mission to accomplish.

Septimus was standing by the street door of the granary, similarly dressed, waiting for him. When he saw Marcus he signaled for him to follow and then went down an alley, waiting until they were well away from the shouting, churning crowd before saying, "There is another entrance in back."

They found it and went inside, first checking to make sure that no one saw them enter. Once through the door they could hear voices, and they moved toward them as their eyes adjusted from bright daylight to the dim, musty interior of the barn. The air was filled with dust motes dancing in the strips of light seeping through cracks in the walls, and the floor underfoot was thick with spilled stalks and threads of corn silk.

"I say we cut their black hearts out," Tiberius was saying fiercely as the two arrived, his ropy hands balling into fists. "Brutus first."

Mark Antony, dressed as a peasant, his black fringe of hair dusted with gray at the temples and his face haggard, nodded at their approach.

"Any trouble getting here?" he asked Marcus.

Marcus shook his head.

"They deserve the same sort of death they gave Caesar," Tiberius added.

Marcus looked at him, measuring whether he could control his rage and use it to best advantage. Tiberius was brave, but he was a wild man when bent on vengeance, as he was now. He had to temper his feelings and think, as Marcus himself was trying to do. If all of Caesar's allies ran into the streets with swords raised they would not last long against the mobs running loose in the city, looting and burning indiscriminately.

Then Brutus and his cohorts would win by default.

"You'll have to find them to kill them," Lepidus said disgustedly. "They're all in hiding, like the sniveling cowards they are."

" 'Sic semper tyrannis,' they cried as they stabbed Caesar," Antony replied quietly. This always for tyrants. "They expected to be hailed as saviors of the republic. When the Senators bolted after the murder they were taken by surprise and now they're terrified that we'll come after them."

"And we will," Tiberius said firmly.

Antony held up his hand. "We have to consider what is best for the country, Tiberius. I want their blood as much as you do. They made sure I was detained at the door so they could catch Caesar alone and not have to deal with me. But plunging into another civil war will not serve our cause. The question is: how can we maintain control of the government and at the same time make sure Brutus and the others pay for their crime?"

"Turn the people against the murderers," Marcus said, speaking for the first time.

Antony looked at him.

"They loved Caesar, as we did. Recall to them how much he loved them in return, how many reforms he enacted for their benefit, how many times he shared the booty of his victories with the people through triumphs and stipends and feasting at the cost of the treasury. The home legions will be with you, too. We each got two-hundred-fifty gold pieces upon our return from the Spanish campaign and the grant of a farm, remember? The ranting and raving of Cassius and Brutus about Caesar's purple gowns and golden thrones and laurel wreaths will not stand against that."

"If only Octavian were here," Septimus sighed. "If we could show that Caesar's nephew endorsed our cause, many of those caught in the middle would come over to our side."

"He is not here, he went ahead to Apollonia with the scouts," Antony replied shortly. "We must act without him and hope that he remains alive long enough to get back home."

"They left his body lying on the floor of the Senate Assembly Hall," Tiberius whispered. "He bled to death there, alone. Finally three of his slave boys carried him home in his litter, one lifeless arm hanging over the side of it and dragging on the ground."

Marcus closed his eyes, trying not to picture it. It was clear that Tiberius had been rehearsing the grisly details over and over with the group, as if they needed more fuel to fire their outrage.

"If we prevail in this I'll make sure those slaves are freed as their reward," Antony replied.

"Artemidorus gave Caesar a note warning him of the danger as he passed in the street, but he didn't take time to read it before he went inside," Septimus said. "It was found with his papers after his death."

"He had many warnings," Marcus replied. "He chose to ignore them, just as he chose to go around without a guard when he knew plots were daily being hatched against his life. It seemed he was tired of taking precautions and wanted to tempt fate and see if it would favor him."

"Casca said he was careless because he thought he was a god," Lepidus said darkly.

"Casca!" Tiberius exploded. "I'll throttle the life out of that snow-topped old crook; we'll see how his fine clothes look when they're wrapped around his neck."

Marcus looked down, thinking anxiously about Julia, hoping that her status as a Vestal would protect her from whatever befell her grandfather. How could he get to her? The Vestals were in seclusion, on Antony's order.

"Tillius Cimber, that snotrag, pretended to ask Caesar a question and then grabbed his shoulders, holding him still for the others to butcher him," Tiberius said darkly.

"Tillius always was a spineless sea creature," Antony said disgustedly. "He'll surface when this is over and claim to have been in Capua when it happened."

"l know he was there, and I'll remember," Tiberius replied quietly. "The physician Antistius, who did the *post mortem*, said that none of the wounds was mortal but the second one in the chest, yet there was so much blood the slaves are cleaning the floor of the assembly hall still. They hacked at him relentlessly until he fell, those pig stickers." His mouth became a grim line. "I'll introduce them to the ferryman myself."

Antony held up his hand. "Enough, Tiberius. Beating it into the ground will not help Caesar's cause now. We must act to preserve what he left us. I think Corvus is right, an appeal to the people is what we need. They are already rising, it seems that the mobs are mostly pro-Caesar. I think I'll give them a little push. Maybe they'll do our work for us."

"What do you mean?" Lepidus asked.

"I'll speak at the funeral, remind the crowds what a friend to them Caesar was. If the environment for the murderers becomes . . . inhospitable . . . we won't have to lift a finger against them. They're all rats; they'll scatter and desert their sinking ship."

"l want to lift a finger against them,"

Tiberius shouted. "I want to crush their heads myself!"

"You will do what I say!" Antony snapped, in a tone which brooked no argument. Tiberius stared back at him, and the others exchanged anxious glances. Antony was the senior military man there, and they did not question that he was in charge, but Tiberius could be a problem when incensed.

They all waited, as the silence grew.

Tiberius finally looked away from Antony, his expression indicating that he disagreed but would obey.

"We must sacrifice our thirst for the satisfaction of personal vengeance in order to gain the greater good," Antony, the consummate strategist, said in a milder tone. "My first objective, as Consul, is to convene the Senate. They will be much more difficult to convince than the populace. After all, the Senators had become so disenchanted with Caesar that these murderers thought they could kill him and be rewarded for it, right?"

Marcus nodded dolefully as the others looked on, waiting for their instructions.

"I will meet with opposition there, but I think I can win them to my side. Self-interest is the governing emotion for most people, and Caesar appointed the majority of the Senators, either directly or through elections which he influenced or controlled. If his edicts are declared invalid they will lose their seats. They won't want new elections; with Caesar gone they won't be guaranteed to prevail, will they?"

Marcus listened admiringly. He had always been in awe of Antony's manipulative turn of mind; he himself was an excellent soldier and military strategist, but Antony's grasp of politics was beyond his, and rivaled Caesar's.

Caesar was dead, but his side might yet triumph.

"Now listen to me," Antony said, putting his left foot up on a storage box and leaning forward on his upraised knee, "this is what we're going to do."

Larthia was saying goodbye to the *capum*, or chief, of the tanners' guild when she heard a disturbance in the crowd behind her. She had spent the afternoon of the previous day in the tanners' booth at the festival of Minerva, and had returned this morning to sign the sponsorship book to conclude the fiscal year for the guild. When she looked around, a distraught man was running amok through the forum stalls, screaming, "Caesar is dead! Caesar is dead! He was murdered in the Senate this morning!"

Larthia stared at him, aghast, thinking that he must be deranged. Verrix, who had been standing outside the booth, moved a few steps closer to Larthia.

"What's going on, Lady Sejana?" the guild Chief said to Larthia.

"This madman is shouting that Caesar is dead," Larthia replied, as the people standing near her all turned to look at the intruder.

The *capum* dropped his book and ran into the street, grabbing the arm of the runner.

"Is this true?" he demanded.

"It's true, it's true!" the man replied. "Down at the Capitol mobs are storming the *curia,* they're on their way here."

"Who?" Larthia said. "Who did it?"

"Brutus and Cassius and old Casca," the messenger replied. "They stabbed him all at once to share the blame. Oh, the father of our country is dead!" He broke free and ran on, still shouting, as Larthia stood rooted, stunned.

Verrix muttered something under his breath and moved to her side as a dull roar escalated in volume at the other end of the forum. They both looked in that direction and saw what seemed like hundreds of people streaming down from the surrounding elevation, all incensed, some screaming, some shaking their fists, many of them carrying tapers although it was broad daylight.

"Let's get out of here," Verrix said to Larthia in an undertone, steering her in the other direction.

"Did you hear what he said?" Larthia whispered. "That man said my grandfather murdered Caesar."

"I heard," Verrix replied, pulling her by the arm, looking anxiously around him for shelter. There was none.

"He knew," she murmured. "He was planning this the night he came to see me and told me to transfer my money from the banks. Casca was planning this all along!"

"It doesn't matter now," Verrix said, glancing over his shoulder at the advancing mob. "You have to get home." He gestured to the bearers urgently. "Dump the litter behind the stall and leave it there."

Larthia looked at him.

"It has your crest on it," he explained. "If these people are pro-Caesar they might not be too fond of any of Casca's relatives right now."

Larthia closed her eyes, then opened

them. When he pulled her along a second time she did not resist.

The slave boys followed close behind them, tearing off their tunic belts with the Sejanus crest stitched on them and tossing them aside.

When they reached the other end of the street Verrix saw another tentacle of the mob coming around the corner. He pulled Larthia into an alley and began to run.

"What's the shortest cut to the Palatine?" he panted to one of the bearers.

The boy pointed, and Verrix shoved him to the front of their little band.

"You go, we'll follow," he said, and the boy darted ahead with his companion. Verrix and Larthia ran after them in silence; when one of Larthia's sandals came loose she pulled it off and dropped it, running on with one foot bare, her skirts clutched in her hands.

The boy turned left, dodging wicker crates of garbage left for collection that evening, and the others weaved after him. When they finally emerged between two buildings the Sejanus house loomed above them, at the end of a long path up the Palatine hill.

Verrix grabbed Larthia's hand, not caring at that moment who saw him.

"Come on," he said. "Once inside the house you'll be safe; nobody's seen you yet." He pulled Larthia along after him, then stopped short as three men emerged from a doorway across the street and spotted her.

"There's the Sejana!" one of them shouted to the other two. "That's Casca's granddaughter."

As one body they turned and advanced on Verrix and Larthia and the two boys, seeing only one man who could oppose them.

Verrix shoved Larthia behind him and didn't wait to be attacked. He ran forward and punched the first man in the stomach as hard as he could. The man doubled up and crumpled to the ground, gasping.

Verrix whirled and kicked his companion in the groin, then tripped him. The third launched himself onto Verrix's back. Verrix hauled his attacker over his head and slammed him to the ground, then kicked him in the jaw when the man had the temerity to move again.

All three stirred for a few seconds more, groaning, and then lay still.

Verrix stood over them, panting, making sure they were out, as Larthia and the slave boys looked on in shock, mouths open, speechless. Larthia had never seen a person move faster in her life; it was all over in several blinks of an eye.

Verrix grabbed Larthia's hand again and dragged her forward with him.

"Let's go," he said. "There may be others coming, we have to get back to the house."

They fled uphill once more, as the sound of the angry mob increased behind them. When Larthia stumbled, her gait uneven because of her lost shoe, Verrix scooped her up without missing a step and ran with her in his arms the rest of the way.

Nestor opened the door to them, and they dashed past him. He watched as Verrix grabbed the yellow ash crossbar from the hall and barred the door with it, then ran into the *tablinum* and looked out the strip window that had a narrow view of the winding descent to the forum.

"There's nobody coming up the hill," Verrix said to Larthia, who was right behind him. She collapsed into his arms. He held her tightly, stroking her hair and looked over her shoulder to see Nestor and the two bearers standing and watching them.

He stepped back from Larthia, who glanced around and said, "It's all right, the immediate danger has passed. But Caesar is dead, and I fear we may become targets of revenge for his murder, as my grandfather was involved in it. Nestor, lock and bar all the other doors. Cato and Domitius, you two stand as lookouts on the back portico and let me know immediately if you see anyone approaching the house. You may go now."

When the servants had left Larthia closed the door behind them and said, "They saw us."

Verrix nodded and said, "I know, but that may be the least of our troubles. Word has gotten around that Casca was one of the murderers. You can't be seen in the town; you have to stay inside here until we see which group wins the struggle."

Larthia sighed, still trying to take it all in; so much had happened in such a short space of time. "I wanted to leave Rome just as soon as you took the message to Julia about where we were going," she said.

He sat on the couch, and she sank onto his lap, drawing her legs up like a child. He noticed that her feet were covered with scratches from their run up the Palatine.

"I'll get to Julia," he said, "but you have to remain here, Larthia. You can't risk attracting attention, these people are crazy. I've seen mobs before, men who were perfectly sane a day earlier get caught up in the frenzy and do unspeakable things."

Larthia shuddered. "You don't have to convince me. Did you see the look on the faces of those three who came after us? Blind hatred, and they don't even know me!"

"They know your grandfather killed Caesar. That's enough for them."

Larthia dropped her head to his shoulder. "Casca was planning this for a long time, Verrix, without a thought for Julia or me. His envy of Caesar was overmastering; it ate him up for years. Caesar was witty and charming and brilliant; my grandfather was none of those things. All he had was money, and in the end it was not enough for him."

"Caesar was ruthless and amoral. He only showed kindness or mercy after he had already achieved his objectives. Don't make a hero out of him now that he is dead," Verrix replied flatly.

Larthia looked up and traced the line of his full lower lip with a finger. "I don't expect you to be one of his admirers," she said. "But he knew how to get people to follow him, he inspired loyalty.

All Casca knows is how to bribe people to get what he wants."

"Caesar was not above bribery; that's one of the reasons he got into such trouble with the Senate."

"He got into trouble with the Senate because he admitted Gauls like you into its ranks," Larthia replied, grinning.

He shot her a disgusted glance.

"It's true. He permitted Gauls to become citizens and then to represent their home districts in the Senate, instead of appointing Romans to represent them as had previously been the custom. Haven't you heard the song the children sing?"

Verrix shook his head.

Larthia struck a pose.

"Caesar led the Gauls in triumph,
Led them uphill, led them down,
To the Senate House he took them,
Once the glory of our town.
'Pull those breeches off,' he shouted.
'Change into a purple gown!' "

Larthia finished singing and checked for his reaction. He smiled at her thinly.

"Very funny," he said.

"I like your trousers." She ran her hand up his leg. "I especially like them off, as the song says." She bent forward to kiss him, and he cupped the back of her head, his fingers sinking into her hair, his mouth exploring hers gently.

There was a knock at the door and Nestor's voice said, "Mistress, I must speak with you."

Verrix slid Larthia off his lap and said grimly, "This time I *am* going to kill him."

Larthia caught his arm. "You promised me you would leave him alone. We have enough to worry about without fighting among the servants."

Verrix subsided and let her pass by him to open the *tablinum* door.

"What is it, Nestor?" Larthia said.

"Senator Gracchus has just sent word with his steward that your kinsman, the poet Helvius Cinna, was murdered on the Via Sacra a short time ago. The mob mistook him for his brother, Cornelius Cinna, who had just delivered a bitter speech against Caesar yesterday. They are now marching through the forum with the head of Helvius stuck on the point of a *pilum*. The Senator urges you to remain indoors and keep your servants closeted with you."

Larthia swallowed, then nodded. "Give the steward a gold piece for coming over

here," she said to Nestor. "And convey my
thanks to the Senator for the warning."

When the old slave had left Verrix said,
"What relation is the dead man to you?"

"A distant cousin," Larthia replied.
"What a shame! He was never interested
in politics, they killed him by mistake.
Cornelius is his twin, allied with Casca's
faction. I guess for the mob it was a close
enough connection."

"Do you think your grandfather would
come here?" Verrix asked.

Larthia shook her head. "No, he had
it all planned. He's holed up somewhere,
his money safe, waiting to see which way
the wind will blow."

"What weapons do you have in the
house?"

"Weapons?" Larthia said softly. She had
never thought about it.

"You must have some spades, picks,
axes, gardening tools if nothing else, that
I can sharpen and give to the slaves to
defend themselves."

She stared at him, her eyes huge. "Do
you think it will come to that?" she whispered.

"I don't know, but we have to be prepared. Tell Nestor to give me the key to
the gardening shed."

"All right." She took his hand and held

it up to her cheek caressingly. "You must be sorry you ever met me; look at the mess you're in now."

He turned his head and kissed her fingers. "I'd rather be in this mess with you than king of Gaul without you."

"Do you mean that?"

"l do. Now come on, let's get those tools."

Larthia followed him out of the room.

For the next several days Rome was in flames and decent citizens kept to their homes with their doors locked. Mark Antony managed to convene an emergency session of the Senate, and the majority of the Senators, while not condoning Caesar's murder, still condemned him as a tyrant. Prepared for this reaction, Antony replied that if Caesar was a tyrant, his edicts must be invalidated and all the Senators he appointed must resign. Faced with the prospect of new elections, the Senators rose en masse and protested, whereupon Antony proposed a compromise: he would forgo vengeance for Caesar, and the assassins would not be prosecuted, if all Caesar's edicts and decrees were confirmed, because Caesar's policies were advantageous to the future of the commonwealth.

This was agreed.

Marcus stood in the atrium of the Senate Hall with Tiberius and Septimus, his arms folded, watching Mark Antony put into practice the first part of his plan. The military men were not permitted inside the Senate chamber, since they had not been elected; non-Senators entered the Senate only on those occasions when they were requested to appear as guests. But from their station near the building's entrance the men could hear everything.

"It went just as he said," Septimus commented.

"He learned his methods from the master," Tiberius replied dryly. "Caesar will never be dead as long as that one draws breath, he's a copy of the original."

"Now he'll bring up the will," Septimus said.

Antony raised his arms to quiet the murmuring crowd of white togaed men, waiting until they had all fallen silent and were looking at him.

"At the request of Lucius Piso, father of Caesar's wife, Calpurnia, I petition all of you for permission to obtain Caesar's will from the Chief Vestal, Livia Versalia, and to make its provisions public, to content the people," he said.

A babble arose from the Senate seats, and Septimus cast a sidelong glance at Marcus. This was tricky. The contents of the will could be controversial.

"We would not want it to appear to the citizens of Rome that we were concealing Caesar's last message to them," Antony added craftily.

The Senators were looking at one another, nonplused. Marcus smiled. They all knew it was customary for high public officials to make bequests to the people in their wills. If the Senate refused to vote a public reading of Caesar's will the citizens of Rome would certainly think they were being cheated.

The measure passed.

"So far, so good," Antony said in a low tone as he joined the men waiting for him. "Now let's get the will before they have too much time to think about it."

They left the Senate hall together.

Julia marched back and forth, toying with her veil and ignoring Margo, who was following her around patiently with a plate of sliced fruit.

"Please eat something," the servant said.

"You've refused breakfast for three days running. You're thinner every time I look at you."

Julia took a slice of apple and stuck it in her mouth, her mind racing.

Antony was arriving at the Atrium soon to unseal Caesar's will, and she was praying that Marcus would be with him. Verrix had come to the Atrium that morning with a message that Larthia would visit Julia the following day, but he had said nothing at all about Marcus.

"Why are you so jittery?" Margo asked. "The civil unrest is subsiding; Antony has the government well in hand. The Senate has voted to implement Caesar's policies, and your grandfather will not be prosecuted for murder. You should be smiling!"

"We don't know the contents of the will," Julia said, diverting Margo from the real source of her agitation.

"You'll find out soon enough. Livia wants all of the Vestals to witness the opening and dispensing of the will to prove that it wasn't altered."

Julia nodded. Danuta had already told her; that was why she was pacing.

"You'd better go down to the recording room," Margo said. "The runner said Antony was on his way."

Julia left her suite and walked toward the

room where the transfer of the will would take place; she met Junia Distania in the hall and the two of them proceeded together. When the women reached their destination Antony, Marcus, and Tiberius Germanicus were standing in the hall with Livia Versalia.

Julia could barely conceal her relief. She had not been able to ask anyone about Marcus, and until she saw him herself she wasn't sure he had survived the recent coup in good health.

His eyes met hers, and she had to look away; everything he felt showed in his face.

"Shall we begin?" Livia said, and they all filed after her into the recording room. As her audience watched she selected a scroll from the stacks lining the wall, broke the wax seal with her thumb, and handed it to Mark Antony.

Antony unrolled it and glanced over it, taking in its contents quickly, and then said, "I have the Senate's permission to read this aloud to the people."

Livia bowed her head.

"May I take this with me?" he asked.

She nodded. "I have kept two copies. Please sign the register."

Antony scrawled his signature in the

spot she indicated, and his two companions did the same.

"I will be reading this from the temple steps before the funeral," Antony said, the will clutched in his hand. "Will you and your women come out with me?"

Livia nodded, and the little band of women in saffron robes trailed after Antony and the two centurions. The Consul and his companions walked purposefully through the passage that led to the Aedes. Julia tried to catch up with the men, but they had already emerged into the sunlight at the temple entrance by the time she stood behind Marcus. She was close enough to touch him, but surrounded by many eyes. She fixed her gaze on his broad, beloved back as Antony began to speak.

A huge crowd, responding to the funeral notices posted in the forum, had gathered in the temple square.

In the last version of his will Caesar had made his nephew Octavian his principal heir, and had left his gardens along the Tiber to the people of Rome to be used as a park, along with three gold pieces to every citizen. But it was the provision that adopted Brutus, one of his murderers, as his second heir, that sent

an angry murmur through the listening
crowd.

"To the forum, citizens, to look your
last upon your best, departed friend,"
Antony concluded, urging the crowd to
gather around the bier, which was being
prepared for cremation. As the people,
buzzing like goaded bees, pushed and
shoved their way toward the forum where
the ivory funeral couch awaited immola-
tion, Marcus turned back to Julia.

"Are you all right?" he asked.

She opened her mouth to answer, but
looked away from him deliberately when
Livia said behind her, "Are you coming,
Julia Rosalba?"

Julia shot Marcus a look of pure de-
spair and turned around obediently.

"Coming," she replied.

Marcus abandoned his attempt to speak
to her and trotted down the steps.

The Vestals followed the mob at a discreet distance and listened to Antony deliver the funeral oration. He reminded
the people of the oath the Senators had
taken to watch over Caesar's safety, and
he enumerated the decrees and honors
which they had voted for the departed
man. He talked about Caesar's victories
and his love of the state, as well as the
perfidy of the assassins, gradually inflam-

ing the fury of his listeners. By the time he showed them Caesar's rent and bloodied gown, they were roaring.

The enraged crowd pressed forward as the soldiers present tossed their arms on the bier and the magistrates set fire to it. Several individuals took up sticks and made tapers of them, taking fire from the cremation couch, then ran out of the forum, intending to burn the houses of the assassins. The mob streamed after them, tripping and shoving in their eagerness to destroy.

Marcus ran up to Livia in the confusion and said, "Come with me, I'll give your women an escort."

The Vestals scurried up the steps behind him as he, with drawn sword, opened the temple door and saw them through it. As Julia passed him he said in an undertone, "Keep yourself safe. I'll find a way."

Julia wanted to stop, but she contented herself with one long look into his dark eyes and then hurried inside with the rest.

By evening it was all over. The houses of Brutus and Cassius were burned to the ground, the Senate chamber was vandal-

ized, and the assassins had fled the city.
The funeral pyre still burned in the forum, casting an orange glow over the adjoining buildings. Stories of the day's
doings filtered into the Atrium, and
Margo was a fountain of gossip, as usual.
Now that the real danger had passed, she
was as eager for each tidbit as a pi dog
for scraps.

"And the house of Brutus is still smol-
dering," she said with satisfaction. "Nothing left but a pile of smoking sticks. Just
what he deserved."

"And my grandfather's estate?"

"His servants doused the flames and
saved it. Casca was not the main target,
anyway; the will made Brutus the focus of
the citizens' outrage."

Julia rose and went to the hall, where
Costia, the laundress, was talking to one
of the kitchen slaves. The laundress
handed Julia a stack of her shifts and
went on with her conversation as if Julia
had not appeared.

"And Brutus' gladiators set upon that
centurion of the first cohort," she said,
"the one who witnessed the unsealing of
the will, and clubbed him to death. It
happened just this afternoon, after the funeral, when Brutus was trying to get away
and . . ."

Julia didn't hear any more; her vision was going dim and there was a roaring sound in her ears. She sleepwalked back into her suite as the servants passed on down the hall. Margo looked up at her and then stood abruptly.

"What is it?" she said, moving toward the younger woman. "Are you all right?"

Julia's eyes rolled back in her head, and she fell to the floor in a dead faint.

Nine

Julia blinked dazedly, realized that she was lying on her couch, and then heard voices above her head.

"I don't know what happened," Margo said to Livia. "She came into the room and passed out. Danuta helped me move her to the couch, then we called you."

Livia knelt next to the bed and chafed Julia's wrists. "I think she's coming around," she said to Margo. Then, "Julia, can you hear me?"

"Yes," Julia whispered. Memory came flooding back on a tide of misery; Marcus was dead and she was pregnant. She closed her eyes again and moaned.

"Summon that physician who's been tending her," Livia said to Margo.

"No," Julia said feebly, trying to sit up.

"Nonsense," Livia said firmly. "We can't have you fainting. You've not been well for some time, since the night of my anniversary as I recall. Margo, send a messenger now."

Margo rose quickly to obey, and Julia knew that her fate was sealed.

She was doomed.

Unless Paris was the worst doctor Greece had ever produced, he would listen to her symptoms, perform his examination, and conclude that she was pregnant. He would certainly tell Livia.

Julia knew that concealing such information concerning a Vestal would mean prosecution for a capital crime.

If Marcus was dead, she didn't mind dying herself, but what about his baby?

Julia's eyes filled with tears, and she turned her face to the wall.

"What's going on, little Rosalba, Livia Versalia is very worried about you," Paris said heartily, pulling back Julia's left eyelid and then letting it fall.

That much Julia knew. Livia was worried enough to relax the rule about allowing physicians to come to the Atrium, but her concern would change to fury when she learned the true cause of Julia's malaise.

"Have you been eating?" Paris asked.

"Yes," Julia said.

"No," Margo replied from a corner of the room.

Julia shot her a look, to silence her.

"She has no appetite, and if she manages to get something down it usually comes right back up again," Margo added, ignoring Julia's mute rebuke.

Paris nodded and turned Julia's head, looking into her ear. Julia wanted to end the charade and tell him the diagnosis, but there was always the slim chance he might miss it.

"I'll have to ask you to disrobe now, madame," Paris said, and Julia rose unsteadily, handing her garments to Margo, who scurried forward to take them.

When Julia was prone once more the doctor examined her more intimately. She closed her eyes when his hands went to her breasts, palpating them, squeezing the nipples; when she opened them again she saw the realization dawning in his face. She knew he felt the same way she did.

He was frightened.

"Step forward, please," he said shortly to Margo, all business now. She moved to the edge of the couch, her eyes flashing to Julia's face. When Paris began to perform an internal examination Julia saw from Margo's expression that she knew too.

Paris stood, wiping his hands on a

cloth, a thin film of perspiration forming on his upper lip. "When is Livia Versalia returning?" he asked Margo.

"Shortly," she replied nervously, as Julia donned her *stola* again.

He nodded. "Excuse me for a moment, please," he said, stepping into the other room. Julia heard the trickle of liquid from a pitcher.

He was taking a drink.

"How?" Margo said, sitting next to Julia on the couch, shaking her head, her eyes bleak.

"The usual way," Julia replied.

"Who?"

Julia didn't answer.

"Was it rape?"

Julia shook her head again.

Margo grasped her hand. "You must tell me, maybe I can help you," she said urgently.

"No one can help me."

"Not even the father?"

"Not even the father."

"Julia, please tell me who it is. I'll go and find him, and maybe . . ."

Livia came into the anteroom of the suite, silencing Margo, as Paris emerged from the bedchamber. When Livia saw the looks on the faces turned toward her she knew the news was grave.

"Is it a fatal illness?" she asked Paris, and Julia thought, In my case it is.

Paris swallowed hard, his face pale. "This woman is pregnant," he said.

Livia looked stunned for a long moment, then expelled her breath in a rush.

"How long has she been in this condition?" she said, her tone flat and uninflected.

"Not long. One moon, maybe two."

Livia turned to Margo. "Summon the physician Antistius to confirm this diagnosis. In the meantime, Julia Rosalba is to be placed under house arrest, confined to her quarters."

Margo murmured her assent reluctantly.

"If Antistius agrees with Paris I will ask the *pontifex maximus* to convene a tribunal," Livia said. "The court will determine the disposition of Julia Rosalba's case, according to the provisions of the Lex Papia."

Livia's voice was as cool as water. She looked back at Paris, who stood rooted to the spot.

"You will be called as a witness, of course, and consider yourself a suspect for *cohabitus.*"

Paris goggled at Livia, aghast. "What are you saying?" he whispered weakly.

"To my knowledge you are the only

man this woman has seen on a regular basis during the last two months."

"I never touched her!" Paris sputtered. "Only in a professional manner, I never . . ."

Livia held up her hand for silence, interrupting him.

"You will have your chance to speak in the proper place and at the proper time."

She swept from the room, leaving Julia, Margo, and the doctor all staring after her.

She had not looked at Julia once.

Julia picked up her *palla* and folded it carefully. She had expected nothing different.

She had broken the rules and must now pay the price.

It was *justitia*.

Justice.

When Larthia arrived at the Atrium the next morning she found that her sister was missing from her suite. She took one look at Margo's red-rimmed and sunken eyes and she knew what had happened.

"Where is she?" Larthia asked, as Junia Distania melted into the distance of the hallway, not wanting to witness the upcoming scene.

"In the *fanum,* under the supervision of the *pontifex maximus* and his wife. They have two Spanish guards stationed outside her door."

"Why didn't Junia tell me?" Larthia demanded, looking after the greeter, who had already disappeared around a corner.

"Livia has ordered all of us not to speak of it to anyone," Margo replied, and broke into fresh sobs.

"Am I forbidden to come in?" Larthia asked, and Margo shook her head, opening the door into the anteroom of Julia's suite.

"She said nothing about it, and she knew you were visiting today, so I suppose it's all right." Margo gestured Larthia to a chair.

Larthia sat and the two women looked at one another, equally wretched.

"Did you know she was pregnant?" Margo asked.

Larthia glanced away from her, unresponsive.

"Couldn't you have helped her?"

"I was trying, I just didn't have enough time! Caesar was murdered, the streets were impassable . . ."

"It doesn't matter; there's nothing to do," Margo said resignedly. "She'll go on trial, they'll find her guilty of *sacriligeum,* and she'll be buried alive." She put her face in her hands and bowed her head.

"Maybe not," Larthia said softly, thinking of Marcus. She had to get word to him.

"How could I have missed it?" Margo asked rhetorically, not listening to Larthia. "I live here with her. I saw she was tired, nauseated . . . late for her issue of blood." She threw up her hands. "I just didn't think."

"It's not the first condition one usually connects with a Vestal Virgin," Larthia said ruefully. "Is Julia's confinement common knowledge?"

"A notice will be posted in the forum tomorrow morning," Margo replied. "The hearings will be public."

"Public?" Larthia echoed. "Oh, no." Julia would particularly hate that.

"It's the law," Margo said. "Though hardly anyone remembers what the law is. It's been seventy years since the last trial of a Vestal for breaking her vows."

"Seventy years!"

Margo nodded. "Livia has been studying the Lex Papia, determining what to do."

"She must be incensed."

Margo knit her fingers together in her lap. "She's taking it very personally. That such a thing should happen during *her* tenure is a stain on her unblemished record. She'll offer Julia up on a plate to salve her reputation."

Larthia sighed.

"You know who the father is, don't you?" Margo said, watching Larthia's face.

Again, Larthia said nothing.

"She had to be meeting him at your house; it's the only time it could have happened."

"Have you said anything about that to Livia?" Larthia asked quickly.

"No, of course not. But it was very foolish of you to help her; you had to know it would end this way."

"I really thought they might get away together," Larthia said softly.

"You may be questioned and possibly implicated," Margo said. "The only way to avoid involvement is for Julia to name the father."

"She'll never do that."

"Old Paris has already been arrested."

"The doctor?" Larthia said alertly.

"Yes."

"Does Livia really think Paris was having an affair with my sister?"

"Probably not, but he was with Julia when she was away from the Atrium. Perhaps he saw or heard something then, and knows something now."

He knows something, Larthia thought worriedly, but not about Julia. She rose slowly, letting her skirt fall in graceful folds to her ankles.

"Do you know if I will be permitted to see her?" Larthia asked Margo.

"No one will. The *pontifex* said she would be allowed no visitors before the trial."

Another ancient ordinance invoked, Larthia supposed. Each religious sect dedicated to a god or goddess had its own chief priest or priestess, like Livia Versalia for the Vestals, but the *pontifex maximus* was the overlord of them all, consulted when the interests of religion and state coincided. He lived with his wife in the *fanum*, or residence, on the other side of the Temple of Vesta from the Atrium, and he would doubtless be presiding at Julia's trial.

"I must go," Larthia said. "Do you know when the hearing will be held?"

"Sometime tomorrow."

"So soon?"

"I don't think Livia wants to waste any time disposing of the offending member of our little family," Margo said bitterly, her throat working.

Larthia bent to embrace the other woman, the closest thing to a mother Julia had known since the age of ten.

"Don't give up hope," she said to her warmly. "I have a plan."

"Work quickly, then. There isn't much time."

"I will."

Larthia left, almost running down the hall.

She had to get word to Marcus.

The Campus Martius was finally quiet; the riots were over and Marcus was satisfied that Antony's faction had won. The Consul had incited the people to behave exactly as he wished, but the victory was not without cost. The Senate chamber was destroyed, the campus was littered with rubble, and Tiberius Germanicus was dead. He had gone off from his companions after the reading of Caesar's will and was caught in the melee at Brutus' house. Brutus' pride of paid gladiators, in trying to defend their master's home as the mob torched it, had beaten Tiberius to death.

And little Appius, the camp boy, had been killed when he was trampled by the crazed herd running from Caesar's funeral to the Senate.

All in all, it was not a bright chapter in the history of Italy's first republic.

Marcus glanced up at the setting sun; his watch was almost over.

He had to find a way to see Julia tonight.

A soldier approached, and Marcus recognized the tribune, Drusus Vinicius.

"There's a slave looking for you," Vinicius said. "From the Sejanus estate. I told him you would be getting off watch soon—Oh, here he is."

Marcus saw from a distance that it was Verrix; the big Gaul was recognizable for his height and yellow hair, a gilded helmet in the gathering dusk.

Marcus waited, watching his approach, and finally Verrix stood before him.

"You know who I am," the Gaul said quietly.

Marcus folded his arms and stared at him balefully, then nodded.

"I have this for you from Lady Sejana," Verrix stated, and handed Marcus a rolled note. It was sealed with the Sejanus crest imprinted in the wax.

"She would have come herself, but there are some who would still not like to see her abroad in the streets," Verrix added. He was referring to those few rabble-rousers who had seized on Caesar's murder as an excuse to do random violence and now refused to go home and stay there.

Marcus broke the seal on the note and read, "Julia is pregnant. She's being held at the *fanum* for trial on charges of unchastity tomorrow noon in the forum. Do what you can. Larthia."

Marcus felt as if he had been dealt a heavy blow to the chest. His breath came short, and he stood staring at the piece of parchment in his hand, rereading it several times, before he looked up at Verrix slowly.

"Do you know the contents of this?" he asked, his voice congested.

"Yes."

Marcus closed his eyes, crumpling the note in his hand, his fingers curling viciously. "They'll be sorry they ever put their hands on her," he said hoarsely.

"Don't storm the *fanum*," Verrix said warningly.

Marcus looked at him, taken aback that this slave should be giving him direction.

"They have her very closely guarded, in a confined space. Neither one of you will survive," Verrix said.

"How do you know?"

"Larthia has gotten all the details. Her house has been full of lawyers all afternoon, discussing the situation and offering advice," Verrix said.

"And that is?"

Verrix was silent.

"Well?" Marcus demanded impatiently.

"There is nothing to be done."

"There is something to be done!" Marcus exploded, pushing past the slave. "I'll cut them to ribbons before I—"

"Then you'll both die."

"I'll have the satisfaction of taking some of them with me, then!" Marcus replied. "And Antony or Septimus will—"

"Mark Antony signed the order for Julia's arrest," Verrix said, causing Marcus to halt in his tracks, then turn and look back at the Gaul.

"Antony is Consul, he reviews all the state warrants, doesn't he?"

"How is it that I didn't know?" Marcus whispered, his expression bleak.

"Only a few people know, the notice won't be posted until the morning. Antony would have no reason to tell you; he doesn't know that you're . . ."

"The instrument of her destruction," Marcus said, his voice a dry whisper. "I pursued her, I seduced her, I delayed taking her away because of loyalty to Caesar, who is dead now and cannot help me or her. What a fool I was! It was all for nothing. Her blood will be on my hands. My fault, all my fault."

Verrix was silent, surprised that he felt compassion for this man who had almost been the instrument of *his* destruction. And Marcus, in turn, was conscious of a burning resentment. The only person he could discuss Julia with was this presumptuous slave who had killed his friend Antoninus, and who was now sleeping with Julia's sister.

"What will you do?" Verrix asked.

A look of steely resolve came over Marcus' face and Verrix suddenly remembered Gaul and what had happened to him and his people.

"Tell Larthia that there is a long night ahead, and I will be busy," Marcus said.

They both looked up as Marcus' relief arrived and Marcus added, "Go. Tell Lady Sejana she can send a message to the barracks if she needs me."

Verrix trotted into the gathering dark, and Marcus set off in the other direction, his hands clenched into fists.

Paris was terrified. He sat in the chair, his hands and feet bound tightly. His eyes moved back and forth, from Livia to the *pontifex* to the gladiator trained in torture methods who had been assigned to this interrogation. The *pontifex*, whose name was Paetus Virgilius Sura, gestured to the gladiator.

The man slipped a thin sliver of Indian bamboo under the already torn and bleeding nail of Paris' little finger.

Paris screamed.

"Who is the man?" Sura said.

Paris continued to whimper and blubber for a while. His audience waited patiently until he had subsided enough to hear the questions directed to him.

"Who is the man responsible for Julia Rosalba Casca's condition?" Sura said again. "You?"

"I don't know, I don't know! I've told you I don't know! I never touched her except to examine her, and I never saw anyone else with her. That's the truth, I swear it."

Sura looked at Livia, who shrugged. They had been listening to this for some time. If Paris knew who Julia's lover was he would have given up the information by now.

Sura sighed. If the law permitted him to torture the woman he would have the warrant for her lover signed already, but the Lex Papia specified that a Vestal was *persona sacra,* untouchable. Evidence would have to be obtained by other means.

"You were meeting with Julia Rosalba in the home of Lady Sejana. Did you ever suspect that any illegal activity was taking place there?" Sura said in a bored tone, phrasing the inquiry differently, trying a new tack.

Paris shot him a look, and Sura sat up alertly.

Maybe now they were getting somewhere.

Livia gestured for the gladiator to move in closer. Paris eyed him warily, drawing back in his chair.

"Doctor?" Sura said.

Paris closed his eyes; he was sweating so profusely that they were stinging from the salt in his perspiration. He liked Lady Sejana. She had been very generous to him, and he didn't want to cause her trouble.

Livia nodded to the gladiator, who picked up Paris' hand immediately.

"I'll tell you!" the doctor said.

Livia and Sura waited.

"I think Lady Sejana is sleeping with one of her slaves," Paris said wearily.

Sura looked at Livia, amazed, then passed a hand over his eyes. This was not what they wanted or expected, but if true it could not be ignored.

"You think?" Sura said.

"I know," Paris said reluctantly. "She as much as admitted it to me."

"Which slave?" Sura asked.

"Her bodyguard, a Gaul. Verrix by name."

"Do you have any corroborating evidence for this charge?" Sura said.

"Ask the other slaves in the Sejana's house. I'm sure they've seen more than I did."

Sura pursed his lips and then waved his hand dismissively at the gladiator. "Take him out and clean him up, then send him home," he ordered.

The gladiator nodded.

To Paris, Sura said, "You will attend the hearing at noon tomorrow in case your evidence is required."

Paris sagged into the gladiator's arms as soon as his bonds were cut, and the bigger man dragged him from the room. When the door opened the guards standing outside it moved aside to let them pass.

"Well, that was another shock," Livia said, blinking rapidly, her eyebrows raised. "*Stuprum* is a matter for the civil courts. I'll contact Mark Antony, and it will be

dealt with at the next Senate session. I
hear the Senators are meeting in the anteroom of the *curia* until the Assembly
Hall can be repaired." Sura pushed back
his chair and stood, shaking his head.
"It's a good thing old Casca has fled the
country. If the failure of his coup against
Caesar didn't kill him, this surely would.
His two granddaughters, one a disgraced
and pregnant Vestal and the other lan-
guishing in the arms of a rutting barbarian slave. The ancient Casca name is
sinking in the mud."

"We still don't know the identity of
Julia's lover," Livia pointed out to him.

"According to the law, in the case of a
pregnant Vestal the identity of the man
need not be revealed in order to prose-
cute the case. *Res ipsa loquitur,* the thing
speaks for itself. If she's pregnant, she
broke her vows of chastity. I just wanted
to bring the man to justice, too, and publicly, in order to prevent this disaster from
happening again."

"Julia's death will do that," Livia said
softly.

Sura looked at her sharply. "Don't feel
pity for her; she violated a sacred trust.
You've seen the records. You know how
infrequently this has happened since the
time of the Etruscan kings. And I must

say I am not pleased that the trial will be taking place under my jurisdiction."

Livia took this for the reproof it was. "Julia was closely watched," she said.

"Not closely enough, apparently. You were permitting her to regularly visit a house which, from the testimony we just heard, is clearly a den of iniquity."

"What!" Livia said, staring at him.

"You heard the doctor. Julia Rosalba's sister is conducting an illegal liaison with a slave, and this sister was the very person you were permitting Julia to visit."

"For the sole purpose of consulting with the physician, *pontifex!*"

"You should have had the physician come to her suite at the Atrium."

"You know that's against the code."

"You brought two physicians to the Atrium when the Rosalba fainted."

"She was unconscious, she could not be moved," Livia said heatedly, incensed that she should have to defend herself. "And I don't see myself as a prison warden. My women view their trust as an honor and find their calling admirable. I didn't think permitting a doctor's visit was issuing a license to fornicate."

"One of your women did not admire her calling very much," he snapped.

"That's unfair—" Livia began

"Enough, Livia," Sura said, in a tone calculated to end the discussion. "Bickering between us will not solve this problem. Only making a public example of this errant Vestal will do so. And that will take place tomorrow."

"And you will attend to the other matter, regarding the widow Sejana?" Livia asked him stiffly, still smarting from his criticism.

He bowed his head.

Livia left the *fanum* without another word.

Septimus was just considering ordering his slaves to canvas the town for Marcus when Castor came into the *tablinum* and said that Centurion Demeter was in the atrium of the Gracchus house.

Septimus thanked him. "Show him in here and then leave us alone please," he added.

Castor bowed and withdrew. When Marcus entered the room Septimus waited until Castor had closed the door behind him and then seized his friend's shoulders.

"Where in Hades were you?" he demanded. "I've been scouring the city for you."

"I had the afternoon watch and then came straight here," Marcus replied.

Septimus searched his face.

"I already know," Marcus said quietly. "How did you find out about it?"

"My father heard it in the Senate; it was all the talk. He didn't know who the Vestal was, but as soon as I heard it, I knew."

"Is your father here?" Marcus asked.

Septimus shook his head.

"Good. I need to use his library, and I don't want him hanging over my shoulder."

"The library? Why?"

"He was a lawyer before he went into the Senate, wasn't he?" Marcus said impatiently. "He must have a copy of the Lex Papia in there, the *pontifex* is using that to try Julia."

"And how will that help you?"

"I won't know until I read it. Let's go."

Septimus led the way to the *libraria* at the back of the house, standing aside as Marcus bent to examine the labels on the bottom shelves.

"Frankly I'm surprised that you're not at the *fanum* right now, cutting off the heads of Julia's guards," Septimus said.

"That was my first reaction."

"What stopped you?"

"A tip from an unexpected source," Marcus replied dryly, extracting a scroll.

"What does that mean?"

"Never mind." Marcus unrolled the parchment and looked it over, then replaced it.

"Have you consulted with Julia's sister? She's had every lawyer in Rome at her house today; she might be able to help you with this."

"I can't go there. If I'm seen, she'll be implicated, and Sura is probably having her house watched by now."

"Implicated in what?" Septimus demanded. "Marcus, what are you planning?"

"I can't read half of this," Marcus muttered, ignoring the question as he held another scroll up to the light of a candle. "Your father writes like an arthritic chicken."

"That's not his handwriting," Septimus said. "It was transcribed by a slave."

"Isn't there a special section for religious law?" Marcus asked, standing on tiptoe to scan the high shelves.

Septimus shrugged.

"You don't know?" Marcus asked, bending again, looking up at him from the floor.

"I'm not a big reader," Septimus replied, with an irony that was lost on his anxious friend.

"Then get Castor in here," Marcus said. "I'm wasting precious time."

Septimus muttered something under his breath, but left the room and came back shortly with Castor.

"Where is the religious law?" Marcus asked, and Castor took him to a corner of the room.

"Lex Papia?" Marcus asked.

Castor stood on a stool and took four scrolls down from a high shelf. He handed them to Marcus, who unrolled the first one on the Senator's desk and bent over it.

"Thank you, Castor, you may go," Septimus said.

When the slave had left he added to Marcus, "I guess now you can see who knows what's going on around here."

Marcus was not listening. He was reading. He scanned the sheets of parchment until he came to the section marked *De virgo vestalis.*

"Here it is," he said to Septimus.

"Does Julia need a lawyer? I don't know what Larthia is doing, but I can get the best," Septimus offered. "My father knows everybody, and we can pay."

"She's not entitled to one, the hearing

tomorrow is a formality, to make an example of her," Marcus answered, his eyes still fixed on the page.

"Are there any exculpating conditions?" Septimus asked urgently.

Marcus didn't answer.

"Any situations in which breaking her vows would be excused?" Septimus pressed him.

Marcus held up his forefinger for silence as he continued to read rapidly.

"Well?" Septimus said.

Marcus rose, his expression set.

"That's what I thought," he said.

"What?" Septimus demanded, bewildered. "What did you think?"

Marcus didn't answer.

He knew what he had to do.

Ten

Julia awoke in the detention cell in the high priest's house before the birds began to sing. The cot had not been used in a long time, and the covers were grainy and dusty. She shook them off and went to stand by the barred window, watching the first lemon light come into the sky.

Perhaps this was her last day of life. She wasn't sure how long it took for the sentence, once imposed, to be carried out, but her death would most likely follow soon after the trial.

Well, so be it. She was content. Marcus was already in Elysium, and she would see him there.

Her only regret was for Marcus' baby. She put her hand on her still flat stomach and thought about the child growing there, the child that would perish before it was even born because of the sins of its parents.

Julia didn't feel very sinful. She knew

she would be held up to public ridicule
today, but she didn't care. Those evenings
in Marcus' arms were worth the years
taken from both of them. And she knew
that before he had died Marcus had felt
the same.

Julia turned back to the room, thinking
about the prisoners who had stood in this
spot before her. Priests who had broken
their vows, abused their privileges, sold
their influence: the detainees for many
years before her had always been men.
And none of them had suffered the fate
that was now to be hers.

She wondered what it was like to be
buried alive. Was suffocation a slow, painful death, as everyone imagined? Or was
it really quite pleasant, like drowning, a
gradual, dreamlike loss of consciousness
that passed uneventfully into death?

She didn't know.

The sun was rising. Half a day would
pass before the trial. She knew there was
no one to help her. Marcus was dead, her
grandfather was gone, fled into exile, and
even if present would have disowned her
for shaming his name. Larthia was doubtless trying, conniving, perhaps bribing,
working behind the scenes, but Julia knew
she had committed the crime from which

everyone turned in horror and for which there was no remedy in Rome.

A disgraced Vestal had no friends.

She sat back down on the edge of the cot and folded her hands in her lap, lacing the fingers, thinking back to the first time she saw Marcus. He'd been so handsome, standing tall and proud at Caesar's side, his dark eyes lingering on her face, bringing the heat up under her skin.

It would be much easier to pass the long morning with pleasant thoughts.

Larthia stood up as Verrix entered the *tablinum*, waiting until he had closed the door behind him before demanding urgently, "Did you get it?"

Verrix reached into his tunic and produced a vial, holding it out to Larthia, who clutched it eagerly.

"What is it?" she asked.

"The Syrian poison, *zarnig*. The Greeks call it *arsenikos*. It works very fast, your sister will not suffer if she drinks this as soon as she is entombed."

"Did you get it from Paris?"

"No, he was not in his shop, no one seems to know where he is. The other physician in the same street, Antistius,

sold it to me. Did you get permission to
see Julia?"

Larthia shook her head, her distress apparent. "That old rule book Livia Versalia
keeps quoting forbids any visitors. I spent
what seemed like an eternity with Livia
and got nowhere. Not with her or anyone
else. This whole city has been for sale for
the last ten years, and suddenly my
money's no good; I can't even bribe a
clerk to get a copy of the charges brought
against Julia."

"They're afraid, Larthia. The whole
government has closed ranks on your sister. She's made them look ridiculous for
holding the Vestals in such awe and reverence, and they want her life in expiation for her crime."

"She didn't want to make anyone look
ridiculous, she was just in love," Larthia
said softly.

"Have you heard from Demeter?" Verrix asked.

"No. He's my only hope now. And if
he fails, I must get the poison to Julia. I
can't stand the thought of her choking,
gasping, clawing the rock walls of her
tomb . . ." She broke off, stuffing her
fist into her mouth, and Verrix put his
arm around her.

"I'll get her the poison," he said. "They

THE RAVEN AND THE ROSE   367

know you're her sister, but they don't know
me. I'll figure some way to do it; don't
worry about it."

Larthia shot him a grateful glance.
"When does the trial begin?" she asked.

"The notice of the hearing is posted in
the forum," Verrix said. "As soon as the
apparitor announces that it's noon they'll
bring her in from the priest's house."

Larthia put her head against his shoulder and he drew her closer, kissing her
hair.

"Is all of this my doing?" she whispered. "Should I have discouraged her,
prevented her from meeting him here?"

"Shh, don't blame yourself. You could
not have stopped them, no more than you
could have stopped what happened between us. Some things are just meant to
be."

"*Destinata*," Larthia said.

"Yes."

"It seems strange to hear a Gaul talking
about fate," she added, smiling sadly.

"Why? Did you think it was a Latin
concept?"

"Give Margo the poison," Larthia said
suddenly, stepping back from him. "She's
Julia's slave, she'll be with her until the
end. Margo will smuggle it to her."

"Are you sure she will help?" Verrix asked.

Larthia nodded. She was sure.

"Do you think you should get ready to go now?" Verrix said gently.

Larthia put her hand to her mouth again. "I wish I didn't have to go," she said. "I wish none of this was happening."

"You must go. It's your last chance to see your sister," he replied. "Be brave for her."

"I'm not brave."

"Yes, you are. Nobody knows that better than I do. Now go." He pushed her toward her bedroom, and with a final glance over her shoulder at him, she left.

Verrix looked after her, his blue gaze somber.

It was going to be a long day.

The spring sun shone brightly as Julia was led from the *fanum* down to the rostrum erected that morning to serve her hearing. On either side of her strode the Spanish guards who had stood outside her cell at the priest's house. Completing the little procession were Sura, the *pontifex,* and Livia Versalia, in the full ceremonial robes of the *virgo vestalis maxima.* Waiting for them on the rostrum was

Mark Antony, who as Consul would make the final decision regarding Julia's fate.

The crowd of civilians in the forum was restive, waiting for the show to begin. To a population which thrived on the bloody spectacle of gladiators fighting to the death and captured enemies being torn apart by wild beasts, the prospect of a virgin sacrifice was enticing. And the fact that her virginity was the issue only added spice to the event.

The rest of the Vestals, in their saffron robes, sat near the rostrum, about to watch their sister undergo a trial which could come to any one of them.

The spectators began to murmur as they saw Julia's slight figure getting larger, coming toward them. But a curious thing happened as she arrived and they got a better view.

They fell silent. They had come to jeer, but when they saw her, hands bound before her with a length of rope, golden-red hair streaming over her slim shoulders, stripped of her robes and dressed in a simple white shift, they found the catcalls dying in their throats.

This was no scarlet woman, and they knew it. This was an innocent young girl who had made a choice, and she was going to die for it.

Mark Antony waited until Julia was positioned with her guards before the rostrum. Then he convened the hearing, using the ceremonial language indicated in the Lex Papia. He was about to begin questioning Julia when he heard a shout from the other end of the forum. All heads turned to see who was disrupting the first trial of a Vestal to be held in Rome since the days of the Gracchi.

Striding toward the rostrum was Marcus Corvus Demeter, the hero of Gaul and Iberia, in full uniform and wearing all his medals, their gold plate glinting in the full sun.

Mark Antony stared at him. What in Hades was Demeter doing here?

Septimus saw his friend and closed his eyes.

Whatever Marcus was about, it was bound to be foolish as well as dangerous.

Larthia felt a fierce surge of hope when she saw Marcus. Maybe all was not lost yet. She reached out for Verrix at her side and squeezed his hand.

And Julia, who had thought him dead, swayed on her feet and would have fallen to the ground had not one of the guards caught her arm.

"What is your business here, Centurion?" Antony demanded, his expression glacial.

"This woman is innocent of the charges brought against her," Marcus said.

"How so?" Antony was beginning to get the drift of what might be happening. And what had happened in the past.

"She is accused of breaking her vow of chastity, and the proof of that crime is her pregnancy, correct?" Marcus said.

Antony nodded briefly, making a gesture which indicated that he should go on.

"She did not break her vow. To do so requires consent. She is pregnant because I raped her, and she is therefore absolved of guilt, according to the Lex Papia."

A cumulative gasp, like a rush of wind, rose from the crowd. Their celebrated soldier, Caesar's favorite, had forced himself on this slip of a girl, this icon of the state? It was too scandalous, too odious, to be true.

Julia watched Marcus, tears running down her face, so full of love for him that she felt as if they were alone in the midst of this crowd. She understood his intent immediately; he was attempting to sacrifice himself for her. The penalty for *cohabitus* for a man of his stature might be exile to Illyria or a sentence to the galleys or the North African mines.

But the penalty for raping a Vestal was always death.

If the tribunal believed him, she would live and Marcus would die.

Antony looked at Julia. "Is this true, Julia Rosalba Casca?" he asked.

The crowd was mesmerized; a falling leaf would have resounded in the forum like a gong.

"No," she whispered, and then, in a louder, carrying voice, "No!"

"Julia, don't do this!" Marcus shouted.

"Silence!" Mark Antony said to him. He looked back at Julia. "Continue," he said.

Julia drew herself up to her full height and said in a ringing voice, "I take full responsibility for my condition. I went with Demeter willingly and would do so again."

Marcus bowed his head in defeat.

"Seize him!" Sura shouted to Septimus and Drusus Vinicius, who were standing at the forum entrance.

Septimus looked at Antony, who sighed, then nodded reluctantly.

As the two tribunes marched toward Marcus he bolted and dashed to Julia, drawing his sword from its sheath and slashing her bonds.

"Run!" he shouted.

The Spanish guards reached for her, but she eluded them, throwing herself into Marcus' arms.

"I love you, I love you," she sobbed, as he tried to push her away, urging her to flee.

The tribunes and the guards fell on them at the same time, separating them, Septimus and Vinicius restraining Marcus as the Spanish guards dragged Livia away from him.

"I will not have this proceeding turned into a circus!" Pontifex Sura called out indignantly, rising from his seat on the rostrum.

"Then change your outdated and punitive laws, old man," Marcus fired back at him, as the tribunes held his arms. "If you didn't keep healthy young girls penned up like *castrati* this proceeding would not be necessary."

Everyone, including Sura, stared at Marcus in openmouthed shock. No one had ever dared to speak to the high priest that way.

Livia looked on in horror. The last thing she wanted was to make these two miscreants sympathetic figures, and she could tell from the crowd's reaction that the onlookers were feeling compassion for their plight.

Antony held up his hand for silence.

"Take the centurion to the Esquiline prison," he said. "He will be tried for his crime when the Senate has composed the warrant."

Marcus was taken from the forum as Mark Antony said to Julia, "Julia Rosalba Casca, you stand convicted of the crime of unchastity in a Vestal, the penalty for which is death by live burial. This sentence will be carried out at dawn tomorrow at the Campus Sceleratus." He waved his arm at the guards, who led her away.

She glanced over her shoulder once at Marcus, then submitted, walking between the two guards back to the *fanum*.

Larthia blinked back tears and said to Verrix, "She was magnificent, wasn't she?"

He nodded soberly, watching the dispersing crowd, looking for Margo, whom he'd met when he'd taken Larthia's message to the Atrium for Julia.

"And so was he," Larthia added.

"Julia's centurion certainly doesn't lack courage," Verrix admitted.

"He should have killed her when he drew his sword," Larthia said softly. "He could have spared her the agony of a slow, painful death."

"I don't think he's given up," Verrix said.

Larthia looked at him.

"She isn't dead yet, is she?" Verrix asked.

Margo emerged from behind the train of departing Vestals, walking slowly after Danuta, her head bowed, her rounded shoulders slumped.

Verrix left Larthia, moving rapidly through the chattering crowd until he was directly behind the Vestal slave.

"Give this to Julia Rosalba when you can," he said, bending to speak directly into her ear.

Margo stopped short and turned to face him, her expression changing when she saw who it was.

"It's poison," Verrix added, as they both shuffled along with the throng. "It will kill her quickly and spare her suffering."

Margo nodded, dropping her hand to her side, keeping it concealed in the folds of her gown. Verrix slid the vial into her palm, and he felt her fingers close around it.

"Thank you," she whispered. "My lady will be grateful." She pushed ahead of him immediately, to put some distance between them, and Verrix dropped back, watching her disappear into the mass of humanity exiting the forum.

When you can't do what you want, he thought, you do what you can.

Marcus lay against the dripping wall of the prison, which was carved out of rock, and plotted his escape. Night was falling, he was disarmed and locked up, but Julia was still alive.

If he could break out of jail and get to the Campus Sceleratus before dawn, he might yet save her.

He sat up and looked around at his fellow prisoners. They were a collection of drunks, vagrants, and petty criminals who had expressed mild surprise to find a centurion in their midst and then had gone back to sleep.

There would be no help from them. He would have to go it alone.

He glanced up as the heavily barred door fixed to the front of the cave swung open and the guard announced, "Consul Marcus Antonius to see the prisoner, Marcus Demeter."

Marcus straightened as Antony bent to enter the cage and then crouched next to him as the gate clanged shut again.

"Well, Corvus," Antony said, squatting on his haunches, looking around at the snoring rabble, "this was the last place I expected you to end up."

"Can you do anything for Julia?" Marcus asked.

"I came here to help *you*," Antony replied.

"Can you spare her?"

Antony sighed and shook his head. "That old hypocrite Sura and Livia Versalia are demanding the letter of the law. Rosalba admitted her guilt in front of the whole city. There's nothing I can do."

"I'd like to immolate that Chief Vestal on her own altar," Marcus said darkly.

"Oh, Livia's a bitch, always has been, but she's powerful. The people love those Vestals; don't ask me why. Some mystique about virgin goddesses, Diana the huntress, who knows. I think it's a barbaric practice, unhealthy, but I'm stuck with the Lex Papia and it says your lady must die."

Marcus said nothing.

"Is there anything you need?" Antony asked.

"To get out of here."

"I can't help you with that, but I can give you your choice of the Chaldaean galleys, the mines in Numidia, or the frozen wastes of Northern Illyria."

Marcus looked away. He wasn't going to

any of those places; if he failed to save Julia he would kill himself.

"I'd choose Illyria," Antony advised. "The galleys will give you one arm longer than the other, and you'll die of heatstroke in the mines. Illyria is cold, but it has its compensations. The Yugoslav women are quite beautiful."

Marcus looked back at him bleakly.

Antony put his hand on the younger man's shoulder.

"I won't make you feel worse by reminding you of the glorious career you threw away on this woman," Antony said. "I was looking forward to your help in rebuilding Rome, and I will miss you, but I'm sure you know that."

"I consider that my time with her was worth the cost," Marcus said.

Antony smiled slightly. "Who would have thought that you of all people would turn out to be a romantic?"

Marcus had to smile in return.

"I fear I am too hard to ever lose my head over a woman that way," Antony added.

"Maybe you haven't met the right woman," Marcus replied, and Antony laughed. He rose, almost banging his head on the low ceiling of the cave.

"Good luck, my friend," he said. "Just

nod your head at your hearing at the sentence you wish to have. I will try to avoid a life term and restrict it to banishment for a period of years."

Marcus nodded. He didn't care, but he knew Antony was well intentioned.

"*Vale*, Demeter," Antony said, as he signaled for the guard. "Farewell."

Marcus watched him bend to get through the gate and then straighten up on the other side, his figure black against the flaming sky.

He then went back to planning his escape.

Larthia looked out at the moonlit night, thinking that when the sun came up again, Julia would die. If Marcus couldn't stop it, no one could, and his attempt had failed. Her sweet little sister, served up as a sacrifice to the Casca name, was now to be sacrificed again, to an ancient tradition revered more than the people whose culture it represented. It wasn't right, it wasn't fair, and Larthia had never felt more powerless in her life.

She turned at a knock on her door.

"Come in," she called.

Nestor entered, carrying a cup of wine. "I thought you might like to have this, mistress," he said, setting it on the table beside her bed.

"Thank you, Nestor,"

"We're all extremely sorry about Julia Rosalba, mistress," he added.

Larthia nodded.

"I hate to disturb you with a domestic matter at a time like this," he said hesitantly, "but the two bearers have been absent from their duties all day."

"Who?"

"Cato and Domitius."

"Oh, yes."

"Since you said you would not need the litter I sent them to the market this morning, and they never returned."

"Well, maybe they've gone off on a lark, you know boys that age," Larthia said dismissively.

"They're usually quite reliable, mistress," Nestor said dubiously.

"All right, if they haven't returned by morning we'll do something about it," Larthia replied shortly. Why is he bothering me with this now? she thought in irritation.

Nestor bowed his head and withdrew. When he left Larthia flung herself on her bed, face down.

It would be the sixth watch before Verrix came to her after everyone was in bed.

How would she last until then?

She felt the bed depress and turned, startled. Verrix was sitting next to her, and she threw her arms around his neck.

"I'm so glad to see you," she whispered, kissing his cheek, the side of his neck. "I was so lonely."

"I took a chance and came early," he murmured, holding her tightly. "I thought you might need me."

"I need you, I need you."

"I'm here."

He lay back on the bed, and she fit herself against his side, resting her head on his chest, the comforting heat of his body spreading to hers.

"Larthia, we have to get out of this city," he said. "Look what these people are doing to your sister. No one is safe if such a thing can happen."

She put her forefinger to his lips. "I know. As soon as I got back from Julia's hearing I wrote a letter to Senator Gracchus, asking him to handle the transfer of my estate to the Sejanus cousins. Once they petition to declare me *nulla* he can step in and settle everything. I made provisions for the old slaves like Nestor to be freed with a bequest, enough to keep them comfortably until they die, and Gracchus will see that the Sejanus brats honor it. The rest of the slaves will transfer with the estate."

"Can you trust this neighbor of yours?"

"Oh, he's as crafty as any of them, but there's no reason for him not to do what I ask. As long as his interests are not threatened, he's honest."

"Then let's go now, tonight," Verrix said.

Larthia was silent.

"What?" he said, looking down at her.

"I have to see Julia tomorrow morning before . . ." She stopped, biting her lip.

"You won't be able to talk to her, Larthia," Verrix pointed out quietly. "Or touch her or say goodbye."

"I know that, but I want a loving face to be the last thing she sees. Can you understand that?"

"Yes. Yes, I understand," he said soothingly, sorry that he had suggested leaving to her. "One day won't matter, more or less. We can wait."

"I can't believe they're actually going to kill her," Larthia said quietly. "It seems like a dream, some awful dream from which I'll awaken and be thankful that the terrors in the night were merely of my own imagining."

"You'll forget it, Larthia. Some day you will hardly be able to recall this time."

"Never."

"It's true. I've seen things in war, terrible things done to my people by the Romans, that I thought would haunt me forever and make me hate forever. But those memories have already receded, enough for me to fall in love with you."

"That took eight years."

"Then eight years from now you'll be free of this. That's not so long. You'll still be young, and I'll still be with you."

"Will you?" she said, looking at him.

"I will." He bent to kiss her, and was pulling her to him when they both heard a loud pounding in the distance, at the front of the house.

"What is that?" Larthia said, alarmed.

"I'll see. Stay here." He got up and walked outside to the portico, vanishing around the side of the house. Larthia put on her night robe and hurried out her bedroom door, running along the hall to the atrium.

Nestor was already there, the front door was open, and several soldiers were standing at attention in the hall.

Larthia recognized Drusus Vinicius and said to him, "What is the meaning of this outrage, Tribune? I was in bed. How dare you intrude into my home in the middle of the night?"

Vinicius, already uncomfortable with his involvement in Julia's hearing that morning, clearly wished he were somewhere else. He felt like he was persecuting the Casca family.

"I'm sorry, Lady Sejana," Vinicius said, "but I have a warrant here for the arrest of one Verrix, a slave of this house, on charges of *stuprum*, illegal carnal relations with a noblewoman."

Larthia, obviously the "noblewoman" in the case, stared Vinicius down until he looked away.

"What evidence do you have for the prosecution of these charges?" she demanded, stalling, hoping that Verrix would see what was happening and get away.

Vinicius gestured abruptly to one of his men, who handed him a scroll. He unrolled it and read aloud, "Charges are brought on the evidence of Paris, one freedman, a Greek physician, resident of the Via Sacra, and two Ligurian slaves of the house of Sejanus, Cato and Domitius by name . . ."

Larthia looked at Nestor.

Now they knew what had happened to the bearers.

"You know you must surrender this man to me, Lady Sejana," Vinicius said, and at that moment Larthia saw Verrix appear behind the tribune.

She gestured for him to go back, and Vinicius saw it. Verrix turned to run, Larthia threw herself into the tribune's path to block him, and Vinicius grabbed her. She screamed and Verrix looked around, saw Larthia being handled by the tribune, and dove for the officer, pulling him off Larthia and wrestling him to the ground. The other two soldiers fell on Verrix. In short order Vinicius was back on his feet and Verrix was restrained by the soldiers.

Larthia stared at the scene in horror.

"Are you all right?" Verrix panted, looking anxiously at Larthia.

She nodded mutely, unable to take her eyes off the sword held at his throat.

"We'll have to add some new charges to this warrant, it seems," Vinicius said, adjusting his cloak.

"Go right ahead," Verrix snarled back at him. "Obviously a noble officer wouldn't understand that I couldn't watch him mistreat a lady."

Vinicius flushed deeply with anger. "There's no lady here," he replied tightly, his compassion for Larthia's plight vanishing in the face of her lover's arrogance.

"Roman ladies don't sleep with their slaves."

Verrix lunged for him again, and Larthia gasped as the sword point sank into the flesh of his neck just below his torque, drawing blood.

"Verrix, please!" she begged him, on the verge of hysteria. "Just go with them and don't make any trouble. I'll get you a lawyer, I won't abandon you, but don't give them an excuse to kill you. Do it for me."

Verrix stopped struggling, and the soldier holding the sword relaxed.

"Where are you taking him?" Larthia asked Vinicius. "Which prison?"

"That's up to the magistrates," Vinicius replied gruffly, not looking at her. "My orders are to bring him to the roundup tonight at the Capitol."

Larthia looked at Verrix. "I love you," she said tenderly, ignoring her audience. "I'll find you."

Vinicius gestured, and the two soldiers yanked Verrix along with them as they departed. The tribune turned to face Larthia then and said stiffly: "I'm sorry about all of this, Lady Sejana."

"So am I. I'm sorry that my sister is going to die in the morning, and I'm sorry that our laws proscribe a relationship that has made me happier than I've ever been in my life."

Vinicius stared back at her stoically, his training preventing him from responding to her as he had to Verrix.

"Oh, go, Vinicius," Larthia said wearily. "I know this was not your idea. Leave me alone."

The tribune turned and marched down her walk, following his soldiers as they took Verrix off to jail.

Larthia went into the house, shut the door, and stood with her back to it, her hands over her face. She felt like screaming. When she was somewhat calmer she looked up and saw Nestor standing there, watching her.

"I was not responsible for this, mistress," he said quietly, his dark eyes grave.

"I know that, Nestor. Now let's not talk about it anymore, I have things to do, and I need you to help me."

He bowed his head and followed her down the hall.

Marcus was watching the guard standing beyond the prison gate, his profile illuminated by the torch in a brass brace hammered into the rock. Prison guards were frequently ex-gladiators who had won a re-

prieve for valorous performances in the
ring, and this man was a bruiser, about as
tall as he was but quite a bit heavier. Marcus was evaluating his chances of taking
him when a new prisoner arrived at the
cave, escorted by a foot soldier and the
tribune, Drusus Vinicius.

"Here's a friend for you, Marcus,"
Vinicius said, shoving the newcomer inside
the gate and then stepping back as the
guard clanged it shut. "I think you know
him."

When Marcus saw who it was he sighed
and shook his head. What next?

"He likes women, too, so you won't have
to worry about him getting next to you
during the night," Vinicius said, laughing,
and Marcus shot him a rude gesture.

Verrix slumped across from Marcus and
drew up his long legs to conserve space.
Marcus waited until the soldiers had left
and then said to him, "What are you doing here?"

"Larthia," Verrix replied glumly.

"*Stuprum?*"

Verrix nodded wearily.

"Who turned you in?"

Verrix shrugged. "They must have evidence, or Larthia would not have let them
take me."

"You can't stay out of trouble, can you, boy?"

"You don't seem to be doing too well yourself," Verrix replied dryly, and Marcus snorted.

"At least I won't wind up in the arena," Marcus said.

"I thought the sentence was crucifixion."

"They won't waste you on the cross, strong man. It will be the arena for you."

"I've been sentenced to the cross before," Verrix said.

"For killing Antoninus, yes, but Casca voided that sentence when he paid your life price. For *stuprum* you'll be sent to gladiatorial school and forced to learn the use of the mask and the trident. You'll wind up entertaining the masses on feast days, trying to stay alive against Thracians and Nubians in order to fight again another time."

Verrix glanced up at the dripping ceiling of the cave, the running walls, the pile of tattered ne'er-do-wells sleeping in the depths of the musty squalor.

"Not if I get out of here," he said.

"Oh, I forgot. You're the escape artist."

"And you could certainly use one. Your lady dies at dawn if you don't bust loose tonight. Do you think you might profit from some help?"

Marcus could barely see his companion in the dim light of the torch outside; the cave was almost black. He knew he didn't like him. The memory of Antoninus was still fresh. But Marcus also knew that the slave was an amazingly resourceful individual who seemed to survive, and even prosper, in any circumstances.

And Julia's sister apparently loved him.

Two sets of hands were better than one. Even if he managed to escape, he still had to get Julia away from her jailers before they carried out her execution.

"What do you have in mind?" Marcus asked.

"Is there only one guard?"

"More than one is not necessary. The only access is that road coming up the hill and it's a sheer drop the other way."

"And the lock?"

"It's a simple turnkey, but the guard always stays outside, he never gets close enough for me to grab his belt."

Both men looked up suddenly as they heard voices outside the cave. Marcus smiled as he recognized one of them.

"What . . . ?" Verrix began, and Marcus silenced him with a gesture.

"Be quiet! That's Septimus, a friend of mine."

"What's he doing?" Verrix hissed.

"Listen!"

Septimus had a leather bottle of wine, and they heard him trying to persuade the guard, whom he knew from Senator Gracchus' gladiator school, to take a drink. This went on for a while, the guard feebly protesting his duty until he finally succumbed to temptation.

"What's going on now?" Verrix whispered.

Marcus crawled into a tenuous position on a ledge, pressing his nose to the grids of the gate, where he could just see the two men conversing.

"Be still and I'll tell you," Marcus muttered. He reported to Verrix as he saw Septimus matching the other man drink for drink until the guard was reeling. When Septimus thought him drunk enough, he walked behind the guard and braced his hands together, lacing his fingers tightly, then struck him on the back of the neck.

The guard toppled like a felled tree, and Septimus snatched his keys. He ran to the cave.

"I thought that Samnian would never go down," he muttered thickly as he unlocked the gate. "He must have the constitution of a Parthian camel. I had to keep him going, and I'm not too steady myself."

"Am I glad to see you!" Marcus said, throwing his arms around his friend.

Septimus stared as Verrix came piling out of the cave behind Marcus.

"Him, too?" he said.

"He's coming with me."

"What are you doing with Larthia's slave?"

"Long story. Will you lock the gate before those dreamers in back wake up?"

Septimus locked up and then refixed the keys to the unconscious guard's belt. He came back to Marcus and handed him a goatskin pouch.

"Forty gold pieces," he said. "That's all I could put my hands on today."

Marcus took the bag and stashed it inside his cloak. "How will you explain this?" he asked, indicating the drunken guard.

"At the moment, I don't know. I'll think of something. It will be as outrageous as I can make it; I never miss an opportunity to give my father another reason to disinherit me." He took off his weapons sheath, which contained his sword and knife, and handed the belt to Marcus.

"You've been a good friend, Septimus. I don't know how to thank you." Marcus buckled on the belt.

"No need. It's my belief that you can

never do enough for the man who's saved your life." Septimus grinned.

"Will you two just kiss each other and get it over with?" said Verrix impatiently. "We don't have much time."

Marcus glanced up at the night sky. It would not be night much longer.

He embraced Septimus again and said, "I'll never forget you, *amicus animae*."

"Go!" Septimus said.

Marcus and Verrix sprinted off down the hill.

Mark Antony was working late in his office at home. He looked up in surprise as his steward admitted a distraught *pontifex maximus* into the torchlit room.

"Paetus Sura, what brings you out at this time of night? Is there something I can do for you?" Antony said, putting aside the edict he was reading.

"Something you can do? Marcus Corvus Demeter has escaped from the Esquiline prison!"

"Is that so?" Antony said, leaning back in his chair, folding his hands at his waist.

"Yes, that's so, and I want to know what you are going to do about it!"

Antony opened his hands. "What can I do about it?" he asked innocently.

"Send a deployment of soldiers after them!"

"Them?"

"Demeter has a Gallic slave with him, the Sejana's lover, accused of *stuprum*. They escaped together."

Antony pursed his lips. "The Gaul has good taste," he said judiciously.

"Is that all you can say?"

Antony sat forward again and picked up the scroll he had been reading. "I think Larthia's sister is prettier, but there's no accounting for individual preference."

Sura stared at him. "Do you think this is funny? Demeter flouted our laws by defiling a Vestal, and now he's at large, probably on his way to rescue that little tart from the death she so richly deserves. At least send reinforcements to the burial site to make sure he doesn't snatch her."

Antony shrugged. "I'm sorry. I don't have the men to spare, there are still pockets of resistance all over the city, conspiracies that might erupt at any moment."

"Are you serious? You can't spare two men?"

"Julia Rosalba will be attended by the Spanish guards assigned to her when she was arrested. Not to mention the formidable Livia Versalia, who is well worth ten of my men on any given occasion. That's enough."

"You're on their side, aren't you?" Sura demanded, eyeing Antony narrowly. "You want them to get away."

"I am on *my* side, *pontifex*, and it is not in my best interest to send my soldiers to an execution when they are needed elsewhere. That is all."

Sura didn't move.

Antony looked up at him. "I said, that is all. And if I find out you have done anything to contravene my wishes in this matter, it will not go well for you, I assure you."

Sura made a disgusted sound and stomped noisily out of the study.

Antony smiled, silently wished Demeter the speed of winged Mercury, and went back to his paperwork.

Eleven

"What are you going to do with that?" Verrix asked, as Marcus stripped off his uniform and rolled it into a ball.

"I'm going to hide it. In case anyone comes after us I don't want it to be a marker for the route we took." Marcus rolled aside a rock and stuffed the red tunic under it, then replaced the rock, kicking dirt around the edge to disguise the fact that it had been moved. He took the woolen tunic Verrix handed him and belted it tightly around his waist. Verrix, now attired only in shift and trousers, looked down the hill at the stable on the edge of the forum.

"Are you sure Postumus isn't there at night?" he asked, peering through the almost unrelieved dark.

"He has a house near the Via Flaminia."

"But he must leave somebody there to make sure no one steals the horses."

"There's probably just a stableboy, Postumus is too cheap to keep a night staff. Come on."

They picked their way down the rest of the elevation, their footing unsure without light to see. Marcus had been tempted to steal the torch from the wall outside the prison, but he knew that it would flash like a lighthouse fire if anyone did come after them.

Going in the dark was slower, but safer.

It seemed an eternity before they were standing in back of the stable. The pungent aroma of many horses confined together and the occasional stomping and neighing of restive animals was punctuated by the rumbling of carts in the street out front.

"Where's the entrance?" Verrix asked.

Marcus nodded to the left. "I wish we could just wake up the attendant and pay for the horses, but if we do that whoever is in there will remember us."

"Let's go," Verrix said.

They crept around to the double doors, which were barred from the inside. On the plain front of the wooden structure they saw a small trap door used for feed deliveries.

"There," Marcus said.

They kicked it in; the stableboy sleeping inside on a bench jumped up at the noise and then shrank back against the wall when he saw the two intruders crawl through the door.

"So much for stealth," Verrix muttered. "He'll be sure to remember us now."

Marcus didn't have time for the niceties; he lunged forward and grabbed the boy's tunic.

"Get me your two best horses," he said. "Now."

The boy stared back at him, his eyes like saucers.

"There's a gold piece in it for you," Marcus added, and the boy, realizing that they weren't going to kill him, bolted down the stable aisle. In short order he was leading two mares to the front as Marcus and Verrix waited impatiently.

"Get me the bridles and blankets," Marcus barked, reaching inside his tunic for the money pouch Septimus had given him. When the horses were outfitted Marcus handed the boy the coin and added, "Now open the door."

The boy obeyed, and as he and Verrix led the horses into the street, Marcus said, "You didn't see anyone. You fell asleep and when you woke up the horses were gone."

The boy nodded vigorously.

During the whole encounter he had not said a word.

"That money will keep him quiet until he hears the first threat," Verrix said.

"It doesn't matter. We'll be long gone by the time Postumus arrives to open his shop."

"Where are we going?" Verrix asked.

"Porta Collina," Marcus replied shortly.

Verrix nodded. It was one of the many gates to the city which stood in the outlying districts and fed the major roads into the forum. This one lay across the Tiber, near the gardens which Caesar had recently given to the public in his will. The fastest route to it was to ride around the flats beyond the seven hills and then enter the city, because the streets at night were so clogged with carts, not to mention the roaming gangs of cutpurses who might also slow, or stop, their progress.

"Let's go," Marcus added.

They led the horses away from the forum, walking with them for several miles until they had left the settlements behind and there was nothing but scrub grass and open fields in view. At Marcus' signal they mounted, riding bareback except for blankets, controlling the animals with their leg muscles.

Verrix was by far the better rider; the Roman army lacked an efficient cavalry, indeed many of its officers could not even

ride, but the Gauls were mounted brig-
ands, able to do almost anything from the
back of a horse. Marcus kept up with his
companion, since he had learned to ride
as a young boy in Corsica, but as he
glanced up at the sky he was glad he had
run into the slave when he had.

He hated to admit it, but Verrix was
an asset.

He kicked the horse's flanks with his
heels and spurred his mount on urgently.

The sky was getting lighter.

"Are you ready?" Margo said quietly. to
Julia, who smiled humorlessly.

"I'm dressed," she said. "I don't think
it's possible to be 'ready,' do you?"

Margo glanced over her shoulder at
Livia Versalia, who was standing at the
door, waiting with the two Spanish guards
to escort Julia from the *fanum*.

"May I have a minute alone with her?"
she asked Livia.

Livia hesitated, then nodded. She
stepped out of the detention cell and
closed the door.

Margo produced the vial of arsenic
from the folds of her gown and pressed
it into Julia's hand.

"I got this from your sister's slave.

Drink it as soon as they seal you in," she whispered. "It will all be over quickly, you will not suffer."

Julia took the poison and tucked it into the bodice of her gown. Then she embraced Margo, holding the other woman close and saying softly, "I love you. I don't think I would have survived my first years as a Vestal if it weren't for you. The only thing I regret about all of this is leaving you behind to live here without me."

"Why did you do it, Julia?" Margo sobbed. "Is anything worth this punishment? Anything?"

"I don't expect you to understand," Julia said gently, stepping back from her. "Just know that I made a free choice to do what I did, and I'm not sorry."

Margo clung to her a little longer, then let her go, wiping her eyes with the end of her sleeve as Livia opened the door again.

"Time to go," she said shortly.

Julia walked forward, a slim figure in her white *stola*, a thin silk *palla* over her arms. Livia and the guards fell in behind her as she left the cell.

The only other witnesses permitted at her execution would be the rest of the Vestals and her sister Larthia.

Two carriages awaited them in the temple square. Livia and Julia sat in one, which was driven by the first guard, and the five other Vestals got into the other with the second guard. As they drove off in the gloomy predawn, the horses' hooves clopping on the paving stones, Julia looked her last at the scene which had been daily life to her for the last ten years. The merchants, loading their stalls to get ready for sunrise, looked curiously at the vehicles as they passed. Those who recognized the Vestal crest might have known what was happening, but most were too preoccupied with presenting their merchandise to give the little caravan more than a passing glance.

Julia reflected with a fitting sense of completion that it was market day.

Livia, sitting at her side, was silent.

There was nothing to say.

Larthia got dressed in the dark, not even bothering to light a candle. She had spent a sleepless night after Verrix was taken, wondering where he was, wondering what her sister was doing with her final hours. She wondered also, briefly, how her own life had come to such a pass, but she didn't have time to waste lamenting recent events.

For Julia she could do nothing except be present as the sentence was carried out, but Verrix needed a lawyer.

Her grandfather's crony Cicero she considered to be a pompous blowhard, overly fond of his own opinions and the sound of his own voice, but he was widely thought to be the best lawyer practicing in Rome. She considered and discarded most of the attorneys she had consulted about Julia's situation; they specialized and were conversant with religious law, which would be of no help to Verrix. The regulations concerning slaves were constantly changing, due to the many foreign conquests which supplied the labor force, and she needed someone who had kept up with the latest developments.

Senator Gracchus would probably know.

But first she had to witness Julia's execution.

She left her room and went into the hall, where Nestor kept torches burning all night long.

The old slave was already up and dressed, waiting for her to emerge.

"Will you have something to eat, mistress?" he asked solicitously.

Larthia shook her head.

"Can I do anything for you before you go?"

"No, thank you, Nestor." Larthia was about to walk past him and then had a thought.

"Nestor, if anything should happen to me, if I should disappear or meet with an accident, there is a letter for Senator Gracchus in my room on my dressing table, already sealed. Will you take it to him if it becomes necessary?"

"Are you expecting any trouble, mistress?" Nestor asked worriedly.

"I don't know. I haven't been the most popular person lately: my grandfather is one of Caesar's assassins, my sister is a disgraced Vestal about to be executed, and my lover has been arrested. Can you understand how I might be concerned?"

Nestor nodded soberly.

"Will you do that for me, then?"

He nodded again.

"Good. Now I must be off. Look after things here for me, and make sure all the servants follow through with their duties."

Nestor extended his hand and pressed a silver piece into Larthia's palm.

"A coin for the ferryman, mistress. For Miss Julia. Please give it to her."

Touched, Julia took the coin and then hugged the old man briefly.

"That's very kind of you, Nestor." She

tucked it into her purse and ran down the hall before she broke down and cried.

Burying the dead with coins to pay the ferryman who bore them across the River Styx to the home of the blessed was an ancient custom. Tradition said that if you did not pay him you were left to wander forever, lost and unfulfilled, in a misty netherworld of troubled souls. It was a fate to be avoided at all costs.

Julia would travel with her fare in hand.

Larthia wiped the back of her arm across her eyes and hurried out the door.

Marcus and Verrix crouched behind an outcropping of rock and peered around at the empty landscape. The horses, tied to a tree near them, munched on grass contentedly, glad of the rest.

"Are you sure this is the right place?" Verrix whispered, struck by the awful thought that Marcus might be mistaken about the location.

Marcus nodded. "I read the law, this clearing is considered sacred for sacrifices. And look."

He pointed. Verrix followed the direction of his finger and saw a huge rock rolled back from a hollow freshly dug into the side of a hill.

"Is that the tomb?" he asked.

"Yes."

"And you call us barbarians," Verrix observed disgustedly, shaking his head.

"Shh!" Marcus said suddenly, grabbing his arm. "I think I hear something."

They both listened intently.

"They're coming," Verrix murmured.

Muffled footfalls signaled the approach of the little procession. Marcus raised his head and saw Julia, her hands bound with rope, at the head of the column, walking between her two guards. Directly behind her was Livia Versalia, trailed by the rest of the Vestals.

He glanced up at the sky. The first thin threads of light were coming into it; entombment would take place when the sun was first visible over the horizon. As Marcus had already explained to Verrix, Livia would first prostrate herself and pray for the acceptance of the sacrifice. When she was flat on the ground and unable to resist, they would strike, taking out the two guards. He doubted if any of the other Vestals would fight them; it was too easy for those women to put themselves in Julia's place.

"There's Larthia," Verrix muttered, as a figure emerged from the trees, all alone, as Livia had specified.

When Julia saw her sister she bowed her head.

Livia knelt on the grass, then lay forward with her head pressed to the ground, her arms extended.

"Get the horses," Marcus said to Verrix. "Now."

Verrix rose and sprinted away, returning a short time later with the two animals in tow. They mounted and led the horses a little closer, until they could hear Livia's murmuring voice.

"I'll take the guard on the right," Marcus said. "Go!"

As the men burst from the trees, all the participants in the ceremony looked around, startled. Before the guards could react, Verrix had slashed the first one with Septimus' knife and the man went down, clutching his arm.

Julia gasped aloud when she saw Marcus, and Larthia shouted for joy.

Marcus attacked the second guard, who offered only token resistance as Marcus dismounted and wrestled him to the ground, holding him there with the point of his sword.

"Cut her loose," he barked to Verrix, who slashed Julia's bonds as Larthia ran to help her sister.

"Do something!" Livia screamed to the

injured guard. "They're going to get away!"

The first guard struggled to his feet, and Verrix whirled instantly, bringing his forearm across the other man's throat and knocking him down again.

Livia rushed at Verrix, who clipped her on the jaw. She crumpled to the grass.

"Larthia!" he called, and extended his hand. She dashed over to him and took it. He hoisted her onto his horse as Marcus said, "Stay down or you die!" to the second guard. The man remained down, and Marcus ran to Julia, who fell into his arms.

"I thought I would never see you again," she sobbed, clutching him.

He held her briefly, tightly, then said, "Come, we have to go. I don't know what Livia has planned; she may have ordered some reinforcements."

They ran to his horse and he lifted her onto it, then jumped up in front of her, as Verrix mounted behind Larthia. The remaining Vestals watched in awe as the two men kicked their horses and galloped out of the clearing, the women behind them clinging to their waists.

"I can't believe that just happened," Junia Distania whispered, still dazzled by the spectacular rescue, as the dust settled behind the departing horses.

"Somebody help me," Livia said hoarsely, dazed and struggling to her feet. Augusta Gellia ran to her side and assisted Livia to stand, offering her arm.

Livia looked around alertly. She saw that Julia and Larthia were missing and the two Spanish guards were still prostrate on the ground.

"Go after them!" she shrieked at the guard who was not bleeding. "What are you waiting for?"

"I'll have to consult Consul Antony for my orders," he replied in heavily accented Latin. He was a mercenary and didn't care if Julia lived, died, or moved to Transpadani.

"You mean go back to the *curia?*" Livia demanded shrilly. "They'll be in Parthia by then!"

"I have no authorization to pursue them, madam," he said in protest.

"I'm giving you authorization! I order it!"

"I take my orders from the Consul," the guard replied stubbornly, staring Livia down, as the other guard watched the byplay, silent.

"Oh, you are useless!" Livia shouted, balling her fists. She looked as if she were about to stomp her feet and tear her hair. Then, suddenly remembering that her women were watching her make a spectacle of herself, she took a deep breath and struggled for calm, forcing herself to behave rationally.

"Let us return to the temple," she said in a level tone. "Pontifex Sura warned me that there might be trouble, but the Consul would not authorize additional men for the burial." She smiled thinly. "Sometimes the magistrates do not take much notice of our ceremonies; they always protest they have weightier things on their minds."

Once she got back to the city, the Consul would surely hear from her.

Marcus and Verrix ran their horses flat out until they had left the city and its environs far behind. The sun was high above their heads at midmorning when Marcus finally gave the signal to stop and rest at a stream, a tributary of the Tiber, which flowed north toward Fidenae. The men dismounted and then lifted the ladies down to the grass under a stand of trees.

"How are you feeling?" Marcus asked Julia anxiously. She had endured many shocks in recent days, not to mention a wild ride on horseback for the last few hours. It was an ordeal for any woman, much less a pregnant one.

"I feel wonderful," she replied, touching his face. "I'm alive, I'm free, and I'm with you."

"All of those things could change if we don't get out of this republic very fast," Verrix said, dropping full length on the grass. Larthia sat next to him, her hand on his shoulder.

"What do you suggest?" Marcus asked him.

Larthia looked at Julia, who seemed to take this instant camaraderie between the two former enemies for granted. Larthia supposed she should do the same.

Prison, like politics, made strange bedfellows.

"I think we should backtrack to Ostia after darkness falls. From the seaport we can take a ship for anywhere in the world," Verrix said.

"Isn't that exactly what they'd expect us to do?" Larthia addressed the question to the others. "For Marcus to go back to Corsica, to his family? It's nearby, and safe."

"They'd expect me to stay on the continent and return to Gaul," Verrix replied.

"Who is 'they'?" Marcus protested. "Antony is not going to send anyone after us."

"How can you be sure?" Julia asked.

Marcus shrugged. "I know him. He thinks the Vestals are an oddity and the laws concerning them ridiculous. He's not going to go out of his way to enforce them, especially against me. He has much bigger plans afoot."

"Livia Versalia has a big mouth," Larthia said ruefully. "She'll be shrieking like a harpy about Julia's escape."

"Antony can handle her."

"What about Sura?"

Marcus snorted. "Antony has enough dirt on that old lecher to shut him up for the rest of his life."

"So you think we can go anywhere we like?" Verrix asked disbelievingly.

"As long as the Senators don't give Antony a hard time about us, and with Caesar dead and the government reorganizing they have enough to do saving their own skins. They won't have the time or energy to worry about ours."

"Then we're free!" Julia said exultantly, still unable to believe it.

"I guess we would be if we had any money," Verrix said dryly, smiling.

"We have money," Larthia piped up suddenly.

The other three looked at her.

"When my grandfather told me to transfer my money to easily transportable items, I followed his advice. There's a cache of jewelry and gold plate waiting for me at the Sejanus *villa maritima* in Neapolis."

"You mean you actually did it?" Verrix said to Larthia, his tone revealing amazement.

"Why not? I may not have been fond of my grandfather, but he always gave me good business advice."

Verrix burst out laughing.

"All of my war booty and army pay is stashed on the farm I was awarded after Iberia," Marcus said.

"Where is that?" Julia asked.

"Lavicum. I pay a couple to live there as tenants, to maintain it."

"It appears there a number of choices," Larthia said, marveling.

"But first we must get as far away from the city as possible," Marcus said, rising. "It would be foolish to stay where any one of us might be recognized." He offered his hand to Julia. "I think we can make Nomentum by nightfall. I have stayed at the inn there. It will suffice, and in the morning we'll buy two more horses and make plans."

Julia rose, and he pulled her into his arms. "I'll take care of you and the little one you're carrying," he said fiercely. "You almost gave up your life for me; I'll spend the rest of mine paying you back."

"There is no debt," Julia whispered. "I love you."

He held her off to smile at her and then lifted her onto his horse.

"Aren't they sweet together?" Larthia said to Verrix.

"Charming. You'll pardon me, but I'm a little more worried about the fugitive slave laws than I am about your sister and her centurion. Consul Antony is not my buddy."

"A fugitive slave case is prosecuted by the slave's owner. Since I am the owner of record, I don't think anybody is going to be looking for you, do you?"

"What about your grandfather?"

"I imagine he has other problems."

"I thought the assassins were pardoned."

"No, the Senate agreed to forgo prosecution for the good of the State, that's a different matter. I don't think Casca will be showing his face around Rome for a while."

"Where do you think he is?" Verrix asked.

"Who cares? He's not with me, that's

all I know, and his reign of terror has been broken. People will not forget Caesar's murder for a long time."

"There's still my prosecution for *stuprum*," Verrix reminded her.

"That's a civil case. If I'm not around to remind everyone of your terrible crime they'll forget about it."

"Let's go!" Marcus shouted from horseback.

"Still issuing orders," Verrix muttered, getting up and pulling Larthia along with him.

"He saved your hide."

"We saved each other's," Verrix corrected, helping her onto his horse.

"The war in Gaul is over," Larthia said to him. "You must be friends now. For my sake, and for Julia's."

He nodded, vaulting up behind her.

Marcus kicked his horse and cantered out to the road, and they followed him.

Antony rose to his feet when Livia Versalia entered his office at the Senate house. Lepidus did also, and the men exchanged glances as Livia stopped before the Consul's ornate desk, clearly in high dudgeon.

"You may go," Antony said to the

scribe sitting next to his desk. "Wait for me in the hall." He nodded to the other servants to leave as well.

"I'll go, too," Lepidus said, striding toward the door. "I'll be in the assembly hall if you need me." He rolled his eyes at Antony as he passed behind Livia's back.

Antony waited for the room to clear.

He didn't want any witnesses to this conversation.

"Please have a seat," the Consul said to Livia, when they were alone.

"I'd rather stand," she replied.

Antony shrugged. "What happened to your face?" he asked, referring to the darkening bruise on her jaw.

"I had an accident. I assume you've heard what occurred at the Campus Sceleratus this morning," she said coldly.

"I heard about it," he replied.

"A prisoner of the State was permitted to elude custody as well as execution, and you are personally responsible," she said accusingly.

He raised his brows. "How so?"

She narrowed her eyes. "I know that Sura told you about the prison escape and asked you for more men to cover the burial. I also know you refused the request."

"That is so."

"You *wanted* Demeter to rescue that little Casca!" Livia said accusingly.

"I wanted all of my men to be available to me in case of civil unrest. That is a very different thing."

"You expect me to believe you couldn't spare one or two soldiers to make sure Julia Rosalba wasn't snatched away? Do you think I am a complete fool? You have made me a laughingstock, and I won't forget it!"

"Are you threatening me?" Antony asked quietly.

"You can take it any way you want!" Livia said, drawing herself up proudly. "I have quite a bit of influence in this city, as you may learn to your cost."

Antony got up from his desk and walked around it to confront her, his expression neutral.

"Now you listen to me," he said, never raising his voice, his eyes locked with hers. "I am not Caesar, the Vestals never did me any favors, and you would do well to remember that the Imperator is dead. I am in charge now, and I regard you and your women as religious fanatics. I wouldn't protest if you were all fed to a pride of Armenian tigers for dinner."

Livia stared at him, aghast, silenced for one of the few times in her life.

"Marcus Demeter is a friend of mine, one of the best and bravest soldiers it was ever my privilege to command. He fought at my side through many bitter campaigns while you were warm and safe in your temple, burning incense and muttering incantations. I don't care if Demeter is sleeping with a Parthian camel, I'm going to do what I can to help him. I couldn't prevent his arrest, since he admitted his guilt publicly, but if you think I'm going to send a military force to chase after him just to save face for you and that hypocrite Sura you are sadly mistaken."

"But Pontifex Sura—" Livia sputtered.

"Pontifex Sura's favorite companion is a twelve-year-old Nubian catamite, and you can tell him for me that if he wants his wife and her wealthy family to know all about his games with that child he can take your side in this situation."

Livia was speechless once more, stunned.

Antony took a step closer to her, and she backed away from him.

"And one more thing, Livia," he said softly. "If you ever threaten me with your 'influence' again, you will find out what it means to make an enemy of *me*. Now get out of my sight before I forget that

I'm a gentleman knight who is duty bound to show deference to ladies."

Livia scurried out of his office, her face chalk white, and Antony looked after her, wondering belatedly if he had been too harsh with her.

Even if he considered her to be half out of her mind, Livia was dedicated to her calling, and that was more than could be said for most people. She was also curiously naive; his comments about Sura had shocked her. Antony knew everything about everybody, and the information about the *pontifex* was a weapon to be withdrawn if Livia dropped her demands. In general Roman men could do just about what they wanted, but Sura was a religious figurehead who had set himself up in judgment over other people. His self-righteousness had made him vulnerable.

Antony sighed. He was a military man and had little patience with these petty officials concerned about protecting their little bailiwicks; if men like himself and Demeter didn't go out to fight Rome's enemies, there would be no bailiwicks for them to protect. But Caesar had romanced people like Livia all his life, and Antony knew he would have to do the same.

He would mend fences with her in the future. Once Marcus was safely away.

They would need each other in the long run.

He opened the door to the hall and called the scribe back into the room.

Senator Gracchus paced back and forth on the mosaic floor of his *tablinum,* his toga sweeping in circles as he turned, glancing up occasionally at his son, who stood before him in uncharacteristic silence. Drusus Vinicius, his cloak hanging from his shoulders, his helmet under his arm, waited near the doorway to the hall, clearly wishing himself somewhere else.

"So you have nothing to say for yourself?" Gracchus finally asked, stopping to confront Septimus.

Septimus was silent.

"Vinicius here says you could be arrested on charges of aiding an escape," the Senator continued.

"I gave the Samnian a few drinks, that's all. If he passed out and then Marcus escaped it's no concern of mine."

His father's face flushed deeply. "The guard was knocked unconscious, he has the broken bones to prove it. Did he hit himself on the back of the neck?"

Septimus shrugged.

"When will the Senate consider the warrant?" Gracchus asked the tribune.

"In the session tomorrow morning," Vinicius replied.

Gracchus nodded. "Thank you for bringing my son home, Vinicius."

The tribune glanced at his friend Septimus sympathetically, then made his escape.

The last few days had been brutal. He had been called upon to do many things in the name of duty, things he would rather have avoided. He was heading straight to the nearest *taberna* to get drunk.

The Senator waited until Vinicius had left the room and Castor had closed the door behind him before he said to his son, "Have you lost your mind?"

"I don't think so," Septimus replied mildly.

"You helped Marcus escape! He was a State prisoner, charged with defiling a Vestal, the daughter of one of the oldest families in Rome!"

"You liked him until he did something that might cause you embarrassment for associating with him. You were always inviting him here; you thought he was a good influence on me," Septimus replied dryly.

"How could I know he would do something as insane as sleeping with a Vestal Virgin?" Gracchus countered incredulously.

"If you were really his friend you'd stand by him no matter what he did."

"Oh, I see. This was a test of loyalty. You proved yourself by behaving just as stupidly as Marcus."

"I don't expect you to understand."

"You're right; I can't understand it."

"I don't desert my friends when they're in trouble."

"He brought this trouble on himself! He has to diddle a Vestal when there are hundreds of available women in the Suburra every night? I saw Cytheris throwing herself at him in my own house. He is a national hero, he could have had anyone!"

"Maybe he doesn't regard women as interchangeable commodities, as you do," Septimus said coldly.

"What is that supposed to mean?" the Senator demanded, his eyes narrowing.

"A man who changes his teenage mistresses every six months might have difficulty grasping an enduring love for one woman," Septimus replied.

His father slapped him.

"What I do in my private life is none of your concern," his father said hoarsely, his voice shaking with anger. "I have spent my entire career upholding the name of my illustrious ancestors, and you have spent your time playing at dice and drinking at parties."

"You have spent your entire career shaking the right hands and paying off the right officials. You've never had a true friend in your life. When Marcus saved my skin in battle, dodging spears and catapult balls to drag me to safety, he didn't stop to think whether it was politically advantageous for him to risk himself for me. All I did in helping him to escape from prison was return the favor. And if you think I was playing knucklebones and guzzling wine during the Munda campaign against Gnaeus, then your baby girlfriends have you more addled than even I have assumed. Thirty thousand men lay dead on that Iberian field while you debated policies in the Senate, came home to a perfectly run house organized by my mother, and spent your evenings playing sex games with your latest pubescent whore. Don't talk to me about manhood and honor, Father. You know nothing about either of those attributes or you would be applauding my actions on the Esquiline hill instead of wondering what they might do to your political future."

The Senator stared at him, too enraged to speak.

"I will be moving out of the house tonight," Septimus added. "I'll stay at the barracks until the army goes on the march. Antony is planning to undertake Caesar's Parthian campaign so it won't be long before I'm out of your hair again. And if I am charged with aiding in Marcus' escape I will not expect any assistance from you with my legal concerns. Mother's father has money, and I'm sure he will see fit to help me. Goodbye."

Septimus stalked out of the Gracchus *tablinum,* and the Senator heard footsteps continue down the hall until his son was out the door.

Septimus' father sat heavily on his couch and put his head in his hands.

The inn at Nomentum was more like a shack, with the upper floor divided into four cells, each containing a bed and a washstand and not much else. Verrix could not stand without putting his head through the low thatched roof, so he stretched out on the wood-frame bed, watching as Larthia undressed, her clothes making a little pile on the floor. When he held out his arms she came into them naked, her silken skin warm and inviting.

There was no conversation for a long while, and then, just when he assumed she was asleep, she said, "I thought I was seeing things when you appeared at the burial site this morning. You and Marcus together, it seemed like a miracle."

"We were locked up together in the Esquiline prison with a bunch of criminals."

"How did you get out?"

"His friend, the tribune, got the guard drunk and knocked him out, taking the keys. He sprung us."

"Septimus Gracchus?"

"Yes."

Larthia laughed. "The Senator will have something to say about that."

"Are he and his son at odds?"

"Let's just say they do not get along very well." She rolled over and propped her chin on his chest. "Where will we be heading in the morning?" she asked.

He ran his forefinger over her open mouth. "Somewhere you're not Lady Sejana and I'm not your slave."

"Beyond the reach of Roman law? That's pretty far, the conquered territories are vast."

"Marcus was talking about Britannia."

"It's a wild place. Lots of warring tribes."

"It sounds like Gaul. And there's an island to the west of it, Hibernia, where even Caesar's legions never reached."

"What's there?" she asked.

"Celts," he replied, and grinned.

"You'd be right at home," Larthia said. He kissed her.

"I don't care where we go," Larthia whispered, climbing on top of him. "I'm tired of being Lady Sejana, it was never very rewarding work. I just want to be with you."

He rolled her under him and began to make love to her once more.

In the next room, Marcus and Julia lay curled together like puppies in a basket, drowsily watching the moon rise through the slit of a window in the wall.

"Are you surprised to find yourself in these luxurious accommodations this evening?" Marcus murmured teasingly, stroking her arm.

"I'm surprised to find myself still alive."

"Did you think I would just let them kill you?" he asked incredulously.

"I knew you were in jail, Marcus; I didn't think you would have much choice."

"Even if Septimus hadn't gotten us out, I would have found a way. Verrix and I were working on it when Septimus showed up, I wasn't planning to sit in that cave while Livia and her minions buried you alive."

"She must be having apoplexy. In her mind making an example of me was the only way to restore her reputation." Julia suddenly started to giggle. "Did you see Verrix punch her?"

"She's lucky it was Verrix. I would have done a lot worse to her."

"She'll be walking around with the bruise until the next *nundina*. I'd like to hear her explanation of it."

"She was coming at Verrix with nails and teeth bared, she looked like a she-cat in heat."

"I guess I've spoiled her glorious retirement," Julia sighed. "Livia had an unblemished career for over a quarter century before my defection."

Marcus made a dismissive gesture. "There will be a new scandal next week. By the time she leaves in two years she'll be revered again."

"I suppose so."

"I can't imagine why you're worrying about her; she didn't give a fig about you."

Julia sat up and studied his face in the

light of the single candle on the wash-stand.

"Do you really think we can get away from Rome without being caught?" she asked.

"If Antony wanted us, we'd be in custody right now," Marcus replied flatly. "He's letting us go. He is a relentless enemy, but he can also be a good friend."

Julia settled back into the curve of his arm. "I want to have lots of children with you," she said happily.

"You've made a good start on it already," he answered, laughing. "But we can always practice for the next one."

"Let's," Julia said, and they did.

WHAT'S LOVE GOT TO DO WITH IT?

Everything . . . Just ask Kathleen Drymon . . . and Zebra Books